GOLDHAMMER
A JAMES FLYNN ESCAPADE

HARIS ORKIN

Black Rose Writing | Texas

ISBN: 978-1-68433-967-9
PUBLISHED BY BLACK ROSE WRITING
www.blackrosewriting.com

Printed in the United States of America
Suggested Retail Price (SRP) $20.95

Goldhammer is printed in Book Antiqua

*As a planet-friendly publisher, Black Rose Writing does its best to eliminate unnecessary waste to reduce paper usage and energy costs, while never compromising the reading experience. As a result, the final word count vs. page count may not meet common expectations.

Author Photo Credit: Laura Burke
Cover Art Credit: Juan Padron

Praise for
GOLDHAMMER

"*Goldhammer* has all the heart-stopping action and biting wit of the first two novels, but at its core, this one is all heart. As Flynn's quixotic ambitions escalate, so does our bond with him and the compelling characters he pulls into his delusions. I love the layers of LA history in this sparkling, hilarious novel, which delivers both Hollywood royalty and a thoroughly modern villain. Bonkers in the best possible way."

—Wendall Thomas,
Anthony, Lefty, and Macavity nominated
author of the *Cyd Redondo Mysteries*

"Orkin writes the Flynn series with such panache that I started to believe the hero actually works for Her Majesty's Secret Service and that all the other characters are crazy. The mental hospital as a cover story is brilliant and Flynn's adventures of derring-do go a long way to pull you in and win you over. The *Goldhammer* escapade only serves to cement the series' place in the hearts of fans."

—Bill Fitzhugh,
Award-winning author of *Pest Control* and *A Perfect Harvest*

"A fast-paced quixotic thriller that would make Miguel de Cervantes and Ian Fleming proud. The third James Flynn novel is a powerful cocktail of suspense, adrenaline and a whole lot of laughs. Orkin has the remarkable ability to keep the reader straddled between a genuine spy thriller and an off-the-wall comedy"

—Joe Barret,
Award-winning author of *Managed Care*

"One of those books that has you laughing and turning pages well into the night."

—Len Boswell,
Bestselling author of *The Simon Grave Mysteries*

"A riotous comic novel that's also a legit page turner. A deftly plotted, swiftly paced thriller."

—R. Lee Procter,
Author of *The Million Dollar Sticky Note* and *Sugarball*

I dedicate this book to my dad. Richard Orkin was an actor, a writer, a scholar, and a very devoted father. He was also the silliest man I ever met. He taught me everything I know about writing comedy and, more importantly, how to successfully navigate the world like a mensch.

ACKNOWLEDGEMENTS

First off, I want to Reagan Rothe for giving Flynn a new home at Black Rose Writing. Next, I need to thank my patient and brilliant editor, M.J. Moores, who helps create the illusion that I actually know what I'm doing.

I'm very thankful to all my early readers who gave me their insights, critiques, ideas and reassurance. In particular, I want to thank Darlene Chan, Dwight Holing, Richard Procter, Dan Jolley, Lisa Orkin, Terry Evans, and Jeff Fisher.

My mom loved to read and laugh and loved physical comedy, whether it was Lucille Ball or one of her kids taking a header. She was always my biggest fan, and her unflagging belief in me actually made me believe in myself.

My siblings and my Uncle Sandy are steadfast supporters and cheerleaders.

My wife, Kim, and my son, Jakob, patiently read much of what I write, including this book in all its many forms. They are my sounding boards and my proofreaders, and I greatly appreciate their love and patience.

GOLDHAMMER

"When life itself seems lunatic, who knows where madness lies?"
—**Miguel Cervantes Saavedra,** *Don Quixote*

CHAPTER ONE

The Corsican wanted him dead.

Of that James Flynn was certain.

Somehow, the assassin had infiltrated Her Majesty's Secret Service as a security officer. Flynn didn't recognize him at first. The killer had put on a few pounds and likely had plastic surgery, but what he couldn't disguise were his eyes. His cold, dark, pitiless eyes. The eyes of a sociopath. The eyes of an executioner.

The only question was when.

When would the Corsican come for him?

He told his colleagues what he suspected, but they refused to believe him. They claimed his name was Thomas Hernandez and that someone else on the security team had recommended him. They also said they fully vetted him. But Flynn wasn't fooled. He tangled with the Corsican before. The man was relentless. A cold-blooded enforcer who started with the Corsican mafia but went on to do contract hits for the Sicilians, the Albanians, the Serbians, and the Russians.

Instead of waiting for the Corsican to come to him, Flynn decided to flush him out. Force his hand. Expose him for who he was and why he was there.

Flynn dressed in black denim and a black turtleneck and waited until 2 a.m. to make his move. He kept to the shadows as he trod the deserted corridors. He had no weapon since lethal weapons of any kind were now forbidden at headquarters. A foolish rule put in place by sheltered bureaucrats who had no clue. Luckily, not even security could carry a firearm at headquarters. All the Corsican had was an expandable baton and a Taser. Even so, the man was lethal enough with just his hands and feet.

1

But then, so was Flynn.

Flynn heard footsteps ahead and ducked into a conference room. He waited and listened as the footsteps drew closer. As they passed the doorway, Flynn peered into the corridor to see the Corsican lumbering forward, quietly peering in room after room. Suddenly, he stopped. Flynn felt a jolt of adrenaline. The air was electric. The silence palpable. Could the Corsican feel Flynn's eyes on him? Flynn knew that scientists have identified a specialized group of neurons in the primate brain that fire specifically when a monkey is under the direct gaze of another. Humans also appear to be wired for that kind of gaze perception. Predators like Flynn and the Corsican can also be prey and have developed a sixth sense to alert them to danger.

The Corsican turned and he and Flynn locked eyes for a moment. Before the hit man could take a step, Flynn took off down the hall in the opposite direction. He heard the footfalls of the Corsican as he chased after him. Flynn had his route all mapped out. Darting down one corridor. Then another. Running until he arrived at a door that led down to the basement and the guts of the building. Flynn had picked the lock after dinner, knowing that this was the night he would lure the Corsican to his end. He had a license to kill and could have used it anytime, but Flynn didn't exercise that power willy-nilly. Only as a last resort. He didn't want the Corsican dead. He needed to know who put the price on his head. Otherwise who ever hired the killer would continue to send hitters until finally one succeeded.

The building that housed HMSS was huge and had a substantial infrastructure. The basement utility plant had mechanical, electrical, HVAC, and plumbing systems that fed water, air, and electricity all through the facility. Flynn moved from massive room to massive room, staying just ahead of the Corsican. He needed to lose him and lay in wait. Flynn was confident in his abilities, but to come at a killer like that head-on didn't make much sense. Why give your opponents any edge at all?

Flynn ducked into a room that housed all the electrical panels, distribution boards, and circuit breakers. Conduit snaked everywhere and Flynn found a metal door secured with a heavy padlock. Using two straightened paper clips, he quickly picked the lock. The door led to an outside area protected by a chain-link fence topped with razor wire. The security fence surrounded three giant transformers and two massive backup generators the size of semi-trailers.

Flynn stood next to the door and strained his ears to hear approaching footsteps over the electrical buzz of the transformers. Faint at first, they moved closer. Careful. Slow. Stealthy. He saw a shoe as someone came through and Flynn took them from behind, using jiu-jitsu to slam them into the ground.

"Whoa, whoa, whoa," said the man Flynn had face down in the gravel.

"Sancho?"

"Get off me, man."

Flynn released his comrade-in-arms and helped him to his feet. Bits of gravel still clung to his face. "I thought you were the Corsican." Flynn's British accent had a touch of Scottish burr.

"His name is Hernandez," Sancho said.

"That's not his real name."

"And I'm telling you, he's not the Corsican."

"Don't let him fool you, my friend. He's not who he says he is."

"Then why'd he call me? He knows I know you. He knows we're friends. He asked me to find you. Talk to you. Calm you down."

"Perhaps he wants to take care of you too."

"Take care of *me*?"

Flynn heard the Corsican call to them, his voice deep and resonant. "You okay in there, brother?"

"We're good," Sancho said.

The Corsican walked in with two other men. All three wore the blue security uniform issued to those who guard HMSS. The Corsican looked at Flynn with his dark, merciless eyes. "You okay, Mr. Flynn?"

"Tell them who you are," Flynn demanded.

"Thomas Hernandez."

"Who you *really* are."

The Corsican rolled his eyes and sighed. "That's who I really am."

Flynn aimed an accusatory finger. "I *know* who you are. Born Stefanu Perrina in Porto, Corsica. Contract killer for the Unione Corse, the Cosa Nostra, and the Russian mafia. Wanted by Interpol for fifty-two confirmed kills."

"I was born in Hacienda Heights."

Flynn glanced at Sancho. "The man is a master of deception. It's kill or be killed with men like him."

The Corsican drew his Taser and the other two guards followed suit.

Sancho raised his hands. "Whoa, come on now. Easy." He stepped in front of Flynn as the Corsican fired. The Taser darts caught Sancho in the shoulder and socked him with fifty thousand volts. He screamed in agony as his whole body seized up and shook. His legs gave out and he fell on his side, helpless and twitching.

Flynn dove behind a generator before the other two guards could fire. Each guard stalked him from a different side. Flynn clambered up over the top and launched himself from above, tackling the Corsican. He wrenched away his reloaded Taser and shot one of the guards in the crotch. The man went down with a shriek as the other guard fired on him. Flynn fell to his knees and the darts parted his hair before hitting the Corsican in the chest. The killer crumpled as Flynn sprang to his feet and pulled the Corsican's expandable baton out of its holster. Flicking his wrist, Flynn fully extended the menacing club and turned to confront the last standing guard.

Someone grabbed Flynn by the arm and Flynn elbowed him in the face. Sancho staggered back, holding his bloody nose. "What the hell, man?"

"Sorry, mate."

Flynn heard a Taser fire and an instant later, two darts hit him in the side. Fifty thousand volts took him to his knees as another guard fired another Taser. Those two darts hit him in the stomach. Flynn lost control of every muscle in his body. And then he saw the Corsican looming over him with his own weapon. He shot the darts directly into Flynn's chest. Right over his heart. Now all three lit him up with electricity. One hundred and fifty thousand volts rocked Flynn as they shocked him with charge after charge until the world faded into a tiny aperture that slowly began to close.

CHAPTER TWO

Jack Parsons, the co-founder of the Jet Propulsion Laboratory, and Scientology founder L. Ron Hubbard were followers of famous occultist Aleister Crowley. Both believed that Devil's Gate Gorge in the Arroyo Seco was one of the seven portals to Hell. The gorge's namesake rock face resembles a devil's head and sits on the far western edge of Pasadena. The two amateur occultists and their followers would hold sex magick ceremonies outside of what they referred to as the Hellmouth, hoping to open the gates of Hell or at the least conjure up a demon or two. Some believe the two friends did indeed open that dark portal. Though, no one has ever claimed to have seen Baal or Beelzebub or any other major demons marching in Pasadena's annual Doo Dah Parade.

Sancho Perez stood frozen outside the front doors of City of Roses Psychiatric Institute. He tried to calm his heart as he worked up the nerve to walk inside. Band-aids covered the scratches on his face. His nose was swollen and his eyes were beginning to blacken. A hand rested on his shoulder and Sancho looked over to see the senior psychiatrist, Dr. Nickelson, smiling at him.

"Mr. Perez!"

"Hi, Dr. Nickelson."

"How are you feeling?"

"Okay."

"Good! Well, don't overdo it. You suffered a severe trauma ten months ago and that incident with Mr. Flynn last night is exactly the kind of thing you want to avoid. Something like that can be very triggering. I appreciate you coming to his aid, but please take it easy today."

"Okay."

Dr. Nickelson told Nurse Durkin to assign Sancho less-taxing duties to start. So, instead of putting him into the daily rotation, she asked him to gather the patients for their midday meal. The very first one he approached was Tom Gavoni. Hollow-eyed and balding, he sat on a couch and refused to come to lunch. "Food is meaningless to me now," he said.

Sancho smiled and raised a curious eyebrow. "Meaningless how?"

"Because I have no need of nutrition. My bodily functions have stopped functioning."

Sancho was struck by how skinny Tom was. Skeletal even. "What are you saying? You don't feel good?"

"I don't feel anything."

"Do you want to see the doctor?"

"The doctor can't help me. No one can help me."

"Why would that be?"

"Because I'm dead." His bulging eyes burned with guilt and despair. Two of his teeth were missing.

"Dead inside, you mean?"

"Dead like deceased. Like no longer among the living."

"Are you saying you're a ghost?"

"I'm saying six months ago I blacked out after a three-day bender and woke up here."

"In City of Roses?"

"In Hell."

"You think you're in Hell?"

"You think you're not?"

A blood-curdling scream ended their conversation. Tom gave Sancho a look like, "*See*?"

Sancho hurried down the corridor to find the source of the screaming. Ear-splitting in its intensity, it echoed off the cinderblock walls and down the halls.

Sancho found the room and entered to find a petite brunette in her early twenties strapped to a hospital bed, her dirty, tear-smeared face contorted with fear. Young and pretty, she reminded Sancho of Emma Watson, that English actress from the Harry Potter movies. She writhed and struggled against the wrist and ankle straps and stared at Sancho with a furious intensity.

"Let me go! Please! Please! They'll kill me!"

"Who?"

She let out an ear-shattering shriek so loud it even woke Mrs. Jakobs, the narcoleptic in the next bed.

"No one's going to kill you," Sancho said with a soothing voice.

"I might," Mrs. Jakobs mumbled.

"Please! Pleeeease!" the young woman begged.

Sancho figured they brought her in sedated during the night shift and she woke up strapped to her bed, not knowing where she was or what was happening. He looked at her chart, noted her name, and patted her hand. "Chloe, look at me. You're going to be okay."

"He wants me dead. He tried once. He'll try again!"

Sancho squeezed her hand. "You're safe here."

"No, no, no, he knows I know! He can't let me live!"

"Who can't?" The voice came from behind Sancho, and it was so deep, comforting, and commanding, it immediately calmed the girl. The accent was British and Chloe stopped struggling to stare.

Sancho knew who it was without having to turn around. "Hey James, no worries, man, I got this."

"She clearly believes someone intends to do her harm."

"She's just confused, dude."

Sancho watched as James Flynn entered the room and approached Chloe's bed. Tall and strikingly handsome, he wore a navy blue, single-breasted, slim cut suit with a light blue shirt and a gray silk tie. It fit him tightly, which only emphasized his wide shoulders and powerful arms. Unlike Sancho, he didn't have a mark on his face. "What's your name, dear?"

"Chloe."

"What a lovely name." Flynn pulled out a pocket square and dabbed her tears. "If I remember correctly, it's from the Greek and harkens back to Demeter. The Goddess of fertility."

"*Dude.*"

"We need to get these restraints off her, Sancho."

Chloe looked at Flynn with big brown eyes brimming with tears, her voice a whisper. "Someone's trying to kill me, doctor."

"James ain't no doctor," Sancho said.

"Who are you then?"

"A friend." Flynn unbuckled one of the straps.

Sancho grabbed his wrist. "You can't be doing that, man."

"We can't very well expect her to protect herself if she's trussed up like a turkey."

Sancho watched with a worried look as Flynn unfastened each restraint. "Durkin won't be happy, dude."

"Is that who strapped her down like this? Nurse Durkin?"

"It was indeed." Durkin's harsh, flat, emotionless voice filled Sancho with fear as he turned to see her standing in the doorway.

The head nurse at City of Roses was as tall as Flynn but considerably wider, tipping the scales at over two hundred pounds. She sported an immense bosom barely restrained by her starchy, white nurse's uniform. Her hair, tied back in a tight red bun, sat atop a wide, meaty face. She directed two icy blue eyes at Sancho and Flynn.

"Mr. Perez, you know the rules. You can't let patients like Mr. Flynn run roughshod over them."

Chloe looked at Flynn with surprise. "Patient?"

"I'm sorry, Nurse Durkin," Sancho said. "But I didn't want to upset her more than she already was."

"Patients need discipline. Boundaries. Without them they feel out of control."

O'Malley and Barker loomed behind Durkin. The two burly orderlies traded smiles as they leered at Chloe's naked legs. Sancho tugged her hospital gown down as Flynn worked on opening her last restraint.

The two goons stepped into the room and pulled Flynn away from the bed. Flynn's jaw grew taught with anger. Sancho got between them and put his hands lightly on Flynn's chest. "Dude, just stay cool."

O'Malley grabbed Chloe by her right wrist and wrenched it back into the restraint. She slapped him with her left hand, leaving a red mark and enraging the big man. Barker caught her arm before she could slap O'Malley again. As she fought to free herself, Barker twisted her arm until she winced and cried out.

"Whoa, whoa, not so rough!" Sancho tried to intervene. Barker elbowed him in the gut, backing him up.

Durkin looked on as Chloe kicked and struggled. "Get those restraints back on her!"

O'Malley bent her arm back and Chloe cried out, "No! No! *No! Let me go!*"

Flynn put his hand on O'Malley's shoulder. "Enough! You're hurting her."

O'Malley tried the same elbow-in-the-gut move he used on Sancho, but Flynn turned just in time and used the bigger man's momentum to pull him back, sweeping O'Malley's feet out from under him. Down he went, his head bouncing off the floor.

Barker released Chloe's wrist to go after Flynn. He was wider, but Flynn stood taller and moved faster. He sidestepped the attack, tripping him. Barker fell and his fat head collided with O'Malley's. Both collapsed in a heap.

Nurse Durkin looked perturbed as Flynn attended to Chloe. "Are you all right?"

Chloe nodded through tears as an angry O'Malley used the hospital table to pull himself up.

Flynn casually kicked it out from under him and O'Malley fell back down, clunking heads with Barker again.

Sancho saw the syringe in Durkin's hand an instant before she injected Flynn in his right shoulder. Flynn tried to jerk away, but it was too late. He glared at her, his eyes flashing with fury. "Nurse Durkin, what did you do?"

"I gave you something to relax you."

O'Malley and Barker scrambled up, their faces red with rage and embarrassment.

Sancho took Flynn by the arm and tried to usher him out of there. "Let's get you back to your room, brother."

"I got this." O'Malley growled, grabbing Flynn by his other arm.

A tug of war ensued before Durkin finally took charge. "Let him go, O'Malley. Get those restraints back on Miss Jablonski." She then aimed her chilly eyes at Sancho. "Perez, take Mr. Flynn back to his room."

Flynn tried to turn around, but he wavered unsteadily as the sedative and antipsychotic cocktail did its thing. "Come on, James. Let's get you to bed before you take a header."

"I was just simply… I was trying… I only wanted…"

"I know, brother. I got you."

Durkin injected Chloe with her own B52 cocktail. Being much smaller, the drugs took immediate effect. She sank back into the bed as Barker and O'Malley tightened the restraints. Her big brown eyes locked on Flynn as Sancho ushered him out.

"He's not a doctor?" Chloe mumbled, her eyes beginning to droop. "What is he?"

"He's out of his goddamn mind," O'Malley said.

CHAPTER THREE

In 1429, the three kingdoms of Okinawa came together as one. The Kingdom of Ryukyu. When King Shō Shin came to power in 1477, he banned the practice of martial arts. The ban continued even after Japan invaded the island in 1609. Rebels secretly practiced the ancient arts and this led to the development of kobudō, a practice that uses common household and farming implements as weaponry. They combined Chinese martial arts with their own existing arts to create what came to be known as Okinawan Karate.

Flynn awoke to the sound of someone belting the title song of Rogers and Hammerstein's *Oklahoma*. One of the older agents, a Miss Doris Frawley, claimed to have placed fourth in 1948's Miss Arkansas pageant. She often started the day with a show tune.

Flynn started the day in a very different way. He slept in a pair of sea island cotton boxer shorts and, upon waking, dropped to the floor to pump out forty press-ups. He would do them excruciatingly slowly. Until his muscles screamed. Turning onto his back, he'd do countless straight leg lifts until he couldn't do another. Rising to his feet, he performed twenty standing toe touches, twenty jumping jacks, and then handstand press-ups, upside down against the wall. From his inverted position, he saw Doris Frawley smiling at him from the doorway.

"You're looking very handsome today, Mr. Flynn."

"And you look lovely as always, Miss Frawley."

The nonagenarian grinned and shuffled off down the hallway, belting out "Oh, What A Beautiful Morning."

Flynn glanced at his roommate, still asleep in his bed. Q headed Q Branch and created all the Secret Service's state-of-the-art gadgetry.

11

Elderly and eccentric, he always slept like a rock. Not even Doris and her exuberant singing could awaken him. Flynn opened his armoire and selected a black karate gi. He slid on the *zubon* and then the *uwagi* and tied it shut in the traditional fashion with a black *obi*.

Sancho still lived at home with his mama, his abuela, and his tata. However early Sancho woke up, his tata was always awake before him, bustling around the kitchen, making breakfast, and getting ready for work. At five foot two, he was five inches shorter than Sancho, but broader and stockier, with a round rock-hard stomach and huge powerful hands. He worked construction and could build anything. Tough as he was, he wasn't the toughest person Sancho knew. That would be James Flynn. Though his abuela came in a close second.

Sancho drove to City of Roses Psychiatric Institute with a belly full of machaca and eggs. His Aston Martin DB 9 Volante turned a lot of heads. Few orderlies could afford such a high-end luxury sports car. In fact, none of the doctors at City of Roses owned anything comparable. Flynn gifted it to Sancho after their first adventure together. He nearly sold it numerous times and recently decided to see what he could get for it. The gas, insurance and maintenance costs were killing him, and it made him uncomfortable to drive such a fancy car. He could bank the money and buy himself a Camry. It was the smart thing to do, but he really enjoyed the looks on people's faces when they saw him behind the wheel.

He found a spot next to some doctor's gleaming Bimmer and headed inside to start his day. After punching in, Sancho made James Flynn's room his first stop. No Flynn. Next, he checked on Chloe. She wasn't in her room either. He bumped into a nurse on the way out, a slender sloe-eyed beauty originally from Jamaica.

"Hey, Wanda, have you seen Chloe?"

"I think she's with Dr. Nickelson."

"She was really upset yesterday."

"She's doing better, but she's still pretty paranoid. Thinks some Hollywood producer wants to murder her," Wanda said.

"No shit?"

"Poor thing OD'd on Demerol and almost died."

"They bring her in on a 5150?"

Wanda nodded. "Yep."

"She looks young."

"She's a baby."

Wanda continued on. Sancho checked the TV room and the activity room and finally found Flynn in the inner hospital courtyard. The outdoor area had raised planters with all kinds of shrubs, flowers, and other greenery, as well as tables for nurses and patients who wanted to take their lunch outside. Exercise classes were often held on the well-manicured lawn, but at the moment only James Flynn took advantage of the fresh air and sunshine.

Flynn often exercised there, and Sancho watched him perform a complicated-looking karate kata. He executed impressive jump kicks and punches, elbow strikes and spin kicks, knife hands and hammer fists. Sancho knew the moves, not because he practiced, but because he loved watching kung fu movies.

Flynn was built like Jean-Claude Van Damme and moved like Bruce Lee. The dude had skills, and Sancho wasn't the only one who noticed. Nurses often took their lunch outside when Flynn practiced. He always worked up a sweat and would often take off his top, revealing a torso packed with muscle and a six-pack that would put Hugh Jackman to shame. Yeah, the nurses knew he was delusional, but he was also movie star handsome and charming as hell.

Flynn finished his kata in "ready position", eyes closed, as he held his breath for a count of two before letting it out. He opened his eyes and winked at the nurses watching him, enjoying their fluttery embarrassment and blushes. He spotted Sancho sitting on a cement bench and smiled.

Sancho waved him over. "How you doing this morning, brother?"

Flynn crossed to him, mopping his face with a hand towel. "I feel good. Fit. What about you, my friend?"

"I'm better every day."

Flynn surveyed his damaged face. "Sorry about the other night."

"No worries, dude. How'd *you* sleep last night?"

"Like a block of cement."

"Durkin dosed you pretty good."

"Yes, I'm a little upset with her and her lackeys. Young Chloe was obviously in distress. I assume our enemies held and tortured her. Was she released as part of a prisoner swap?"

"Man, she's here because she's not in her right mind."

"Of course she isn't. Not after what she's been through."

"It was nice of you to help her, dude, but look at me. You really need to stay out of Durkin's way."

"Does Durkin believe that Chloe's been brainwashed and turned against us? I understand the need to debrief her, but that's no reason to treat her like a traitor."

Sancho worked hard not to roll his eyes. "All I know is you need to keep away from her."

"Durkin?"

"Chloe."

"You have a kind soul, Sancho. I applaud your empathy. Often compassion is seen as a weakness in our line of work. But we have to remember what we're fighting for. We can't become the monster to fight the monster."

CHAPTER FOUR

Flynn needed a mission. He couldn't remember the last time he'd been operational. He was built for war. For taking the fight to the enemy. Too much inaction dulled the senses. Boredom sapped his energy and blunted his battle readiness. He worked hard to stay in condition, so when the call came he'd be ready. After all, he was a Double-0. The sharp tip of the spear. Those at the top needed to unleash him. Nothing made him feel more alive than risking life and limb. Danger made life more vivid, food and drink more delicious, the touch of a woman more exquisite.

His lack of recent action allowed the Corsican to get the better of him. Why the killer let him live was a mystery. It's possible Flynn wasn't his ultimate quarry. Perhaps Flynn's pre-emptive attack derailed his plan to take out another target. Could it have been Chloe?

Flynn knew in his bones that Chloe was in danger. Yes, the torture she suffered created post-traumatic stress and sometimes that could result in paranoia, but that didn't mean she wasn't at risk. He needed to debrief her. As an expert interrogator, he knew he could discover the truth.

After changing out of his gi and showering, Flynn put on a black polo shirt, taupe chinos, and gray suede chukka boots. He found Chloe in the lounge area with a few other agents and operatives enjoying some much-needed R&R—reading and playing cards and watching the telly. She must have finished her debriefing with the powers that be because she looked exhausted. Apparently, they decided she was no longer a threat to herself or others as they'd removed the restraints.

She sat on a couch next to another agent. Ty was Black, young, rotund, energetic, and volatile. He had a teenager's intensity. Flynn appreciated his passion.

"Fact is Tupac ain't dead. Homeboy faked the whole thing. Look at the evidence. Suge Knight paid three million for a private cremation and the bastard who did it disappeared. Poof. Gone. Tupac only had a hundred grand in the bank when he supposedly died. Didn't own no property. How's that possible, right? Homie made millions."

"Ty?"

"Hey James."

"Mind if I have a word with Miss Jablonski."

"Who?"

"Chloe."

"Who?"

"The young lady you're talking to."

"What's her name?"

"Chloe."

"We're kind of in the middle of a conversation, brother. Talking about Tupac. Brother faked his own death."

"You can pick it back up later. I just need a few minutes with her. It won't take long."

Ty glared at Flynn and held the stare before finally acquiescing. "Fine. Gotta take a leak anyway." He lurched to his feet, hiked up his baggy shorts, and made his way out.

Flynn sat on the couch next to Chloe and studied her for a moment. Her eyes were half-lidded, her pupils huge and unfocused. Her chin drifted to her chest, her head bobbing as she went in and out of consciousness. No wonder they didn't bother to strap her back in. They had her in chemical restraints.

Flynn put his hand on her knee. "Chloe? Can you hear me?"

She moved as if underwater, slowly turning her head, fighting the sedation as she looked at Flynn. "They drugged me with something."

"Try to focus. Look at me."

She struggled to push away the fog. "They...they don't believe me."

"Don't believe what? That you're in danger?"

Tears filled her eyes. "They think I tried to kill myself."

"Tell me what happened."

Her voice was slurred, her tongue thick. "It wasn't me. It was him."

"Who?"

"Goldhammer."

"Sounds German. Who does he work for?"

"He's a big producer."

"Of what?"

"Movies," she mumbled.

"Ah, brilliant cover."

"He wants me dead." She trembled and started to cry.

Flynn squeezed her hand. "Breathe. Relax. It's okay. You're safe now."

"Don't think so."

"No one can touch you here."

"He can. He can buy anyone. Go anywhere. He's Goldhammer."

"With that kind of reach it sounds like he might have ties to SMERSH."

"Who?"

"SMERSH. It's a portmanteau of Smiert Spionam. Death to Spies. Coined by Stalin himself in 1942."

"I don't understand."

"You say he masquerades as a movie producer?"

She nodded. "He's won like three Academy Awards."

"Which allows him to travel anywhere and meet anyone. Were you sent to seduce him?"

She shook her head. "What? No! What are you talking about?"

"Goldhammer. How did you meet him?"

"At a party. I was working for a caterer."

"That was your cover?"

"My job. He asked if I was an actress and I said, yeah, and he said he was producing a movie and asked me if I wanted to audition."

"And you said yes?"

She nodded and started to shake and cry again. Flynn held her hand and tried to comfort her. "It's okay. You did the right thing."

She fought the sedation to find the right words. "I don't think I did. He wanted me to audition for him in his hotel room. I knew that wasn't right. I knew he was up to something, trying to get me alone in his hotel room. I thought I could handle him. I thought this could be my shot. My big chance."

"To get what you were after?"

"Yeah, but I think he drugged my drink. And he's so big. I couldn't fight him." Her voice cracked. "I couldn't fight him."

"But you obviously escaped."

"Hours later. I snuck out while he was sleeping. The next morning, I told my brother what happened and he wanted to go to the police. I said no way."

"Because you didn't want to blow your cover?"

"Because I knew they wouldn't believe me, but he called them anyway."

"And what did the police do?"

"They told me I needed proof that it wasn't consensual. They said without that there was nothing they could do. That it was my word against his."

"I assume that didn't sit well with your brother."

"No." Chloe shook her head. "The next day, Tyler went to Goldhammer's office and caught him outside his building. Screamed at him. Called him a pervert. Said he'd go to the press."

"And after that?"

"Tyler wouldn't let it go. Starting posting on social media. He even tweeted we had evidence. That I recorded the whole thing on my iPhone."

"Did you?"

"No."

"So what did *you* do?"

"I didn't do anything. I just wanted to put it behind me. Forget it ever happened. So I went back to work."

"With the caterer?"

Chloe nodded. "That's where I met Avi. At a party in Beverly Hills. He said he was a cinematographer. He was so charming and I was feeling so shitty, it was nice to have someone like that pay attention to me. Two nights later, I met him for drinks at the Chateau Marmont. But I think he roofied me because I woke up in the emergency room and I don't even remember how I got there. They said a maid found me in one of the rooms. Said I OD'd on Demerol. But I don't use that shit. I don't touch it."

"And you think this Avi tried to kill you?"

"I do." Her voice cracked. She started to cry again.

"That night when you were in Goldhammer's apartment. What were you looking for?"

"What do you mean?"

"Before you snuck out. Were you searching for codes for an offshore account in the Caymans? A microdot with the schematic of some sort of high-tech weapons system?"

"What are you talking about?"

"What are *you* talking about?"

A shadow fell across Flynn. He looked up to the imposing presence of Nurse Durkin. "Mr. Flynn, don't you have an appointment with Dr. Nickelson?"

"I thought that was at two?"

"It's two fifteen."

"It's funny how time gets away from me sometimes."

"Yes, and now it's time for you to get away from Miss Jablonski." Durkin hovered, staring down at him over her impressive and immovable bosom. "On your feet, Mr. Flynn."

Flynn stood and met Nurse Durkin eye to eye. "Nurse Durkin, perhaps you'd be kind enough to grace me with your given name. We've known each other for quite some time now and I feel we needn't be so formal. You could call me James and I could call you—"

She clapped her hands together twice to shut him up. "Dr. Nickelson is ready for you, Mr. Flynn. Let's not waste his time."

Flynn offered Chloe a rakish grin before making his way from the room.

CHAPTER FIVE

The 5th edition of the Diagnostic and Statistical Manual of Mental Disorders defines a delusion as a false belief that persists despite all evidence to the contrary. They can be persecutory (a belief that one is going to be harmed by an individual, organization or group), referential (a belief that gestures, comments, or environmental cues are directed at oneself), grandiose (a belief that the individual has exceptional abilities, wealth, or fame), erotomanic (a false belief that another individual is in love with him/her), or nihilistic (a conviction that a major catastrophe will occur). Because cognitive functions are otherwise intact in someone suffering a delusional disorder, it has been described in the literature as a "partial psychosis."

The senior psychiatrist at City of Roses felt relieved and exhausted. Extricating himself had proven more difficult than he imagined. After twenty-two years, he and City of Roses had become one. One intertwined, hopelessly entangled knot of codependency. Enough was enough. His adventure with Flynn eleven months ago convinced him he needed more. More adventure. More excitement. More surprises. More variety. He'd fallen into a deep, deep rut and climbing out took everything he had. This old bird needed to leave the nest.

When Dr. Robert Nickelson looked in the mirror, he saw a tired, careworn face, and thinning auburn hair shot with gray. That morning, he put on his usual wrinkled khakis and well-worn tweed jacket and arrived at the office knowing that this was the day. His next to last day at City of Roses. So when he handed James Flynn's file to his replacement he experienced both immense relief and an underlying sense of anxiety.

The *new* senior psychiatrist at City of Roses was twenty years younger and stood half a head taller. He had a black goatee streaked with gray, gun metal Giorgio Armani eyewear, and a clean-shaven head. His eyes were shrewd and cold and for a moment, Nickelson suffered a stab of regret. He hoped Dr. Michaels would treat his patients with the proper care, respect, and kindness they deserved. Nickelson knew that some, like Nurse Durkin, considered him too kind. Too soft. Too forgiving. Well, too late now. He made the decision, tendered his resignation, and now would be on to a new life. At sixty-five, he was newly single and had no ties or responsibilities. His wife left him. His kids were grown. In some ways, he was back to where he was at age twenty-seven. On his own.

He sat behind his desk and watched as Dr. Michaels perused the documents inside the file folder. "Mr. Flynn can be very charming." Nickelson picked up a pen and scratched the back of his neck. "Often, he seems quite rational, but don't be deceived. He never wavers from his delusion. Never. If anything at all contradicts that imagined reality, he will immediately come up with some rationalization to explain that inconsistency."

"I've read about him, of course. For a while Mr. Flynn was all over the news."

"Much of that was wildly exaggerated."

"Quite an interesting case."

"Quite an exceptional person," Nickelson replied.

"So, his parents were killed in a car accident when he was ten?"

"Yes, and as he had no other living relatives, he went into the system."

Michaels nodded and continued to read. "Nine foster homes over a period of seven years. He certainly had a time of it."

"I've treated hundreds of delusional patients over the years, but Mr. Flynn is in a class by himself."

"He believes this hospital is Her Majesty's Secret Service?"

"And that he's a Double-0."

"With a license to kill?"

"Yes, though he's never seriously hurt anyone," Nickelson said.

"No?"

"Well, no one here at the hospital. He's had run-ins with some of the patients, and the orderlies have had to restrain him at times. There was an incident last night, but for the most part he doesn't often act out or exhibit any violent tendencies. Durkin, the head nurse, might disagree, but she likes to maintain strict order, and Flynn can be a disrupter."

"So his early trauma and abandonment triggered the development of a delusional persona?"

"Basically, yes. He became the most powerful person he could imagine. As an adolescent he was an obsessive fan of 1960s espionage films."

Michaels grunted and nodded and continued to read until he came upon something that surprised him. "He seduced a nurse?"

"More than one actually."

"Sociopaths can often be master seducers."

"He's no sociopath. Flynn can be very empathetic. He often tries to protect the more vulnerable patients and follows a strict personal code of conduct. He can be flirtatious, but never pushes himself on anyone. In fact, he keeps a certain distance which only seems to fuel the attraction."

"So why does he think he can't leave this place?"

"As far as he's concerned, he can leave whenever he wants. And has. Multiple times. But he always returns."

Michaels's eyebrows went up at something he saw on the next page. "He's been a patient here for eighteen years?"

"One of a handful in long-term care."

"I assume you've challenged this delusion?"

"Many times. I've treated him with antipsychotics and antidepressants. Cognitive behavioral therapy. Transcranial magnetic stimulation. One-on-one psychotherapy. Group therapy. It's all in the file."

"Fascinating."

"I've grown very fond of Mr. Flynn, however, so I will check on him now and again. Not to look over your shoulder, but to keep another constant in his life. I hope that's all right."

"Personally, I have no problem with that, but we'll have to see how that works therapeutically. Perhaps to start, you should keep your distance so he can learn to rely more on me."

Flynn strolled into Dr. Nickelson's outer office with a grin. Miss Honeywell, his assistant, glowered at him. "You're late, Mr. Flynn." Honeywell, an unsmiling African American woman in her fifties, took a bite of a bear claw and directed Flynn to a chair against the wall. "Have a seat. I'll let him know you're here."

Flynn, instead, sat on the edge of Honeywell's desk, much to her obvious consternation. "Don't be like that, Honeywell. I know you're happy to see me."

"You want to make me happy? Get your skinny ass off my desk." Honeywell hit the intercom. "I have Mr. Flynn to see you, Doctor."

"Send him in."

"Have you ever seen Paris in May, Miss Honeywell? That's when the Jardin du Luxembourg is in full bloom. The perfect place for a romantic stroll and picnic. A crusty baguette, a wheel of brie, a bottle of wine, and thee."

"You are working my last nerve, Mr. Flynn." Honeywell pushed Flynn off the edge of her desk. "More walking. Less talking."

"Pretend all you want, my dear. I can see how you really feel." Flynn offered Honeywell a goodbye smile, but she actively ignored him, typing something into her computer.

Flynn entered Dr. Nickelson's office.

"Mr. Flynn, so good of you to finally join us."

"Sorry I'm late, N. I was interrogating our agent released in that prisoner swap."

"Excuse me?"

"Miss Jablonski. She appears to be in some sort of danger."

"Yes, well, I think she's out of danger now."

"I'm not sure she is, sir. The person after her is an immensely powerful individual. The evidence suggests he may have ties to SMERSH."

"Well, luckily, Miss Jablonski has agreed to stay with us indefinitely. So you needn't worry."

"I'm not worried, sir. I'm simply being cautious. In fact, I'm beginning to wonder if Miss Jablonski was the Corsican's quarry."

"There is no Corsican, Mr. Flynn. His name is Mr. Hernandez."

"The man is a master of disguise, sir. And one of the most dangerous men in the world."

"Yes, well, I'm afraid after last night's episode, Mr. Hernandez has tendered his resignation and filed a claim with worker's comp. I don't think he'll be returning."

"At least not in that guise. But we must remain vigilant." Flynn's gaze flickered to another man sitting on the couch.

"I'd like you to meet Dr. Michaels," Nickelson said.

Michaels rose and shook Flynn's hand. "Good to meet you, Mr. Flynn."

"Good to meet you too, sir."

"Michaels is my replacement. I'm retiring."

"*Retiring?*"

"It's time. But rest assured, Dr. Michaels has a great deal of experience with... those such as yourself... and I'm sure you two will get on very well."

"I look forward to working with you, Mr. Flynn." Michaels motioned for Flynn to sit, but Flynn stayed standing. "I'm here to help."

"As are we all. I'm more than ready to go operational again. There must be threats against us in the world. Whether it's a megalomaniac with a loose nuke or a madman with a biological weapon, let me do what I do, sir. Let me take the fight to the enemy."

"Can we put a pin in that and continue this conversation later? I need to get settled and find my bearings. I just wanted to introduce myself."

"Yes, sir. Perhaps I can help you hit the ground running." Flynn turned to Nickelson. "I must say, sir, I'm sorry to see you go. We've made quite the team, you and I."

"Indeed, we have. Thank you, Mr. Flynn."

"Thank you, sir." Flynn nodded once more to Michaels before heading back out into the anteroom. Honeywell didn't look up, but continued to type away on her computer.

"So N is leaving?"

Honeywell grunted in the affirmative.

"Are you going with him?"

"No, I'll be working with Dr. Michaels. Someone needs to show him the ropes."

"There's no one better than you, Honeywell. Without you, this place wouldn't be the same."

"Uh huh," she said as she kept her eyes on the screen and her fingers on the keyboard.

"I'd miss you terribly if you were to leave."

"Uh huh."

"Wouldn't you miss me?"

She didn't bother looking up as she continued to work, her voice flat with sarcasm. "Terribly."

CHAPTER SIX

The trip to the emergency room went by in a blur. The bright lights in her eyes, the nausea, the needles, the nurse shaking her awake, asking her questions she couldn't answer. Chloe couldn't think. Couldn't breathe. It was like drowning. Dying. So cold. Shivering.

Waking up that first morning in restraints terrified her. Trapped. Helpless. She didn't know where she was or how she'd gotten there. Did someone kidnap her? Was she a prisoner? Waves of nausea and dry heaves racked her body. She screamed for help, but no one came. No one heard her. So she kept screaming, shrieking until her voice shredded. Finally, someone showed up. That young Hispanic orderly. He looked so scared. He just stared. Afraid to do anything until Flynn appeared. Flynn was the only one who believed her. She didn't normally go for older men, but he carried himself with such confidence and charm, and seemed so reasonable and calm. It stunned her to find out he was off his rocker.

At least, she wasn't strapped to that bed anymore.

When she told Dr. Michaels that she hadn't taken any Demerol, that someone had tried to kill her, he looked at her like she was crazy. Asshole doctors. Always so arrogant. Her dad was a doctor. An orthopedic surgeon. So full of himself; so condescending. When she told him she wanted to be an actress, he just closed his eyes and shook his head. Everything she ever did disappointed him. He felt the same way about her brother. He didn't know for a fact that Tyler was gay, but he suspected it, and didn't hide his disappointment in his only son's lack of machismo.

Their mom was a hardcore Catholic. Polish Catholic. Full of shame for herself and her kids. She wouldn't let Chloe pierce her ears or wear any makeup or jewelry other than a crucifix. Skirts or shorts could be no higher than two inches above the knee. She couldn't wear tube tops or tank tops or open-toed shoes. Nothing that would get a boy to notice her. When her mom caught her at the mall wearing a crop top and a pair of cut-offs, she called her a slut and dragged her home, embarrassing her in front of all her friends. She couldn't date until she was eighteen, and even then, she had a 9:00 p.m. curfew.

She knew her brother was gay from the time he was ten. Their mom was oblivious, and their dad made it his mission to turn him into a man's man. He forced Tyler to play Little League and Pop Warner football, even though it was obvious he had no interest in either one. His dad spent hours throwing baseballs and footballs at him, and sometimes Tyler would even catch them.

They grew up in Kenosha, Wisconsin. Snap-on Tools, Jelly-Belly, and Jockey International had their world headquarters there. Tourists could visit the Kenosha Sculpture Walk or attend the annual Cheese-A-Palooza. Chloe decided at age ten that she would leave K-Town as soon as she could, certain that she and her brother were destined for greater things.

They bonded over music, movies, fashion, and reality TV shows like Project Runway and The Bachelor. They both loved old MGM musicals, and would stay up late and watch them on Turner Classic Movies. As her father didn't want to pay for Tyler to attend a university out-of-state, he enrolled in the University of Wisconsin at Parkside in Kenosha and majored in business—at his father's urging. Chloe followed him there. She wanted to major in theater, but her father refused to pay the tuition unless she changed her major to something more practical.

After graduation, Tyler finally moved out and came out and took a job as a bartender at Club Icon, Kenosha's most popular gay bar. That was a bridge too far for their parents. From that point on, they refused to talk to him or even acknowledge his existence. The day after Chloe graduated with a degree in communications, she and Tyler packed their meager belongings into his late model Corolla and moved to California, hoping to find a way into the entertainment business.

On her second day at City of Roses, Chloe sat alone at a cafeteria table and stared at her breakfast. Runny scrambled eggs and two slightly burnt pork sausages. Afraid of who might decide to sit next to her, she looked over at the cafeteria line with trepidation. A tall, chubby, bearded, balding guy with a lazy eye wouldn't stop staring at her. Normally, someone will look away if you catch them staring, but not this guy. This guy just stared harder. After getting his food, he headed in her direction. She considered getting up and dumping her breakfast, but didn't want to piss him off. He had angry eyes and a weird smile, and right before he reached her table, someone swooped in and took the chair he was about to occupy.

The chubby guy looked put out and pointed at the chair. "That's where I was gonna sit."

The young chola who hijacked the chubby guy's chair looked to be about the same age as Chloe. Short and round, with a pretty face and long black hair, she reminded Chloe of a more voluptuous version of Selena Gomez. As pretty and petite as she was, she didn't take any shit.

"Too bad, Chuck."

"Fine." He pointed his chin at another chair at the table. "I'll sit here then."

"No, I don't think so. Sit your ass somewhere else."

Chuck and the chola locked eyes and until finally he clenched his jaw, moved off and found another table. The pretty Latina took a bite of toasted bagel. "I'm Valentina."

"Chloe."

"You okay?"

Chloe nodded, but tears filled her eyes. Valentina put her hand on Chloe's and that opened the floodgates. Chloe blushed, embarrassed, but Valentina didn't let go of her hand. "You don't gotta pretend with me, girlfriend."

Chloe nodded and tried to talk, but she was crying too hard to get any words out. Valentina just held her hand and waited until the wave of emotion passed. Valentina handed her a napkin and Chloe blew and wiped her nose.

"Thank you," she whispered.

"It's okay. I've been there. And it's a shitty place to be."

"I don't even know how I got here."

"Sure you do."

"I don't."

"Word gets around. You're on a 5150. Just like me."

"But I didn't try to kill myself."

"It's nothing to be ashamed of and the sooner you deal with it, the better off you're gonna be."

Chloe shook her head. "No, it wasn't like that. *I'm* not like that. Why doesn't anyone believe me?"

"Because denial ain't just a river in Egypt. It's hard to admit. It's humiliating."

Chloe stared at her tray of food and felt like throwing up. "I can't eat."

"The food sucks, but if you don't eat, they'll notice."

"Who'll notice?"

"The nurses. The doctors. They got a point system going and if you want out, you gotta play their game."

"What if I don't want out?"

"Then you really are cray cray."

"James Flynn believes me."

"Yeah, I wouldn't brag about that, chica."

"Why? Because he's crazy?"

"Because he was probably just hitting on ya."

"Seriously?"

"Don't take it personally. He hits on everybody. Every female in here. And not just the young ones. Anybody with a vagina. From twenty-five to eighty-five. Nothing better than watching him light up those old ladies."

Chloe smiled at that. "That's kind of sweet."

"Yeah, they go crazy for him."

Chloe blushed and smiled, lowered her voice, and leaned in. "He *is* kind of hot."

"I know, right? That's part of why he gets a pass. That and that fact that he doesn't push it. You aren't into it; he backs right off. Too bad he's such a nut."

"Why's he in here anyway?"

"Maybe you should ask him."

Chloe looked up to see Flynn coming right towards them. Two other patients followed; the big black kid who wouldn't shut up about Tupac Shakur, and some skinny-looking geezer with big plastic glasses and a mop of curly white hair.

Flynn set down his tray and sat on Chloe's right. "Good morning! I see you've met Valentina. I hope you don't mind if we join you?"

"Not at all," Chloe said.

The other two patients sat on either side of Valentina, crowding her a little, which clearly irritated her.

Flynn pointed to the big black kid. "I believe you already met Ty. And this other fine gentleman is Q. Q meet Chloe."

Q offered Chloe a cursory nod, his eyes huge behind the thick lenses of his plastic glasses.

"Good to meet you, Mr. Q," Chloe said.

"Not Mr. Q," Flynn corrected. "Just Q. It's a designation. More of a job title than a name."

Chloe marveled at the mound of food on Ty's plate. Pancakes swimming in syrup, scrambled eggs, bacon, sausage, a pile of home fries, and two buttermilk biscuits covered in white gravy. Flynn's plate, on the other hand, held two slices of bacon, a single hard-boiled egg, and one slice of toast with jam.

"Do you know what Q stands for?" Flynn asked.

"I do not." Chloe looked across the table to see Valentina smirking at her.

"Quartermaster. He's the head of Q branch. As such, he creates all our high-tech equipment and weaponry. Jet packs. Gyrocopters. Cigarette missiles. Submarine cars."

Chloe wasn't sure how to respond to that. "Wow... that's... wow."

Valentina grinned and tried not to laugh.

Oblivious to Valentina's reaction, Flynn continued. "Q, can you tell us what you've been working on lately?"

"Something called a cortical modem." Q carefully cut off a piece of waffle and dipped it in syrup. "Basically, it's a direct neural interface that connects a computer with a human brain."

"Bullshit," Ty mumbled through a mouthful of scrambled eggs.

"Yes, I agree it sounds preposterous, but that's what's Q does," Flynn explained. "He makes the impossible possible. What else, Q?"

Q chewed and swallowed his bite of waffle before continuing. "A psychoactive microbe that allows for remote control of someone's brain using transcranial pulsed ultrasound."

"Mind control?"

"In a manner of speaking."

Ty shook his head. "Can't believe you're listening to this fool."

"There are more things in heaven and earth, Horatio, than are dreamt of in your philosophy," Flynn replied.

"Who the hell's Horatio?" Ty asked.

"He's in Hamlet," Chloe said.

"Exactly right!" Flynn smiled with delight. "You really are an actress, aren't you?"

Chloe beamed.

Valentina laughed.

Q pulled a tiny can of Binaca Blast breath spray out of his pocket and held it up for everyone to see. "This is my latest innovation."

"Breath spray?" Chloe asked.

"Truth Spray. It blocks neural receptors, reduces inhibitions, and creates a state of extreme suggestibility."

Ty swallowed his last bite of pancake. "Old man, you're crazy."

Q looked at Ty with irritation, held the Binaca blast up to his face, and sprayed.

Ty screamed, clawing at his eyes. "Oh, shit! What the hell!"

Valentina scraped back her chair to get out of the way as Ty flailed around.

"Tell me the truth, Ty!" Q shouted.

"Truth is I'm gonna kick your motherloving ass!" Ty lurched to his feet blind, bumping the table, knocking every drink on its side. Q sprayed Ty right in the eyes again and Ty howled like a banshee. "Ah, Jesus!"

Flynn snatched the Binaca Blast out of Q's hand before he could spray Ty a third time. A blind Ty lunged for Q, tripped over Valentina's chair, and smacked face-first into the linoleum. Flynn vaulted over the table and held him down, holding him tight while Q scurried to safety.

"Gonna kill that asshole!" Ty screamed.

Sancho rushed over to help Flynn restrain him. Not an easy task as Ty weighed more than both of them put together. "What the heck's going on here?" Sancho demanded. "Why's Ty going after Quentin?"

"A misunderstanding," Flynn explained.

"What's that minty smell?"

"That's me, man! That's me!" Ty shouted, tears streaming down his face.

"Breathe, Ty, breathe!" Flynn instructed.

"Let me go!"

"First, you calm down," Sancho said.

"I'm fine! I'm fine!" Ty tried to pull himself free. "I'm good! Let me go! *Let me go!*"

"You sure?" Flynn asked.

"I'm good."

"You promise?"

Ty took a big breath and let it out. He dropped his shoulders and lowered the volume on his voice, consciously calming himself. "I promise. *I promise.*"

"Okay, I'm going to let you go."

"Good. Okay. Thank you."

Flynn released Ty's beefy arm and he immediately wrenched himself free from Sancho and raced out of the cafeteria after Q.

CHAPTER SEVEN

The man on the radio sang with a Texas twang about girls looking prettier at closing time. A woman sat curled in the front passenger seat, her head turned to one side, asleep. From where he sat in the back he could only see the side of the woman's face. He wore Keds and his little legs dangled off the edge of his seat. In his hands he held a Dodger blue baseball cap. The driver had two fingers on the wheel as his head slowly dipped. Bright lights blazed through the windshield. The man snapped awake and wrenched the wheel to the right, spinning it hard, hand over hand. Tires squealed and skidded. The woman awoke in a panic, blinded by the light. She screamed, terrified.

Flynn awoke with a start as the scream from the dream melded with another equally terrified shriek. Still in a fog, he threw off the covers and dropped his feet to the floor. Early morning light filtered through the dusty window into the room he shared with Q. The old man snored away, oblivious to the alarming screams echoing down the hallway.

Flynn threw on a navy polo and some chinos, slipped his feet into well-worn Ferragamo loafers, and hurried into the corridor. At the far end, Barker and O'Malley dragged Chloe around the corner. He chased after them, adrenaline now surging through his bloodstream. He collided with Ty as he stepped out into the hall to see what all the commotion was about. Big as he was, Flynn just bounced off him.

"Who the hell's yelling?" Ty shouted as Flynn maneuvered around him and sprinted after Chloe. He rounded a corner, dodged a surprised ninety-two-year-old Doris Frawley, bolted through the uninhabited activity room, and hurried past the empty cafeteria.

Flynn's loafers slid on the linoleum as he rounded one last corner just as the security door at the far end of the corridor slammed shut. The heavy door muffled the sound of Chloe's screams.

Through the wired glass window, O'Malley and Barker handed a struggling and silently screaming Chloe to two large men in dark suits. A petite woman, wearing a bright red power suit, stood at the reception counter next to Nurse Durkin and filled out paperwork.

Flynn charged ahead, but Sancho came out of nowhere and blocked his path forward. Flynn tried to step around him, but Sancho grabbed his arm.

"Whoa, whoa, take a breath, brother. Chloe's okay."

"Then why is she screaming like a bloody banshee?"

"Because she wants to stay here."

"Then why isn't she?"

"Because her family wants her released."

"Her family?" Flynn looked skeptical.

"Yeah, they sent that lady lawyer to sign her out."

"How do you know that woman was sent by her family?

"Who else would send her?" Sancho asked.

"Who do you think?"

"Dude, I have no idea."

Flynn pushed past Sancho and hurried for the door.

"James, listen to me, man! There's nothing you can do."

Flynn tried the door. Locked. He pounded on the wired glass and Durkin gave him a dirty look.

"Where are they taking her?" Flynn demanded.

Sancho gently tried to pull Flynn off the door. "Another hospital, maybe. Some fancy private treatment center? Who knows? Maybe they're taking her home."

Flynn hammered on the glass. Durkin looked furious. She glowered at Sancho and motioned for him to get Flynn away from the door. Sancho grabbed Flynn around the waist and tried to drag him off, but Flynn was solid muscle and immovable.

"James, come on, man! Durkin's gonna have my ass."

Durkin said something to Barker and O'Malley. They helped the two men in dark suits hold Chloe motionless. Durkin injected her with something. The effect was instantaneous. Her flailing grew weaker and soon she stopped screaming. Her eyes lost focus, her body grew limp. The woman in the red power suit said something to the men in black and they carried Chloe out.

"Durkin is being made a fool!" Flynn shouted, hammering on the glass.

"You're not getting through that door, dude! All you're doing is pissing Durkin off!"

"Exactly!" Flynn agreed and pounded even harder. The petite woman in the red suit glared at Flynn before following her two lackeys through the automatic doors.

Flynn hammered with everything he had. Durkin shouted orders at Barker and O'Malley. They nodded and moved for the security door as Durkin buzzed it open.

Grinning and looking for payback, they rushed Flynn like two tackles trying to sack a quarterback. Flynn stepped to one side to avoid the attack, grabbed Barker by the forearm, and used his momentum against him. He executed a perfect Aikido throw and smashed him into O'Malley. They both crashed into Sancho as Flynn slipped through the door a second before it slammed shut.

Durkin planted her feet wide and held up her hands to block him. Flynn slid on the slippery linoleum like a baseball player heading for home. He shot between her beefy thighs, the top of his head skimming the bottom of her starchy, white nurse's dress. Once past her, he leaped to his feet. She turned, but Flynn was already through the double doors, darting after Chloe and her abductors.

• • •

Chloe wanted to struggle, but she had no control of her body. Whatever Durkin injected her with took the fight right out her. She had no idea who these people were. Not the woman who claimed to be her family's lawyer or the two burly men who held her arms so tight. They dragged her towards a big black Lincoln Navigator SUV. Inside she was screaming, but on the outside she was silent. Numb.

Limp. Paralyzed. They would take her away in the black SUV and no one would ever see her again. This was it. She knew it. She was dead.

The burly man in black on her left suddenly lost his grip as something slammed into him. He hit the ground hard. A dark blue blur shot past and crashed into the other man. He bounced off the SUV and fell to the pavement.

Flynn whispered into Chloe's ear. "I'm getting you out of here."

The woman in red's eyes grew wide at the sight of Flynn. The moment seemed to stretch as time had no meaning in her benumbed condition. The lady lawyer had curly red hair and a middle-aged face taut with Botox. Maybe that's why her eyes were so wide. Or maybe she was just terrified.

The lady handed Flynn her car fob without hesitation.

He opened the passenger door. Chloe's feet left the ground as Flynn lifted her into the shotgun seat. She was grateful, certain she couldn't accomplish that under her own power. He fastened her seatbelt before hurrying to the driver's side and sliding behind the wheel.

Chloe rested her face against the passenger window and watched the burly men in black scramble to get back on their feet. Flynn locked the doors and fired up the engine. One man grabbed onto the door handle as Flynn flattened the gas. He held on for a few feet and fell hard. Bouncing. Rolling. The redheaded woman shouted something as they pulled away. Finally, exhausted from all the activity, Chloe slumped, closed her eyes, and let herself sleep.

· · ·

Flynn squealed out of the car park onto Del Mar Boulevard and made a left on Rosemead. He cut a hard right on Colorado Boulevard and headed east for Santa Anita Racetrack. He wanted to park the big black Navigator in a place no one would find it—a parking lot with thousands of cars. Flynn had found himself in that very car park before on other forays from headquarters. He knew he could easily find another car there to borrow, and that's exactly what he did once the punters arrived.

He wanted something anonymous, and when he saw an elderly horse racing aficionado climb from his silver BMW M5, he figured the old man would be at the track most of the day. Flynn arranged to bump into him, and artfully pickpocketed his keys.

He roused Chloe awake and helped her into the new car. She looked dazed and confused as they pulled out of the car park.

"Where are we?" Chloe looked around.

"Santa Anita."

"Where?"

"Doesn't matter."

"I feel so sleepy."

"Durkin shot you up with something."

"Why was she helping them?"

"She obviously believed that red-haired woman was one of us."

"Us?"

Flynn shook Chloe on the shoulder. "Chloe, look at me. You need to focus."

"I'm trying to." She looked out the window. "Where are you taking me?"

"Somewhere safe. Her Majesty's Secret Service has clearly been infiltrated."

"What are you talking about?"

"The red-haired woman. Did she give you a name?"

"Kesselman."

Flynn nodded. "She must work for Goldhammer."

Chloe rubbed her eyes and tried to focus. "We have to find my brother."

"Agreed. He's likely in danger. Do you know where he might be?"

"The Chinese Theatre."

"On Hollywood Boulevard? Does he work the concession counter?"

"Not exactly," she slurred before slipping into unconsciousness.

CHAPTER EIGHT

Grauman's Chinese Theatre opened in 1927 with the premiere of Cecil B. DeMille's The King of Kings. *The exterior resembles a giant pagoda. Two Ming Dynasty lions guard the main entrance and two gigantic red columns flank a massive Chinese dragon carved from stone. Protected by 40-foot-high walls and copper-topped turrets, the forecourt is home to the cement hand and footprints of Hollywood's greatest stars. Douglas Fairbanks and Mary Pickford were the first, but everyone from Gene Kelly to Jeff Bridges to Robert Downey Jr. have left their mark.* Shane, Breakfast at Tiffany's, Mary Poppins, *and* Star Wars *all had their premieres there. Over four million tourists from all over the world visit the Chinese Theatre every year. Like religious sojourners seeking a sacred experience, they hope to connect with the magic and manufactured memories of the Hollywood dream machine.*

Flynn found a parking spot on Selma a few blocks south of Hollywood Boulevard. He didn't bother feeding the meter or even locking the car.

Chloe seemed less sedated. All the worry about her brother filled her with anxiety. Even with her hair disheveled, her face pale and devoid of makeup, and dressed in a t-shirt and baggy sweatpants, Flynn found her stunningly attractive. There was a steeliness beneath her softness. A determination that Flynn found admirable. Still she appeared disoriented. "Where are we?"

"Two blocks south of Hollywood Boulevard. Not far. Follow me."

Flynn walked the streets of Hollywood before and knew it wasn't the glamorous place most tourists imagined. He couldn't exactly remember when he left London or how or why the Secret Service stationed him in Southern California, but that wasn't surprising. After all, he suffered many traumas in his adventures, physical and psychological. Nearly spun to death in a centrifuge. Poisoned to the point of having to start his own heart with a portable defibrillator. Once he spent fourteen months being tortured and brainwashed in a North Korean prison. They tried to break him and nearly succeeded. Because of that, sometimes he couldn't tell which recollections were real and which were half-remembered nightmares.

He attributed this to PTSD.

When he started as a young officer in the Royal Navy, they called that sort of psychological distress "shell shock" or "battle fatigue" and many saw it as a sign of weakness. Sufferers were sometimes put on trial for desertion and cowardice, and faced a firing squad. Now it seemed better understood, yet part of Flynn still saw the affliction as a personal weakness. Something that had to be pushed down, fought against, and overcome. He couldn't wallow in fear or emotion.

Too many people depended on him.

People like young Chloe, clearly in danger from dark forces who wanted her dead. The same enemies that threatened her, threatened the very integrity of Her Majesty's Secret Service.

As Flynn led Chloe up the filthy sidewalk to Hollywood Boulevard, they passed car parks and seedy apartment houses. The boulevard itself had been gentrified in recent years. Investment reclaimed the main drag and rebuilt the area around the Chinese Theatre, but just two blocks away, the desperate and disenfranchised were barely held at bay.

A wide range of pedestrians packed Hollywood Boulevard—locals, tourists, drunks, addicts, thugs, and runaways. But office workers, shopkeepers, elderly retirees and teenagers playing hooky also walked *The Walk of Fame*. The terrazzo sidewalk was black and shiny with chips of marble, quartz, and granite. Five-pointed brass stars decorated each square and bore the names of actors, directors, musicians, and even fictional characters. Some names were familiar to Flynn. Others were famous decades in the past, lost to another time. Mickey Rooney. Alan Ladd. Tallulah Bankhead. Alvin and the Chipmunks. Walter Matthau. Ernest Borgnine. Boris Karloff.

Flynn noticed Chloe staring at the names as they walked past ticky-tacky tourist shops selling t-shirts and baseball caps, snow globes and other bric-a-brac. They passed Ripley's Believe It or Not, the Egyptian Theater, and the Hollywood Wax Museum before finally crossing Highland Avenue and arriving in front of the Chinese Theatre, now part of the Hollywood and Highland Shopping Center.

• • •

Chloe didn't see her brother, but she did see throngs of tourists. Tyler once told her that fifty million tourists visited Los Angeles every year. She imagined that most of them eventually ended up at the Chinese Theater, walking in the hallowed footprints of Clark Gable and Marilyn Monroe.

No wonder she aspired to be an actress from such a young age. Every star on the *Walk of Fame* was once an ordinary, anonymous person. They came to Hollywood to get noticed, get famous, achieve greatness. Immortality. She too came here to prove to the world that she wasn't just another nobody. She knew the odds of hitting it big as an actress were miniscule. Still, she couldn't shake her dream of being bigger than life.

The glamour of what she thought Hollywood would be collided violently with the reality. The smell of cigarettes, marijuana, body spray, and B.O. assaulted her as she moved through the hot crush of bodies.

Normally, there were many costumed characters standing on the *Walk of Fame* in front of the Chinese Theater. They took tips for pictures. One dollar. Five dollars. Ten dollars. That was how her brother made most of his money. Unlike Chloe, he didn't aspire to be an actor. He had writer/director ambitions. On weekends he worked at a comic book store on Melrose, but during the week he was Captain America.

Chloe didn't see Captain America or many of the other street performers who normally frequented the area. Not fat Spiderman or skinny old Superman. Not shabby Batman or frayed and tattered Elmo. Not tubby Darth Vader or tiny Godzilla. She only saw a plump, middle-aged Wonder Woman and a Cookie Monster.

Wonder Woman posed with a group of smiling Chinese tourists. Once they paid her, Chloe sidled up next to her. "Hey, Jules, have you seen my brother?"

"He went to the memorial."

"Memorial?"

"For Dave. I'm about to head over if you want to come with me."

"What happened to Dave?"

"Heart attack. Died right here on *The Walk of Fame*." She pointed up the sidewalk. "He collapsed right next to Christopher Reeve's star."

"Shit. Really?"

"I wasn't here. Didn't see it. Just heard about it. EMTs came and carted him off, but they said he was probably dead before he reached the hospital."

"Where's the memorial?"

"Mosaic. A local church right up the boulevard."

Chloe searched for Flynn and saw him standing stock still over a pair of hand and footprints. He put his feet over the footprints as he stared rapt at the name signed into the cement. She stepped closer to see what name held his attention so intently.

Sean Connery.

She called to him. "Flynn?"

He looked up, disconcerted and disoriented. "Yes?"

"I know where my brother is."

"Good." He nodded and pulled himself together. "Where?"

"Close. We're going to follow Wonder Woman."

Mosaic was just two blocks away. Thousands in donations had transformed the former night club into a non-denominational house of worship. Jules explained that the pastor at Mosaic built his church to help the homeless (and hopeless) of Hollywood. The junkies. The runaways. The hookers. The costumed characters. The name Mosaic was inspired by the congregation's diversity. Even those broke, broken, and fragmented could come together to create something beautiful.

Chloe followed Wonder Woman inside to a packed sanctuary. Hundreds waited for the start of Dave's memorial. Chloe spotted her brother on the raised platform that served as the stage.

Tyler wore black calf-high boots and red gauntlets, blue tights, and a snug red, white, and blue Spandex top with a silver star on the chest. A soft blue leather helmet covered his head and his mask had a big silver "A" emblazoned across the forehead. Even though he didn't make for a very tall or a very buff Captain America, Tyler carried himself with confidence, chest out, back straight, selling the look as best he could.

Chloe caught his eye and waved. Tyler looked livid and angrily motioned her over. Flynn followed as they moved through all the street performers taking their seats. A diminutive Darth Vader. A threadbare Cat in the Hat. A portly Chewbacca. A not-so-incredible Hulk.

Tyler shouted to Chloe, clearly furious. "What the hell happened to you? I've been worried sick!"

"I'm sorry."

"I filed a missing person's report with the police."

"It wasn't my fault!"

"I thought you were dead!"

"Can we talk about this somewhere more private?"

"Later. Right now, I have a eulogy to do. But I'm not done with you."

"Sorry about your friend."

Tyler's anger faded to sadness at the reminder of why they were there. "He was only fifty-five."

"I didn't know you two were so close."

"You better find a seat."

Chloe nodded. "We'll talk after."

"Damn right we will."

Tyler turned on a boom box sitting on the podium and the theme from the 1978 Superman movie blasted from the speakers. Heroic and rousing, powerful and inspiring, it served as a processional while the last of the costumed characters located their seats.

Chloe and Flynn found chairs in the back behind an elderly Freddie Kruger and a weeping Joker, his tears melting his smeary makeup.

Tyler stood at the lectern and flicked off the boombox. He tapped the microphone to make sure it was on. The *tap, tap, tap* echoed throughout the now silent sanctuary.

Wiping away a tear, he said, "Faster than a speeding bullet. More powerful than a locomotive. Able to leap tall buildings in a single bound. It's Superman! Strange visitor from another planet who came to earth with powers and abilities far beyond those of mortal men. Superman! Who can change the course of mighty rivers! Bend steel in his bare hands! And who, disguised as Dave Merkly, a mild-mannered Superman fan, became the first and greatest costumed hero on Hollywood Boulevard. He inspired us all to fight a never-ending battle for truth, justice, and cold hard cash, which is, in fact, the American way."

The auditorium erupted with ecstatic applause. Not until it died down did Tyler continue.

"Dave was my friend. My teacher. My mentor. He taught me how to be a hero. How to stand on the *Walk of Fame* all day long, keep up my energy and enthusiasm, and give those tourists what they came for. A glimpse of greatness. A connection with their childhood dreams. For them, for all of us, Dave *was* Superman. I remember him telling me how his father never believed in him. How he would slap him around and call him a loser and tell him he would never amount to anything. He told Dave he was nothing and would always be nothing. But Dave proved him wrong, didn't he?

"Like Superman, he came here from another planet—Dayton, Ohio. And after arriving here with nothing, became the greatest, most powerful superhero of all time. Thousands of tourists have posed with him, and his picture hangs on walls and refrigerators and mantels on every continent on Earth. Dave appeared in music videos and on the Jimmy Kimmel Show, in front of an audience of millions. He always said if you're in it to win it, you gotta stick with it. And Dave did. Through good times and bad. And some of those bad times were horrible. Homeless. Broke. Hungry.

"One time they arrested him after a fight with the old Elmo, even though all he was trying to do was help him. He helped us all. Showed us the ropes. Hell, he invented the ropes. He once told me he suffered from social anxiety disorder, but when he put on the costume, he no longer had to be himself. He could be who he wanted to be. He could have super strength. He could fly. He could be invulnerable. Bulletproof. Nothing could touch him. Nothing could hurt him." Tyler hit the button on the boombox and the Superman theme filled the room. His voice broke as he shouted over the music. "Why? Because he was *Superman!*"

CHAPTER NINE

In 1853, Dr. David S. Burbank, a dentist from Waterville, Maine, joined the Great Migration westward and ended up in Pueblo de Los Angeles, the owner of 9200 acres that cost him a little over $9000. He became the largest sheep rancher in Southern California and his ranch house stood where the Warner Brothers backlot stands today. To increase the value of his ranch, he sold the Southern Pacific Railroad a stretch of right-of-way for one dollar. Settlers streamed into California and in 1886 he sold his property to a group of land speculators for $250,000. One year later, the town of Burbank was born.

Chloe told Flynn how to find her and her brother's apartment in Burbank. "It's on Pass Avenue, just up from Warner Brothers."

"Got it." Flynn pulled the silver BMW away from the curb and headed west for Highland.

Chloe then told Tyler where she'd been for the last three days. He sat next to her in the back seat and listened with a mixture of shock, sadness, and anger as she told him the tale of her involuntary commitment.

"Goddamn Goldhammer."

"He's a monster."

"Jesus Christ!" Tyler wiped away an angry tear and pointed at Flynn. "So this guy saved your life?"

"He got me out of there."

Tyler caught a glimpse of Flynn's steely eyes in the rear-view mirror. "Thank you for saving her."

"No thanks are necessary. Just doing my job."

Tyler looked back at Chloe and leaned in close. "So who is he? Some kind of doctor?"

"He's a patient."

It took a moment for Tyler to process that. "At the mental hospital?"

"That's the cover," Flynn explained.

"Cover?"

"It's not a real hospital."

"It's not?"

"No."

"What is it?"

"A field office for Her Majesty's Secret Service."

Tylor nodded and smiled as if that made perfect sense, leaned in close to Chloe and whispered. "Seriously?"'

"He's a little... delusional," she whispered back.

"A little?"

"He was the only one who believed me."

"What are you two whispering about?" Flynn eyed them in the rear-view mirror.

"Brother and sister stuff," Chloe said.

Tyler looked distraught. "This is all my fault."

Chloe squeezed Tyler's hand. "It's not on you."

"I couldn't let it go. I had to keep pushing. Make that asshole pay."

"You were just trying to protect me."

"Instead, I almost got you killed."

"Well, it's over now."

"How is this over? He tried to kill you. What if he tries again?"

"We'll leave L.A. We'll disappear."

"From someone like Goldhammer?" Flynn interjected. He merged the BMW onto the Hollywood Freeway. "With all his vast resources? I don't think so."

"Are you *trying* to scare me?"

"We need to expose him," Tyler said.

"Expose him?"

"It's the only way. Make you so high profile he can't touch you. He has this huge merger in the works with Globalcom. Some sort of leveraged buyout. The FTC has to approve it, and any bad publicity might sink it."

"So, you wanna go to the press?" Chloe sounded skeptical. "He has powerful friends. People who own newspaper chains and TV networks. What makes you think the press will go after him?"

"I'm not suggesting the L.A. Times or CNN."

"Where then?"

"I have that friend at the L.A Weekly."

"Jenna? Isn't she a restaurant reviewer?"

"Yeah, but she has an MA in journalism."

"Who's going to believe the L.A. Weekly?"

"If the L.A. Weekly tells the world what happened to you, it'll get posted on Twitter and picked up by Perez Hilton and TMZ. Once it goes viral, the major news outlets won't be able to ignore it."

Chloe caught Flynn's eye in the rear-view mirror. He nodded. "Normally, I'm not one for pussyfooting around, but going after a man like Goldhammer directly could prove difficult. What your brother's suggesting might be the best route in the short run. Goldhammer's friends in high places may abandon him if we show him for what he is."

"A sexual predator?" Chloe asked.

"And a cowardly and gormless wanker."

• • •

Ten minutes later Flynn parked the silver BMW across the street from an eight-unit, two story blue stucco apartment building. He looked up and down the street, searching for any possible threat.

"Jesus, I'm exhausted. I can't wait to get out of this outfit." Tyler pulled at the spandex clinging to his chest.

"Me too." Chloe sighed. "I really need a shower."

"You'll have to wait just a bit longer." Flynn climbed from the car. "They could be watching the place."

"Who?" Tyler asked.

"Goldhammer's men, of course. Toss me your keys and I'll do a quick reconnoiter."

"Seriously?" Tyler whined.

"Better safe than sorry." Flynn held out his hand.

Tyler handed them over. "It's apartment four on the second floor."

Flynn slammed the car door, waited for traffic to pass, and crossed the street. The apartment house was a typical 1970s stucco monstrosity. Flynn quickly made his way up a cement staircase to the second floor. The door to apartment four appeared to be ajar. He stood to one side, his back against the blue stucco, and gingerly pushed opened the door with his foot. He waited and listened. Nothing.

He peeked through and found the dingy, one-bedroom apartment turned upside down. A disemboweled futon lay next to a slashed and shredded bean bag chair. Tufts of white cotton, shredded foam, and polystyrene covered the floor. Every drawer and closet hung open. Clothes and papers, magazines and torn apart books lay scattered about. What were they looking for? Clearly, Chloe neglected to mention what it was she stole from Goldhammer. Did they find it here? Or did she still have it hidden about her person?

Flynn headed back to the second-floor landing, caught Chloe's eye in the car below and beckoned them up. They both climbed from the Bimmer just as a large black Lincoln Navigator screeched to a stop, nearly running them both over. Out jumped four dangerous men in dark suits: swarthy, wiry, clean-shaven, and highly trained.

If they were surprised to see Chloe guarded by Captain America, they gave no indication. Tyler stepped forward and one of them kneed him in the groin. As Tyler grabbed his injured gonads and doubled over in pain, his assailant followed the knee strike with an elbow to the back of the head.

Flynn charged down the stairs and into the street, right into the path of a speeding food truck.

The surprised driver of the *Buddha Belly* truck swerved and took out two of the operatives in black before crashing into the Navigator.

The two operatives still standing turned to Flynn. They stepped over Tyler writhing on the ground and drew their weapons. Incapacitated as he was, Tyler had the wherewithal to grab one of his attackers by the ankle as Flynn ducked behind the *Buddha Belly* truck.

Chloe crouched behind the BMW, her eyes wide with terror.

"Give it up, man," one of the operatives shouted. "We don't want to hurt you. We're just here for the girl!"

"The girl isn't going anywhere," Flynn replied, noting their Israeli accents.

"Get that *ben zona!*" the other operative said.

They tried to flank him by going around both sides of the *Buddha Belly* truck, but Flynn opened the driver's side door and climbed inside. The Asian man driving jumped into the passenger seat and then out the door, running off down the street.

The operatives followed Flynn inside the truck and chased him into the back-kitchen area. Flynn waited, popped up, and used a plastic squeeze bottle to shoot a stream of Huy Fong Hot Chili sauce directly into their eyes. They screamed and dropped their guns and clawed at their burning eyeballs as Flynn pushed past and scooped up both Glocks in the process.

Out on the street, the other two operatives were back on their feet, waiting outside the rear door for their friends. Instead, Flynn, looking unflappable, held a Glock on each of them.

"Guns on the ground. Now!"

They complied.

"Chloe! Tyler! Back in the car."

As Chloe and Tyler climbed back in, Flynn shot out the tires of the Navigator. The operatives ran for cover. Flynn jumped in the driver's seat, fired up the BMW, and hit the gas.

Flynn watched as their assailants receded in the rear-view mirror. "Are you hurt?"

Chloe shook her head. "No."

His Captain America mask askew, Tyler looked at Flynn with one eye. "What the hell was that?"

"That was him," Chloe said, her face flushed, her heart racing. "The tall one! He was the one who roofied me."

Tyler looked back out the rear window even though there was nothing to see.

"They were looking for something." Flynn caught Chloe's gaze. "They tossed your apartment."

"Looking for what?" Chloe asked.

"You tell me."

"How should I know what they were looking for?"

"Obviously, they believe you took something valuable from Goldhammer."

"I didn't take anything!"

"Jesus Christ," Tyler muttered. "Maybe they were looking for your iPhone."

"Because you told them I took a video!"

"Are you sure you didn't take anything else?" Flynn asked.

"I didn't take anything!" Angry tears filled Choe's eyes.

"So, what do we do now?" Tyler muttered.

"Now we find Tyler's friend. The one who works for the L.A. Weekly."

CHAPTER TEN

In 1949, the Communist Party took power in China, the Soviet Union detonated its first atomic bomb, and Death of Salesman won the Pulitzer Prize. That same year, used car salesman Norm Roybark opened the first Norms diner near the corner of Sunset and Vine in Hollywood. Eight years later, Norm opened another Norms on La Cienega. This one featured a brightly colored futuristic architectural style. Rhythm guitarist for the Go-Go's, Jane Wiedlin, worked at that Norms in the late '70s. To avoid freaking out the elderly Jewish diners from the Fairfax district who frequented the restaurant, she often wore a dark wig to cover her cobalt blue hair.

Chloe ordered a veggie omelet. Tyler went for the Belgian Waffle. Flynn asked for black coffee, bacon, two scrambled eggs, and whole wheat toast with marmalade. At 10:00 a.m. Norms was still surprisingly busy. The clientele ran the gamut from barely awake alt-rockers to cops and truck drivers to unemployed screenwriters typing away on laptops.

As they waited for Tyler's journalist friend to arrive, Chloe commented on Flynn's beverage of choice. "You don't drink tea?"

"I'd rather drink a cup of mud. It's one of the main reasons for the downfall of the British empire."

"Seriously?"

"It's nasty swill and I avoid it at all costs."

Tyler pointed towards the door. "There she is."

Chloe hadn't seen Tyler's friend for a few weeks. A fireplug of a girl full of energy, fueled by espresso and anger at the status quo, Jenna moved fast and with purpose; her black leather ankle boots clip-clopped across the linoleum. She wore a distressed khaki jacket and ripped and faded jeans. Her black t-shirt displayed a Tree of Life symbol and her curly dark hair had streaks of premature gray.

Tyler had met Jenna at U of W's campus LGBT center in Kenosha. They immediately bonded and reunited here in Los Angeles soon after Chloe and Tyler arrived. Chloe knew Jenna had a crush on her, and Tyler thought it was hilarious how Jenna always asked Chloe to join them on their outings. That dynamic kept things between them awkward, but Chloe could handle that. Plenty of guys also mooned over her with unrequited crushes.

Jenna smiled at Chloe and offered her a shy wave.

Chloe smiled back and saw Tyler give her a wry look. Jenna sat next to Tyler, directly across from Chloe. She eyed Flynn with curiosity. "Who's this?"

"I'm James." Flynn reached across the table to shake her hand. Jenna shook, but Chloe detected irritation and jealousy.

Jenna looked sideways at Tyler, taking in his Captain America costume. "Do you wear that stupid outfit everywhere?" She then looked back at Chloe and took in her ratty sweats and t-shirt, messy hair and makeup free face. "Must be some crazy shit going down if you're walking around in public dressed like that."

After Jenna ordered flapjacks, Tyler and Chloe explained the situation with Goldhammer. Flynn randomly inserted the odd comment and bizarre assertion as Jenna struggled to take it all in. Jenna's pancakes arrived and she doused them in syrup, cut them into squares, and began pounding them down. Between bites, she looked at Flynn. "So, you're a mental patient?"

"Actually, no, that's just my cover."

"For what?"

"For my Double-0 status at Her Majesty's Secret Service."

Jenna nodded, took that in, looked sideways at Tyler, before returning her gaze to Flynn. "Is Chloe a Double-0 too?"

"No, but she does work for the service and was captured by our enemies. They tortured and brainwashed her, and even though we managed to get her back, I fear they may have infiltrated our organization."

Jenna was trying not to smile. "And why's that?"

"They tried to kidnap her before she could tell us what it is she knows."

Jenna gave Tyler a long look as she slowly chewed her pancakes.

Chloe patted Flynn's hand. "James is the only reason I'm here. If not for him, I don't know where I'd be."

"As weird as he is, Flynn's a good dude," Tyler added.

Jenna nodded. "Goldhammer has a history of this kind of perverted shit. There's been all kinds of rumors over the years, but nothing's ever stuck. He has a legion of lawyers and either sues his accusers into bankruptcy or pays them off and makes them sign an NDA. Plus, he's part owner of this private security outfit. Black Star. It's run by former Mossad operatives."

"Mossad?" Tyler asked.

"The Israeli Institute for Intelligence and Special Operations," Flynn said. "Possibly the most dangerously effective intelligence agency in the world. It's second in size only to the CIA. They collect intelligence and execute counterterrorism operations around the world. It is exempt from the constitutional laws of the state of Israel, and its director answers only to the Prime Minister. There are various units within the organization and I've worked with many of them. *Metsada's* purview is sabotage. *Kidon* belongs to the Caesarea department and they are master assassins. More dangerous than SMERSH."

Jenna raised an eyebrow. "Smoosh?"

"SMERSH. Soviet Counter Intelligence," Flynn explained.

"Anyway"—Jenna gave Tyler another pointed look— "Goldhammer uses Black Star to investigate and discredit his enemies. Journalists. Accusers. Anyone who gets in his way. They compile psychological profiles focused on their personal and sexual histories. They use threats and coercion, and even go undercover to manipulate and create situations for blackmail."

"Like that asshole who roofied me," Chloe said.

"Exactly," Jenna said.

"I just saw him outside our apartment. He had a gun. He tried to grab me. If not for Flynn..."

"Too bad we couldn't capture him." Flynn pulled out the tiny can of Binaca Blast. "I would have used this on him."

"Breath spray?"

"Truth spray."

Jenna looked at Tyler and rolled her eyes. Chloe reached out and grabbed Jenna's hand. "So, can you do this? Write about what happened to me?"

Jenna looked at Chloe's hand on top of hers and then into Chloe's eyes. "I can, but I'd feel better if you had some solid proof. Tyler tweeted that you secretly taped the whole thing on your iPhone. Is that true?"

"No."

"That was bullshit?"

"It was a rage tweet. I was trying to get a rise out of him." Tyler hung his head.

"Shit. So, you have nothing?"

"We have this." Flynn produced a black wallet and plopped it on the table. "I took it off one of the men who attacked us."

Tyler laughed. "When did you have time to do that?"

"Around the time I scooped up his gun." Flynn held up the Glock and Jenna nearly jumped out of her skin. Tyler pushed the gun down into Flynn's lap, but not before the elderly couple at the next table saw him brandishing it.

"You gotta get rid of that," Tyler said.

"I think not." Flynn slid the weapon back into his belt. "Those Black Star operatives are well-armed and we need to be able to defend ourselves."

Chloe opened the wallet and looked over the man's credit cards. He had both a California and Israeli driver's license. She also found a picture ID from Black Star and set it on the table. "How's this for proof?"

Tyler picked up the card. "Yosef Ohana. Is this the guy who roofied you?"

Chloe studied the card. "Yep."

"Looks like Ohana lives in downtown L.A," Tyler tapped the edge of the card on the table.

Flynn nodded. "Part of Black Star's stateside contingent. They have a satellite office in Los Angeles."

Tyler handed the card to Jenna. "Is this enough evidence to get started on an article?"

"I can write it, but I can't guarantee my editor will publish it. If it turns out he doesn't have the balls, I'll post it on my blog."

Chloe raised an eyebrow. "Your blog?"

"I get 20,000 unique visitors a month."

"Aren't they looking for restaurant reviews?"

"Eyeballs are eyeballs." Jenna finished the last of her pancakes. "So, after you got home from Goldhammer's hotel room, you called the police?"

"I did."

"But they didn't do shit," Tyler added. "Said it was her word against his."

"They didn't send you to the hospital for a rape kit?"

Chloe shook her head. "I asked about that, but they said it was too late. I showered as soon as I got home. I couldn't stand his stink on me. I had to get him off me."

"There's no DNA evidence?"

"No, but even if there was, couldn't he just claim it was consensual?"

"He could try, but he has a pattern of this kind of behavior. If we can publicize your case, maybe other women will come forward."

"Where's Goldhammer from?" Flynn asked.

"New Jersey," Jenna replied.

"He's not German?"

"Goldhammer's not even his real name. His real name Goldfelcher."

Tyler laughed at that. "Goldfelcher? No way."

Chloe looked confused. "What am I missing?"

"You don't know what a felcher is?"

"Should I?"

"It's a guy who comes in someone's butthole and then sucks the semen out."

Flynn gagged a little on his coffee. "Excuse me?"

"Look it up in the Urban Dictionary." Tyler shook his head and laughed. "No wonder that asshole changed his name."

Chloe giggled. "Jesus."

Tyler looked at Jenna. "You write something like this, aren't you worried he's going to come after you too?"

"I hope he does. It's hard to make your name in this town. Something like this could put me on the map. Plus, I hate entitled shitheads like him. They think they can take whatever they want. They don't care who they destroy." She squeezed Chloe's hand. "When I think about what he did to you, I want to take Flynn's gun and blow his balls off. But since I can't do that, I'll do the next best thing. Castrate him metaphorically. Maybe once I do, others will step up too."

The waitress came by with the check and Flynn used one of Yosef Ohana's credit cards to pay for their breakfast.

CHAPTER ELEVEN

At its grand opening in 1923, the Biltmore Hotel was the largest hotel west of Chicago. Three thousand movers and shakers celebrated its opening. Cecille B. DeMille, Mary Pickford, and Myrna Loy were among the celebrities who sipped champagne and hobnobbed with the elite of Los Angeles. In 1929, before the stock market took its tumble, Germany's Graf Zeppelin passed over the hotel on its around-the-world trip sponsored by William Randolph Hearst. For a time, the hotel housed the world's largest nightclub, and in the late 1930s, hosted the Academy Awards. After serving as an R&R facility during World War Two, it became famous as the last place anyone ever saw aspiring movie star Elizabeth Short. Dubbed the Black Dahlia, a lady walking her three year old daughter discovered her mangled corpse in Leimert Park. Even though the LAPD interviewed over one hundred and fifty suspects, her murder remains unsolved to this day.

Chloe felt underdressed in the Gallery Bar and Cognac Room at the Biltmore. The lavish watering hole sported hand-painted frescos, high ceilings made of stamped brass, and Venetian glass chandeliers. She sat at the dark granite bar and eyed the marble angels that flanked the tall glass shelves filled with high-end liquor. Chloe sipped one of their signature cocktails, a Black Dahlia, made with citron vodka, Chambord, and a splash of Kahlúa in a martini glass.

Her sweats and t-shirt were gone, replaced by tight black skinnies, a black V-neck top, a light gray cardigan, and suede boots. Still, she looked casual compared to most of the patrons.

She sat next to Flynn as he ordered a martini from Greg, the bartender. "I prefer my martini in a deep champagne goblet."

"As you wish, sir."

"Hold on. Three measures of Gordon's, one of Grey Goose, and a half measure of Kina Lillet. Shake it until ice cold, then add a large thin slice of lemon peel."

"Interesting."

"I like my martinis large and very strong and very cold. Shaken. Not stirred."

When they left Norms, Tyler suggested they stay at a cheap motel he knew about on Western Avenue. But one look at the blocky Roxy Hotel and Flynn raised a skeptical eyebrow.

"You want to stay here?"

"It's sketchy, but that's kind of the point. No one's going to look for us in this anonymous shithole."

"This looks like the sort of place where serial killers torture and murder their victims."

"Exactly."

"We'll catch syphilis from the TV remote if we aren't eaten alive by bed bugs."

Chloe nodded. "He has a point."

"It's all we can afford," Tyler replied.

Flynn shook his head. "I disagree. I believe we should set our sights higher."

"Well, where do you want to stay? The Biltmore?"

"Excellent idea," Flynn replied.

If the Biltmore's front desk clerk was surprised, he didn't show it when Flynn, a frazzled-looking Chloe, and Captain America showed up to check in. Flynn didn't have a reservation or any luggage, but he did have Yosef Ohana's credit cards and driver's license. Flynn didn't look much like him, but he exuded so much confidence and savoir faire, the desk clerk didn't bother to look too closely.

Flynn reserved the VIP Suite; a three thousand square foot, three-bedroom, three-bathroom retreat with a living room, a formal dining room, a library, and a baby grand piano. Floor-to-ceiling windows overlooked Pershing Square below.

Chloe loved it and couldn't believe Flynn had the audacity.

Tyler thought he was crazy. "We're going to stick out like sore thumbs, man."

"Not after we go shopping," Flynn countered.

"Shopping?"

"For new clothes and toiletries."

Chloe laughed at that. "What if Ohana cancels his credit cards?"

"He won't."

"How the hell do you know that?"

"Because he'll want to see where we use them. They'll want to try and track us down."

"Track us down?" Tyler pulled off his Captain America mask. "They can track us down?"

"Yes, but not immediately." Flynn joined Chloe on the couch. "I also booked us into hotels and motels in Santa Monica, Pasadena, Studio City, Laguna Beach, and Del Mar using this very same credit card. It'll take them some time to suss out exactly where we're staying. In the meantime, we can rest up and plan our next moves."

Tyler looked at his sister. "This fucker is crazy."

Chloe grinned and sat back on a sumptuous couch, clearly enjoying her surroundings. "Said the guy dressed like Captain America."

. . .

They each took a long shower, followed by a shopping excursion to the Los Angeles Fashion District. Chloe found a few fashionable yet practical outfits. Flynn picked up a Brioni tuxedo and two slim cut suits, a Zegna in charcoal gray and a black Armani. He also selected a few more casual outfits, including black jeans, a black turtleneck, and a black leather jacket. Tyler, inspired by Flynn's fashion sense, didn't go as formal, but bought a few high-end designer outfits. They enjoyed an elegant dinner at Water Grill across the street from the Biltmore, where Flynn ordered a dozen Kumamoto oysters and Chilean Sea Bass. Tyler went for the Mahi Mahi, and Chloe feasted on Red King Crab.

Sated, happy, and a little tipsy, they stopped at the Gallery Bar and Cognac room for a nightcap. Flynn sat on Chloe's left and Tyler sat on her right. She watched her brother lick the salt off the rim of his margarita.

"Tyler, are you okay?"

"I'm good. I'm great."

"You're also drunk."

"A little bit."

"Maybe you should go to bed?"

"Why? You want a little alone time with James?"

"Don't be stupid."

"Don't *you* be stupid." Tyler leered at Flynn.

"He can hear you, you know."

"I can," Flynn said.

"So what? I got nothing to hide. You're a good-looking man. Do you go both ways?"

Flynn smiled. "Afraid not."

"So, you're strictly straight?"

"I like women, if that's what you're asking."

"Like my sister?"

Flynn contemplated Chloe. "She is quite beautiful."

"She is, isn't she? I mean, look at her."

"Stop it," Chloe said.

"It's true. All my straight friends always fell in love with you."

"And all my girlfriends mooned over you."

"I loved flirting with your friends."

"They loved it too."

"Because they knew I wasn't talking to them just to get into their pants. Unlike most straight dudes." Tyler pointedly looked at Flynn as he unsteadily climbed off his stool. "Do you know this place is haunted?"

"The Biltmore?" Chloe asked.

"Yeah. The ghost of a nurse haunts the second floor, and on the ninth floor there's a little girl ghost who runs up and down the halls." Smiling at Flynn. "Do you believe in ghosts?"

"I believe in what I can see."

"And what do you see?" Tyler asked.

"Someone drunk off their ass."

Tyler nodded and drained the last of his drink. "Which is why I'm going to bed."

"I'll come with." Chloe climbed off her stool. "James, maybe you should get some sleep too."

"I'm going to keep watch for a while. Just in case. You can't be too careful."

Chloe stepped closer and kissed Flynn on the cheek. He smelled so good. Like leather and soap, musk and citrus. She lightly touched his arm. It felt solid as a rock. She knew she shouldn't be attracted to him, but when she looked into his eyes, he seemed so sure of himself. So strong and kind and reassuring. She felt safe with him. "Don't stay up too late."

Flynn nodded and squeezed her hand.

Tyler stumbled off and Chloe followed. She glanced back at Flynn one last time and watched as he sipped his martini and offered the bartender a complimentary nod.

CHAPTER TWELVE

On an expedition to New Spain, Franciscan missionary Juan Crespí discovered a small river coursing through a verdant paradise in the area known as Alta California. In his journal he wrote, "Should a town be needed in this location, this site shall be called Our Lady Queen of Angels." A small pueblo was established in 1781. Jean-Louis Vignes, a French adventurer and vintner driven from Hawaii when Queen Ka'ahumanu banned all alcohol production, settled in Pueblo De Los Angeles and planted cabernet and sauvignon blanc vines on 104 acres. By 1849, he became the largest producer of wine in California. Citrus groves, freight depots and factories followed. The flood of workers led to the founding of Little Tokyo to the west and Chinatown to the north. Today, Los Angeles is the second largest city in the United States. From sixteen thousand souls in 1850 to almost four million today.

Rather than wait for Yosef Ohana to come to them, Flynn decided to turn the tables and take the war to him. The address on his California driver's license was only a few blocks away, which is why Flynn decided to stay at the Biltmore. He finished his vodka martini and turned to leave, catching the eye of a beautiful blonde. He smiled at her and she smiled back. Hers wasn't the only eye Flynn captured as every woman in the room watched with interest and disappointment as he left the Gallery Bar in his slim fit navy blue Zegna suit.

He headed across the ornate lobby, under the high wood-beamed ceilings and crystal chandeliers, past the oak-paneled walls, and through the bronze double doors. After handing the attendant his ticket, he stood at the edge of the circular driveway and waited for the arrival of his stolen silver BMW.

Once behind the wheel, he plugged in Ohana's address and headed for the ex-Mossad agent's Los Angeles residence. Minutes later, Flynn parked his M5 at a parking meter across the street from a sleek residential tower. He checked the address on Ohana's license and matched it to the address on the gleaming 33-story cobalt blue apartment complex. After locking his car, he waited for the traffic to slow and hurried across the street.

He looked through the lobby windows to see a uniformed security guard standing sentry just inside the sliding hydraulic doors. Another guard sat on a stool by the elevators. Behind the reception desk, a frowning, officious-looking concierge loomed.

A zaftig thirty-something redhead wearing black leggings, a maroon sweater, and flip flops walked outside tethered to a tiny Pomeranian. The tiny, fluffy animal sniffed the base of a street lamp as her owner looked on.

"Let's go, Winky. What's the problem?" Her voice was raspy and Flynn detected a New York accent. "What are you waiting for? Poop already!" The little dog just stared up at her. Irritated, she pulled out a cigarette and planted it between her lips. Next, she patted her pockets, looking for matches or a lighter. "Shit," she mumbled.

An instant later Flynn startled her by flicking the spark wheel of his battered, gun-metal gray vintage Ronson. Cupping the flame, he lit her cigarette. This unexpected chivalry startled her and she stumbled back, bumping into her Pomeranian, who proceeded to bark. The woman seemed fearful at first, but Flynn's charming smile disarmed her.

"Sorry. I didn't mean to startle you."

"No worries. You just kind of came out of nowhere."

"I do apologize."

"No apology necessary. I guess I'm not used to guys in L.A. being so, you know, gallant."

"I detect a New York accent."

"Guilty. I'm from Brooklyn originally. Been here a year now."

"How do you like it?"

"Weather's nice."

"Indeed. I'm a recent transplant myself."

"No shit. I noticed. I like the accent. Very posh."

"I'm looking for an apartment and I was thinking that this place might just be perfect."

"It's not Downton Abbey, but it's not bad."

"I have a friend who lives here and he was going to show me around."

"A girlfriend?"

"No, just a friend. At the moment I'm as single as can be."

She took that in and put out her hand. "I'm Michelle."

"James." Flynn took her hand and kissed it. She just about swooned. He squatted down near the Pomeranian and scratched the top of its head. "And who is this adorable little fluffball?"

"Winky." Winky sniffed Flynn's hand and Flynn scratched her under the chin. "Wow, she's usually not that friendly. Especially to men." Winky looked up at Flynn and proceeded to poop. "Finally," Michelle said.

She picked up Winky's mess with a little plastic bag, tied it up, and headed back through the hydraulic doors. Flynn continued to talk to Michelle as they walked through the modern elegant lobby with its polished marble floors and light gray granite walls and columns. A long gas fireplace burned with a completely gratuitous flame, as fireplaces were hardly a necessity in the Southern California climate.

Flynn continued to converse with Michelle as he followed her to the lift. "Women from New York and London are very different than those you meet in Los Angeles."

"How so?"

"They're grounded. More authentic. Less concerned with appearances. More concerned with what's real."

"That's true of the men too," Michelle said.

"So, you're not seeing anyone here in L.A. at the moment?"

"I go out now and then, but the guys here are either self-involved assholes or just plain insane. The one time I did get serious, the son of a bitch ghosted me." Michelle gave Winky a tug to get him into the elevator.

Flynn followed her inside. "Some men are intimidated by a woman who knows what she wants and isn't afraid to ask for it."

"I just don't like all the bullshit."

"I know exactly what you mean, Michelle." Flynn saw the security guard looking at him as the elevator doors closed.

"What floor's your friend on?" Michelle asked.

"The top one."

"The penthouse?"

"Apparently, he does quite well for himself."

"What business is he in?"

"He does what I do. He's sort of a… problem solver."

"Like a corporate consultant?"

"Something like that. How are the amenities here?"

"Unbelievable. There's a gym. A yoga studio. A club room. A rooftop pool and outdoor lounge with barbecue grills. It's pretty nice."

The lift stopped at the tenth floor and Flynn held the door, but Michelle hesitated and said, "Since you're new in town, I was thinking maybe you'd like to get together for coffee or something sometime."

"A woman who knows what she wants and isn't afraid to ask for it."

Michelle blushed and grinned. "If you're interested."

"Why wouldn't I be?" Flynn said.

She blushed deeper. "I'm in apartment 1005."

"1005. I won't forget."

"Oh, shit. You probably should have gone to reception first. My fob won't take you to the penthouse."

"Will it take me to that rooftop pool? Because I can tell my friend to meet me there."

"That'll work." Michelle put her fob over the sensor and hit the button for the rooftop pool.

Flynn bent down and petted Winky on the head. "Good to meet you, Winky."

Winky made a low grumbling sound and Michelle laughed. "Good to meet you too, James."

"Likewise," Flynn replied.

Flynn could tell Michelle didn't want the elevator doors to close, but finally she let go and Flynn rode the lift to the rooftop.

He found an outdoor lounge with a luminous blue swimming pool, decorative planters, cabanas, canvas umbrellas, and multiple fire pits surrounded by outdoor sofas. The lights of downtown L.A. blazed in all directions.

An apartment tower with wide balconies rose above the pool area. At the top, Flynn could see what he assumed was the penthouse. The sounds of the city surrounded him. Traffic and beeping horns, drunken shouts, and distant sirens. Late as it was, a few of the luxury apartments were dark, but most were not.

Flynn quickly scaled the gray granite I, caught the upper edge, and pulled himself up. Once on top, he used the architectural window details to make his way to the lowest balcony. Leaping atop a glass balustrade, he clambered higher, jumping, and climbing from balcony to balcony, muscling his way up to the top. Exhausted and nearly spent, Flynn finally arrived at the glass balustrade enclosing the much larger penthouse balcony.

Climbing up and over, he dropped down and stayed still, frozen in place. A few lights glowed inside the apartment, but Flynn didn't see anyone walking about. He checked the sliding glass door for alarm system sensors, but found nothing. The door was unlocked and slid open silently. Apparently, Ohana didn't expect a threat from this direction.

Flynn crept inside, trying not to make a sound. He stopped. Listened. Looked around. Dark gray area rugs covered the hardwood floors. The walls were gray as well and devoid of art. All the kitchen appliances were stainless steel, as were the sconces and other lighting fixtures. The floor-to-ceiling windows in the living room offered a striking view of the city.

Flynn searched the apartment, looking through cabinets, closets, and drawers. A hall closet housed an arsenal, most of which was standard issue for Shayetet 13, a highly decorated special ops unit of the Israeli Defense Force. With all his downtime at headquarters, Flynn had researched most of the world's elite units and knew what weaponry each relied on. He didn't take everything in the closet, but he did take the Ari B'Lilah combat knife, the Benelli semi-automatic combat shotgun, the Bullpup assault rifle, and extra ammo for the

Glock 19 he'd already nicked. While checking out the night vision goggles, a suspicious thud reverberated on the other side of the apartment.

Putting the larger weapons down, he made his way up a hallway and followed the source of the sound. Finding a closed door, he put his ear up to it—running water and tuneless whistling.

Whoever was washing shut off the water. The shower door squeaked and the tuneless whistling returned as the person on the other side of the door dried themselves. The doorknob rattled. Flynn ducked into a nearby bedroom just in time. Heavy footsteps approached. Flynn held the Glock ready as a hand reached inside the room and fumbled for a light switch. A distant cell phone rang and the person hurried back down the hall in the other direction.

Flynn crept from the bedroom and down the hall and listened as Ohana answered his cell phone. "Yeah?" After a moment of silence Ohana responded, his voice urgent and tense. "Where?" He listened again and then said with some surprise. "The Biltmore's only three blocks from here." Ohana quickly cut off whoever he was talking to. "Right, right, right, well, I'm the closest. No, no, I'll wait for backup. But hurry your ass over there." It was clear he wanted to hang up, but the person he conversed with apparently wouldn't shut up. "Okay, okay! I'm going!"

Flynn waited for Ohana to come back to the bedroom, but he didn't. So Flynn stepped around the corner to see him staring at the open closet door and the Benelli on the floor. Ohana was totally naked and powerfully built, hairy and muscular with broad shoulders.

"Mr. Ohana?"

Ohana's closely cropped hair matched his beard. He didn't seem all that surprised to see someone pointing a gun at him. "You?"

"Back away from the Benelli please."

"How the hell did you get in here?"

"What difference does that make now?"

He took a step towards Flynn. "You're that *manyak* mental patient."

"Move and I will put you down like a rabid dog."

Ohana offered Flynn a friendly smile. "Come on, man. Don't be crazy."

"I have a license to kill and I will not hesitate to use it."

Ohana raised his hands. "Whoa, whoa, whoa, nobody has to get hurt here."

"I agree. Tell me what I need to know and no one will."

"Can I at least put some clothes on?"

"You can cover your body once you bare your soul."

"Brother, I don't know who you think I am, but—"

"What does Chloe have that Goldhammer wants?"

"What?"

"You heard me. What is he after? Is it the video? Or did she take something from him even more valuable?"

"Who's Chloe?"

The Glock boomed and Flynn put a bullet in the floor inches from Ohana's naked foot.

"Hey, hey, what the hell?"

"Get on the ground, face down, spread eagle."

"*What?*"

"Do it!"

"Fine! *Fine!* Just don't shoot me." He kneeled down and then lay flat on the floor in front of Flynn.

"How many are on their way to the Biltmore."

"On their way where?"

"*How many?*"

Ohana lifted up his head and looked Flynn hard in the eye. "Too many for you to—"

The Glock boomed and Flynn put another bullet in the floor, this one nicking Ohana's left ear. "Ow! *Mamzer!* You shot off my damn ear!"

"How soon will they get there?"

Ohana's intercom buzzed and Flynn turned at the sound. Ohana grabbed the edge of the area rug and pulled it out from under him.

The gun boomed as Flynn fell back, his head bouncing off the hardwood floor. The naked Israeli jumped on top of him. Flynn fought back, but the ex-Mossad agent knew how to grapple. He had both hands on the Glock and tried to wrench it away. Flynn struggled to hold on as the Israeli kneed him in the groin and then pressed his forearm into his throat. The world faded as Flynn's brain screamed for blood and oxygen.

Ohana wrestled the gun away and held it to Flynn's head, but before he could pull the trigger, Flynn grabbed the barrel and twisted it around. The gun boomed. A bullet grazed Ohana's shoulder. Flynn drove his knee into the Israeli's groin before headbutting him in the nose.

Ohana rolled off him and staggered to his feet. Flynn scrambled up. The Israeli raised his weapon. Flynn executed a near perfect inside crescent kick, slapping the Glock from Ohana's hand. It flew across the room and crashed through the sliding glass window, bouncing off the balustrade before landing back on the balcony.

The naked Israeli leaped over his coffee table and couch and ran across the broken glass to snatch up the gun. He turned to aim it. Flynn caught him square in the chest with a flying side kick. The Israeli fired and missed as he toppled backwards over the railing and plummeted into the bushes below. Flynn looked over the edge and saw no movement.

He could taste blood in his mouth as he hurried back through the apartment. Flynn put the Benelli and the Bullpup in a duffel bag and made his way to the front door. The intercom buzzed and Flynn opened the door to find the large security guard from the lobby. The guard immediately put up his hands when he saw the Glock.

Flynn took the guard's sidearm and keys and handcuffed his right arm to his left leg. He left him lying on the hallway floor and pushed the button to summon the elevator. The doors opened almost instantly. Stepping inside, Flynn hit the button for the lobby and watched the guard staring at him helplessly as the elevator doors slowly closed.

CHAPTER THIRTEEN

Chloe opened her eyes to find Flynn sitting on the edge of her bed, watching her sleep. He reached down and cradled her face. Chloe took his hand and placed it on her breast. Flynn gently kissed the corner of her mouth. Chloe pulled him close and kissed him hard. She reached to unbutton his shirt. Suddenly, it was off and so were the rest of his clothes and they were together in each other's arms. His musky masculine scent made her head spin.

"Chloe," he whispered. "Chloe." And then his whispers grew louder and more insistent, and soon they weren't whispers at all. "Chloe? Chloe! *Chloe!*"

Chloe opened her eyes. Flynn stood over her bed, leaning down and shaking her by the shoulder.

"What?"

"Get up. We need to go."

Stunned and disoriented, she searched for her phone on the nightstand. "What time is it?"

"Time to go!"

"Go where?"

Tyler stood just behind him, frightened. "Away from here. They're coming for us."

"Who?"

Flynn pulled her into a sitting position. "Get up and get packed. We don't have much time."

Fear pushed away the fog. She was up and packed within fifteen minutes. Five minutes after that she, Flynn, and Tyler rode the elevator down to the lobby. They rolled their new luggage across the marble floor and towards the front doors.

All three double doors opened at once and six black-suited operatives entered the Biltmore. Flynn motioned for Chloe and Tyler to head back the other way. "Move!" They took off running with their rolling suitcases bumping behind them.

Flynn led them into a ballroom, past an elegant sign on an easel welcoming them to the Katz and Weinblatt wedding reception.

The Emerald Ballroom bustled with hundreds of guests, laughter, loud conversation, and klezmer music. A five-piece band played on an elevated stage in front of a dance floor surrounded by dozens of tables with impressive flower arrangements. The ostentatious wedding reception came complete with a ten tier Disney-themed wedding cake topped with Cinderella and Prince Charming, a chocolate fountain, and a massive ice sculpture featuring two intertwined hearts with the names Josh & Rachel.

After helping a college friend with her nuptials, Chloe became a reluctant expert and knew this shindig cost upwards of $40,000. She stopped to stare and marvel at the stupid extravagance.

Flynn pulled her out of her reverie by pushing her behind one of the travertine columns. She peeked out as three black-suited operatives entered the reception. Flynn scanned the ballroom, searching for a way out.

"There. Over there." He pointed at an exit on the far side of the room. "Stay close."

Flynn moved through the maze of tables and Chloe followed him along with Tyler, hoping against hope the operatives wouldn't see them. Just as they crossed the edge of the dance floor the band began to play Hava Nagila. All the guests leaped to their feet and clapped in time to the music, blocking the way ahead.

The band leader said, "Everyone up! Join Rachel and Josh on the dance floor!" And then he began to sing. "Hava Nagila! Hava Nagila! Hava Nagila! V'nismecha!"

A chunky seventy-something bubbie with bright red hair grabbed Flynn by the wrist and pulled him into the dance line as everyone did the Horah. A pimply faced fifteen-year-old took hold of Chloe and dragged her onto the dance floor as well. She spotted Tyler across the way, shoulder to shoulder in the hora line, kicking his feet to the beat.

The hora line moved around the ballroom, pulling more and more people into the dance, including two of the black-suited Black Star operatives. One of them was Ohana. He caught Chloe's eye across the dance floor. He smiled, his faced scratched up and decorated with a bandage on his forehead. Ohana's smile faded when he saw Flynn, six dancers down the line from Chloe. The operative tried to extricate himself but the old man dancing next to him wouldn't let go of his hand.

The undulating circle surrounded the bride and groom and lifted them into the air on chairs. They laughed and bobbed as the guests holding the chair legs struggled to keep them level. The bride wasn't small. As her weight shifted, the chair nearly toppled.

Flynn leaped into the breach, grabbing one of the legs from an elderly man barely pulling his weight. Ohana made his move, breaking free of the line, reaching under his jacket. Chloe saw a shoulder holster and the black butt of a gun as Ohana moved across the dance floor.

Flynn was reluctant to let go of the chair leg, but he had no choice, and when he reached for his gun, the chair and the bride teetered sideways. Fear and surprise filled the voluptuous bride's face as she fell on top of an even more surprised Ohana. The whole crowd collectively gasped as the bride and the chair smashed Ohana into the portable disco dance floor. No one noticed his gun skitter away or Flynn scoop it up. They were too busy watching the groom leap out of his chair to reach his fallen bride.

The crowd panicked as aunts and bubbies, uncles and zaydies, distant cousins and their plus-ones stampeded in all directions. Flynn, Chloe, and Tyler managed to grab their suitcases and roll past the buffet table.

Chloe saw the other two Black Star operatives moving towards them through the crowd. She glimpsed a gun in one of their hands as they pushed their way through the wedding guests. Flynn shoved the massive ice sculpture of the two intertwined hearts. It crashed to the ground, exploding into a million ice shards that scattered across the dance floor.

Panicked guests slipped and fell on the slick surface. The two operatives were moving too fast to slow their momentum and tripped over all the fallen bodies. Others fell on top of them, trapping them under family and friends of the bride and groom.

Chloe followed Tyler and Flynn out a side door into a corridor that led to the main galleria. They raced across the lobby for the front doors and saw three other operatives exiting another ballroom.

"Run!" Flynn shouted. They did, but so did the operatives. Flynn stopped, turned, and drew his gun, but instead of aiming at the operatives he shot out the chains on one of the massive crystal chandeliers. A single chain snapped and the chandelier fell, catching on the remaining two chains before they broke as well. The chandelier plummeted. The operatives dove for cover. It hit the floor and exploded into nearly as many pieces as the ice sculpture.

Flynn took Chloe's arm and pulled her toward the doors. Tyler followed them outside to the circular driveway. A parking valet approached, but Flynn had no intention of waiting for them to retrieve his stolen M5. Instead, he shot out the tires of a black Lincoln Navigator parked at the curb and wrenched opened the door to a limo parked just in front of it. The driver looked irritated until he saw the gun.

"Out!" Flynn ordered.

The driver jumped out with hands up and backed away.

"Keys!" Flynn demanded and the driver tossed him the key fob.

Chloe noticed the words "Just Married" scrawled across the limo's rear window.

"Get in!" Flynn shouted and they did, bringing their rolling suitcases with them.

Chloe looked out the back window. The Black Star operatives ran outside just as Flynn hit the gas. The cans tied to the back of the limo made a deafening clatter as they rocketed away from the Biltmore.

• • •

Five minutes later, Flynn pulled the limo up behind a Mercedes in the valet line at the Mayan Night Club. The people waiting in line to enter the club smiled and applauded as Tyler and Chloe climbed from the rear of the town car. Everyone assumed they were newlyweds and Flynn used the momentary distraction to snag a fob off the key rack at the valet station. Instead of heading into the club, they searched the nearby car park. Using the fob, they found the Lexus it belonged to and within minutes they were on their way out of downtown L.A.

Flynn parked at the 24-hour Walmart Super Center in Burbank and they spent the rest of the night asleep in the car. All three awoke to the sound of a shrieking baby and barking dog one car over. They used the rest rooms inside Walmart for their morning ablutions, exchanged the stolen Lexus for a stolen Dodge Grand Caravan and breakfasted at the Original Tommy's Famous Hamburgers on San Fernando Road. It was Tyler's suggestion. Flynn was not impressed. The coffee tasted burnt and Flynn opted for the BELT sandwich. Bacon, egg, lettuce, and tomato on whole wheat bread.

Chloe claimed she wasn't hungry and sipped on a diet Coke. Tyler tucked into a Double Chili Cheeseburger. Chloe wouldn't look Flynn in the eye. He reached over to touch her hand and she pulled away. "Are you okay?"

"Okay? You want to know if I'm okay?"

"Obviously, you're not."

"No, I'm not fucking okay."

"It's all right." Tyler tried to calm her.

"All right? Are you kidding me? What are we even doing?"

"Maybe you should eat something," Flynn said.

"Maybe you should shut the hell up."

"I know you're angry."

She started to cry and angrily wiped away her tears, smearing her eye makeup. "We have no money. Nowhere to go."

"Because *you* threw away Ohana's credit cards."

"Because they were using them track us down!"

"Of course. That was all part of the plan."

"Someone's trying to kill me and who do I have to help me? Gay Captain America and a goddamn mental patient." She sobbed and covered her face, her shoulders shaking.

"Come on now, Chloe, you need to buck up." Flynn patted her on the hand. "It's always darkest before the dawn. Keep calm and carry on."

Chloe threw her diet soda in his face.

Flynn looked down at his sopping wet suit, wiped his dripping face, and smiled. Tyler laughed.

"Feel better now?" Flynn asked.

"No!" She threw the empty paper cup at him and it bounced off his head.

Tyler's phone vibrated. "Hello?" He listened and grinned, his eyes growing wide with excitement. "Wait, let me put you on speaker."

"Can you hear me?" It was Jenna, Tyler's reporter friend.

"We can hear you," Tyler said.

"I talked to my editor."

"And?"

"He wants to talk to Chloe."

"Seriously?" Chloe said.

"He's interested, but he has some questions."

"What's his number?"

"No, not on the phone. He wants to meet you in person."

"Why?"

"He wants to look you in the eye and hear your story for himself. Make sure you're not crazy."

"Okay. When does he want to do this?"

"Today. Soon. He thinks it could be a big story, but he wants to make sure you're reliable. Crossing someone like Goldhammer isn't something he takes lightly."

"So, should I bring her into your office?" Flynn asked.

"No, he wants to meet somewhere a little more anonymous. He suggested Huntington Gardens in Pasadena. There's a ceremonial teahouse in the Japanese Garden area. Let's meet there."

"When?"

"As soon as you can get there."

CHAPTER FOURTEEN

Henry Edwards Huntington traveled to San Francisco in 1892 to work for his uncle Collis on the transcontinental railroad. Two years after Collis shuffled off this mortal coil, Henry moved his headquarters to Los Angeles, where he financed and built the electric railway system known as the Red Car. He had extensive landholdings in Southern California, one of which was the former 500-acre San Marino Ranch. In 1913, he married his uncle's widow, Arabella, and together they amassed a massive library and art collection, and built the most impressive botanical gardens on the west coast. They died within three years of each other and in 1928, the fifty-million-dollar art collection, the world class library, and the one-of-a-kind botanical garden were all opened to the public.

Chloe loved the Huntington Gardens. Tyler discovered it six months after their arrival in Los Angeles, and they spent many a day wandering through its lush gardens, perusing the art in Henry Huntington's former mansion and all the galleries built to house his collection. Chloe considered it a refuge. A place to escape filled with nature and beauty, a world away from the sprawl of L.A. It reminded her of a grand English estate. She adored roaming from garden to garden and museum to museum. She hadn't been in months and was grateful to meet Jenna's editor there.

She would tell him everything. Put it all out there. Let him see that she wasn't crazy. But in order to convince him of that, Flynn couldn't be there. If he went off on one of his paranoid rants, the editor would soon know that he was nuttier than a five-pound fruitcake.

Flynn parked near the front of the Huntington's vast outdoor lot, but before he could open the door of their stolen Dodge Caravan, Chloe put her hand on his knee. "I think you should stay here."

"Where?"

"Here."

"In the car?"

"Just to keep an eye out in case someone followed us."

"No one did."

"Just in case."

"I can't let you go in there alone."

"Tyler can come. I'll be fine."

"No, I should be there to talk to Jenna's editor as well. I believe I could add some credence to your story."

"I don't want you to come."

"Don't be ridiculous."

"I appreciate what you've done for me. I really do, but you can't follow me everywhere forever. Eventually, I'm going to have to do this on my own."

"Chloe—"

"Please. Let me do this."

Flynn sighed and finally nodded. "Fine. But if I see anything out of the ordinary…"

"Then you will come to my rescue." Chloe kissed Flynn on the cheek and looked at Tyler. "Ready?"

They used the last of their cash to pay their way into the gardens. A walkway led down a gentle slope lined with terraced flower beds and a shallow stream that emptied into a rectangular pool. Chloe smelled the lavender before she saw it along with yarrow, kangaroo paw, and California poppy. A few puffy clouds drifted across the bright blue sky. Too bad she had to ruin such a beautiful day by remembering and recounting that terrible night.

The California Garden led to the Palm Garden and the Jungle Garden with its high forest canopy and understory of trees and shrubs and climbing vines. The path followed a stream and a waterfall which led to the lily ponds. Croaking frogs accompanied the splashes of koi.

They made their way through the Australian Garden and all the Eucalyptus trees, the blooming acacia, melaleuca, and blue hibiscus.

Tyler led the way up a winding path through a bamboo forest to a serene and elegant bonsai garden. Chloe especially loved the bonsai. She found something so peaceful and centering about them. A stone stairway led down to the Japanese Garden with its koi ponds, natural wood moon bridge, and traditional Japanese Tea House.

Jenna stood on the other side of a small crowd peering into the open teahouse. Tyler smiled at her and she smiled back, but it was a tense smile that set Chloe on edge. Jenna waved them over away from the crowd and they all stood beneath a stone sculpture of a dragon.

"Where's your editor?" Tyler asked.

"He couldn't make it," Jenna said, her eyes nervously darting about.

"Couldn't make it? Why the hell not? He's the one who chose this place." Chloe picked up on Jenna's anxiety. "What wrong, Jenna? What's going on?"

"I'm really sorry."

"So, we'll reschedule." Tyler waved the problem away. "It's a pain in the ass, but it is what it is."

"I don't think that's what she's sorry about," Chloe said.

Jenna took Chloe's hand, her eyes brimming with tears. "They promised me they wouldn't hurt you. He just wants to talk to you."

"Who?" Chloe demanded.

Tyler grabbed Jenna by the shoulder. "What did you do?"

"Not me. My editor. He called Goldhammer."

"*Jesus Christ.*"

"I'm sorry."

Tyler grabbed Chloe by the arm. "We gotta get the hell out of here."

"Too late." Chloe watched four black-suited Black Star operatives closing in on them from all sides. Ohana was the closest. He offered them a ferocious and victorious smile.

• • •

Flynn fiddled with the radio in the stolen Dodge Grand Caravan as he kept an eye on the front entrance. He pushed the different presets. A

Christian Contemporary station played *You Will Never Run Away*. Flynn frowned and tried another preset that played an oldies station. The Band's rendition of *Devil with a Blue Dress*. Flynn sighed and tried a third preset, which sent him to a country station.

Don't the Girls All Get Prettier At Closing Time filled the minivan with its exuberant honky-tonk piano and guitar. Mickey Gilley sang with an energetic Texas twang. A bitter and brutal heart-stopping dread filled Flynn. His heart raced and he couldn't catch his breath. He tried to change the station, but felt paralyzed, stricken with a sense of impending doom. Dizzy and light-headed, his chest constricted and tight, he wondered if he was having a heart attack.

He attributed this rush of anxiety to PTSD, but he couldn't place the significance of the song. He just knew it was rooted in something tragic and terrible. He finally managed to jab the start/stop button, killing the engine as well as the music. It didn't immediately kill the anxiety. He still couldn't catch his breath.

That was when he saw Chloe. He recognized her by her black V-neck top and light gray cardigan. Ohana pulled her along by the arm. Two other Black Star operatives had hold of Tyler. A fourth ran point and led them away from the front entrance into the car park.

When Flynn started the Dodge Grand Caravan, the same song still played. Terror once again incapacitated him. Frozen in place, immobilized and helpless, he watched Ohana and his team spirit Chloe and Tyler away.

"Bloody hell," he mumbled as he steeled himself against the rising panic and poked at the pre-sets. The oldies station blasted out *Who'll Stop the Rain* by Creedence Clearwater Revival. Flynn hit the gas, backed out at high speed, nearly took out a pair of Asian grandparents. He turned the wheel, hand over hand, spun out in the gravel, and tore off after Chloe. He sped around the car park, searching aisle after aisle, but he didn't see her anywhere.

"Never should have let her go alone!"

He cut a hard right up another aisle and nearly collided with a black Mercedes-Benz SUV speeding from the other direction. Flynn swerved, barely missing it. Ohana, sitting in the passenger seat, grinned at Flynn, elated by his victory.

Flynn jammed on the brakes and pulled a tactical evasive maneuver; one he'd only ever practiced in training simulators. Q dismissed them as video games, but Flynn found them quite useful.

He pulled a J-turn by jamming the Grand Caravan into reverse, punching the accelerator, and spinning the steering wheel hard to the right while simultaneously hitting the brake. The minivan did a 180, perhaps the first 180 in minivan history, and Flynn rocketed after them to the driving beat and screaming guitars of CCR.

He caught sight of the Mercedes GL navigating its way at high speed through the Huntington car park, swerving around gaggles of school children, and elderly ladies driving massive Chryslers and Buicks left to them by their late husbands.

Flynn kept the gargantuan SUV in sight and followed as they blew past the guard gate at high speed. The Mercedes raced up Allen Avenue, cut left on California Boulevard, and made a hard right on Hill. Ohana screamed through the yellow light at Corson. Flynn had no choice but to run the red. Cars slammed on their brakes to avoid him as he swerved around them, barely missing bumpers, and chased Ohana onto the West 210 motorway on-ramp.

Once they were on the 210, Flynn dropped back, giving them plenty of room while still keeping them in sight.

Meanwhile, John Fogarty's throaty growl continued to echo in Flynn's head, asking again and again, *who'll stop the rain*?

CHAPTER FIFTEEN

There are more movie stars per square mile in Malibu than anywhere else in the world. For over eighty years, celebrities of all stripes have flocked to that exclusive stretch of Southern California beachfront. The first stars moved there in the 1920s. Douglas Fairbanks and Mary Pickford were followed by Lana Turner and Gary Cooper. Pioneering surfers snuck in to take advantage of the epic waves that pounded the Malibu coast, and in 1959 the movie Gidget *turned the isolated enclave into "surfer central". Today Malibu Colony is home to superstars like Leonardo DiCaprio, Bill Murray, and Tom Hanks. Drive ten miles north on Pacific Coast Highway and you'll find the homes of Pierce Brosnan and Steven Spielberg. Carbon Beach is where billionaires like Oracle founder Larry Ellison and movie moguls like David Geffen and Jeffrey Katzenberg all maintain their stupidly massive estates.*

Chloe sat in the back of the black Mercedes GL next to Ohana. Her brother sat one row up, squished between two huge Black Star operators. The fourth member of the team sat in the driver's seat and maneuvered the massive SUV up Malibu Canyon Road.

She watched the sun set over the ocean. Bright orange and red clouds filled the deep blue sky. As they turned right onto Pacific Coast Highway, they passed the whitewashed buildings of Pepperdine University. Surfers on Puerco Beach peeled off their wet suits and packed up for the day. Rugged bluffs rose on the right as they headed north past Solstice Canyon.

Chloe wondered what Goldhammer could possibly have to say to her. That asshole violated her. Used her and threw her away like she wasn't even a human being. Then this bastard next to her nearly killed her on that original asshole's orders. Why would Goldhammer even bother talking to her at this point?

Maybe they were taking her to somewhere rugged and remote where they could shoot her in the face and bury her in some anonymous hole. Chloe's hands trembled. She should have fought back. She should have screamed for help. She should have brought Flynn.

She wiped away an angry tear and caught Ohana staring at her. "What?"

"No one wants to hurt you."

"Bullshit."

"He just wants to talk to you."

"Yeah, that's what Jenna said."

"It's true."

"Do you know what he wants to talk to me about?"

Ohana shook his head. "That's above my pay grade."

"You are so full of shit. You're right in the middle of this. You shot me up with Demerol! You tried to kill me!"

"If I wanted you dead, you'd be dead. And if that whacko boyfriend of yours hadn't gotten in the way, this would all be settled by now."'

"He's hardly my boyfriend. And anyway, aren't you supposed to be some kind of special ops badass? If he's such a whacko, how'd he get the drop on you?"

Ohana's eyes flashed with anger. "He didn't."

"Then why do you look like you've been run over by a bulldozer?"

Tyler laughed at that. The operative next to him shot him a look.

"We'll be there soon," Ohana said, his voice flat as he looked out the window. "Enjoy the ride."

Chloe kept her eye on the road signs as they headed north. After they passed Latigo Canyon, she figured they were headed for Point Dume. A fitting name for the place that might be the end of the road for her and Tyler. Instead, they pulled onto a private road, which cut along the bluffs overlooking the beach at Paradise Cove.

Two huge entry gates opened. They continued through and followed a gray cobblestone lane flanked by lush tropical landscaping.

Their destination was the circular driveway of a sprawling contemporary-style estate. The driver opened Chloe's door. She climbed out, followed by Ohana. The home was constructed of poured concrete and walls of glass. The warm light from inside created a sharp contrast to the night sky.

Ohana led the way inside the spectacular two-story entry. A dramatic crystal chandelier dangled through the center of a sweeping circular staircase. Marble floors complemented white walls adorned with abstract art. Chloe could see wide open living areas with floor to ceiling windows that looked out on a glowing aquamarine infinity pool. The lights of Malibu and the California coast twinkled below.

A tall, attractive woman in a flowing black and white dress made her way down the circular staircase. She offered Chloe a welcoming smile and extended her hand.

"It's a pleasure to meet you. I'm Marta Karpenko. Mr. Goldhammer's personal assistant." She had just the trace of an Eastern European accent.

Chloe stared at her hand, unsure what to do. "I'm Chloe."

"I know. He's been expecting you."

"Where are we?" Tyler asked.

"Mr. Goldhammer's Malibu Estate. *Mar de Amor*."

Tyler translated with a smirk. "Sea of Love?"

Marta's pleasant expression didn't waver. "Would you two like to freshen up before you meet with Mr. Goldhammer?"

"No, but I do need to pee," Chloe said.

Marta's smile faltered for just an instant. "Follow me."

• • •

The bathroom was bigger than Chloe and Tyler's entire apartment. All gleaming white with a round domed skylight, marble countertops, marble floors, and a freestanding hammered copper bathtub with a gleaming nickel interior. The enclosed shower stall could hold the entire cast of Les Miz. The toilet had a heated seat and a built-in bidet that bathed Chloe's surprised butt with a stream of warm water. After washing her grimy hands and face, she stared at herself in the mirror.

Anxiety squeezed her heart. She didn't want to go out there. Didn't want to see Goldhammer again. But knew she couldn't delay the inevitable.

She opened the door and found Marta, Ohana, Tyler, and one of the other Black Star operators waiting just outside. Chloe pointed over her shoulder with her thumb. "That's some bathroom,"

Marta smiled. "Follow me please." She led the procession through the house and Chloe glanced into each room as they passed. She saw a large screening room and a bigger gymnasium.

The place was massive and Chloe marveled at the size of it. "How big is this place?"

"*Mar de Amor* sits on three acres and has over 10,000 square feet of living space. There are twelve bedrooms and fourteen bathrooms."

"So how many people live here?" Tyler asked.

"Mr. Goldhammer lives here alone at the moment. Though there are six servants who live in a separate servant's quarters as well as a small security force and, of course, me."

Marta led them through a wall of glass doors to a lavish outdoor living area with the aquamarine infinity pool, two blazing fire pits, sculptures, hardscape lighting, and several elegant seating areas. A waxing crescent moon shrouded by clouds reflected off the vast blackness of the ocean. The lights of Santa Monica glowed to the south, but Goldhammer himself was nowhere to be seen.

A splash disturbed the water behind her and she turned to see a ghastly sight. Rising up from a steaming, turquoise Jacuzzi, Goldhammer emerged like a huge white sea creature, dripping wet and completely nude. Chloe looked away and saw Tyler make a face. Marta smiled beatifically as two tiny Mexican maids helped Goldhammer into a large, white terry cloth robe. One maid planted a cigar in his mouth. The other lit the end. Goldhammer puffed and padded across the patio, his bare feet slapping against the travertine pavers.

He looked exactly as she remembered. A blubbery, moon-faced man with a fake tan and a receding hairline. A barrel-shaped torso sat atop a pair of short, hairy legs. He maintained a fashionable gray stubble and had huge, capped teeth. Dark circles and bags hung below his beady brown eyes. She would never forget those rapacious peepers. If eyes were truly the windows to the soul, Goldhammer's were windows to a dark, bottomless hole.

He smiled at Chloe and motioned to one of the seating areas with his cigar. "Let's talk."

He sat on an L-shaped sofa and patted the cushion next to him. Chloe sat as far from him as she could on the opposite side of the L-shape. Tyler took the cushion beside her, sitting between her and Goldhammer. Ohana remained standing next to Marta.

Goldhammer studied Chloe silently. It unnerved her.

"What?" she finally blurted. "What do you want from me?"

"I feel like we got off on the wrong foot, you and I."

Chloe couldn't help but laugh at that. "Are you fucking kidding me?"

"As is often the case with those who possess an extraordinarily high IQ, I've been told I'm on the autism spectrum. As such, I'm not always able to pick up on social cues. If I overstepped, I do apologize."

"Overstepped?"

"I thought what we had was consensual."

"Consensual?" Tyler was irate. "You're blaming what you did to her on autism?"

"I'm not blaming anyone. Sometimes two human beings can experience vastly different realities."

Unable to sit for another second, she bolted to her feet. "I know what you did to me!"

"What you *think* I did."

"What I *know* you did it!"

"You also think I tried to have you killed."

"I OD'd on Demerol! I don't use that shit! Your boy here shot me up with it!" She glared at Ohana.

"I'm not a mob boss, Chloe. I don't have people killed. I don't disagree that things went too far and mistakes were made, but hurting you was never my intention. All I wanted was for you and your brother to stop spreading false rumors about me."

"Why not just sue me?"

"That would only have given the rumors more oxygen."

"You were worried about your deal," Tyler said. "Your leveraged buyout. The merger with Globalcom. You knew that kind of negative publicity could sink the whole thing."

Goldhammer puffed on his cigar and leveled his gaze at Tyler. "Tens of thousands of people depend on me. Employees. Stockholders. I have a fiduciary duty to this company. This proposed merger will turn Goldhammer Incorporated into the largest media company in the world. If the government rules against our deal, do you know how many jobs will be lost? How many billions? Not just by me, but by retirees, stockholders who depend on those dividends?"

"So, you sent your thugs after her because you were worried about the little people?"

"I asked Black Star to find kompromat on your sister. Ruin her reputation. Having her OD was their idea. They wanted her admitted to a mental hospital so no one would take her seriously as a believable witness. But they went too far. Even for me. Which is why I sent my lawyer, Ms. Kesselmen, to facilitate her release."

Chloe's face flushed with anger. "So this is what? An apology? You had these assholes kidnap us and scare us half to death just so you could say you're sorry?"

"When your brother was harassing me on social media, he claimed you had hard evidence. A recording you made with your iPhone. Though that reporter at the L.A. Weekly told her editor just the opposite. She claims it never existed. I just need to know the truth."

Chloe glanced at Tyler sitting next to her and then at Goldhammer. "The truth is —

"The truth is —" Tyler interrupted her. "She turned on her iPhone's camera the moment she walked in the door. She knew about the rumors and suspected you might try something."

Chloe gave Tyler a "what the hell look", but he just kept his eyes on Goldhammer.

"So why didn't you tell this to the police?"

"We did, but they didn't want to hear it. They said it was an illegal recording. That California has a two-party consent law and that it wasn't admissible in court. But we know the real reason, don't we? The powers-that-be protect the rich and famous and rest of us are on our own."

Ohana moved for Chloe. "This iPhone? Do you have it on you?"

"Do you think we're stupid? It's somewhere safe," Tyler said.

"Not your apartment." Ohana directed his next sentence to Goldhammer. "I tossed it top to bottom. If it were there, I would have found it."

Goldhammer's expression grew dark as he turned his gaze on Tyler. "Why did you lie to the reporter?"

"Because we weren't sure we could trust her."

"I see," he said, nodding. "Okay, then." He directed his gaze back to Chloe. "Bring me this recording and I will deposit a half a million dollars in your bank account."

"What?"

"We'll call it up-front money for agreeing to co-star in my new television show."

Chloe was stunned. "A half a million dollars?"

Tyler looked equally gobsmacked.

"It's time we put this unpleasantness behind us."

Tyler raised a skeptical eyebrow. "What's the show?"

"It's called *Bombshells* and it's about an elite force of female special ops. Your sister would play Domino, a former Olympic gymnast and martial arts master who is also an expert hacker."

Chloe couldn't help but smile at that. "Seriously?"

"Yes, but only if you give me your iPhone and any other copies you have of that recording."

Chloe didn't know what to say. She had no recording and Tyler knew it and now she was screwed. What choice did she have but to come clean? She started to open her mouth, but Tyler cut her off before she could. "You'll get the iPhone *after* you deposit that upfront money in my sister's bank account and *after* you publicly announce her as the star of your new show."

"I don't think so."

"That's the only way we're doing this. Otherwise, what's to stop you from reneging? That recording is the only leverage we have."

Goldhammer focused his flat gaze on Tyler and then on Chloe. His beady eyes bored into her so intently she thought she might scream. Finally, he offered her an infinitesimal nod. "I can live with that."

CHAPTER SIXTEEN

Flynn followed the Mercedes GL at a discreet distance as he tailed it from one side of Los Angeles County to the other. Luckily, the Dodge Grand Caravan he stole had just enough gas to make the trip. Flynn listened to a lot of classic rock as he followed the black SUV on the Ventura Freeway before cutting south through the Santa Monica Mountains.

The canyon road had far less traffic, so Flynn hung farther back as he took the tight corners on the twisty two-lane highway. The Eagles sang "Hotel California" as he edged around steep cliffs and breathtaking vistas, past rugged chaparral with clumps of purple sage, buckwheat, and stands of coast live oak. After passing through two short tunnels, he followed the Mercedes GL towards the setting sun and the vast expanse of the Pacific. He passed the sprawling campus of Pepperdine University and headed north on the Pacific Coast Highway. Dusk turned to darkness as the SUV turned left onto a private road.

Flynn made an illegal U-turn and doubled back. He parked on PCH and followed down the private road on foot. Up ahead, the Mercedes pulled through two impressive gates. He ran to catch up and slipped through the gates before they closed. Flynn stayed hidden in the shrubbery and shadows as he made his way up the long cobblestone drive.

The Mercedes parked in front of an impressive estate that he assumed belonged to Goldhammer. Ohana and his men led Chloe and Tyler inside. Flynn moved closer and watched through the glass window as a tall, attractive woman gracefully greeted them.

Two of the Black Star Operators stayed outside and waited in the Mercedes. Presumably, Goldhammer had his own security force on the premises. Flynn noticed an inconspicuous security camera near the front door. He assumed such cameras were everywhere. He'd have to be careful if he wanted to maintain the element of surprise.

Leaving the Glock 19 holstered, Flynn unsheathed his Ari B'Lilah tactical knife. Ari B'Lilah means *Lion by Night*. Twelve inches long and sharp as a razor, it was forged for Israel's most elite counter terrorism units. Flynn kept low and used the Mercedes to hide from the cameras. He stabbed the knife into the rear left tire. The air hissed out slowly and loudly, but not loud enough to penetrate the silent interior of the Mercedes. Flynn snuck off before the tire lost too much air and the vehicle listed to one side. He made his way around the side of the house, staying in the shadows behind shrubs and planters until he heard some voices, one of them Tyler's.

"That's the only way we're doing this. Otherwise, what's to stop you from reneging? That recording is the only leverage we have."

A long pause ensued.

"I can live with that," an arrogant and self-satisfied man replied. "What about you, Ms. Jablonski? Is this agreement amenable to you?"

Flynn didn't recognize the second voice and wondered if it belonged to Goldhammer. It sounded imperious and high-pitched. Creeping closer and keeping behind a large steel planter box, he laid eyes on the tall beauty and Ohana. Chloe sat next to Tyler on a white L-shaped couch and stared at a stocky, middle-aged man wearing a terry cloth robe and smoking a cigar. *Goldhammer?*

Chloe looked at Tyler and then back at Goldhammer. "I guess so."

"Good. Mr. Ohana will drive you home so you can pack for your trip to Las Vegas. You and your brother both will be my guests for the TCA Press Tour."

"TCA?"

"The Television Critics Association. It's at Caesars Palace. I'll be announcing all my new shows and I can introduce you as my new discovery. But you need to understand who is in charge here. From this point on, what I say goes. Is that clear?"

Chloe sat there silently.

"Yes or no, Miss Jablonski. Make up your mind. We can't sit here all night. I do have other plans this evening."

"Change of plans," Flynn said as he rose up from behind the planter and trained the Glock 19 on Ohana. "Mr. Ohana, would you please take your weapon and carefully put it on the ground?"

Ohana hesitated, but Goldhammer had no interest in being in the middle of a gunfight. "Do what he says, Mr. Ohana. Before someone gets hurt."

"Gingerly, Mr. Ohana," Flynn added. A furious Ohana complied, gently setting his SIG-Sauer semi-automatic on the ground. "Now kick it closer to Chloe. Do it." Ohana followed Flynn's instructions. "Okay, Chloe, pick it up and point it at Mr. Goldhammer."

Chloe regarded the pistol as if it were radioactive. "No thanks. I'm good," she said.

Flynn glanced at her brother. "Tyler?"

Tyler looked perturbed. "We're not in any danger here, okay. Goldhammer apologized for his asshole behavior and just put an offer on the table."

"An offer?"

"A very generous offer, so would you please put the gun down?" Tyler raised his eyebrows.

Flynn shook his head. "You can't take the word of a sociopath, Tyler. Goldhammer will say and promise anything to get what he wants."

Goldhammer narrowed his eyes at Flynn. "Is this the mental patient?" He then glanced at Ohana. "Did you let this lunatic get the drop on you again?"

Flynn grinned at Ohana. "Is that what he thinks I am? A mental patient? I wasn't sure that cover would hold. Frankly, I thought it far-fetched, but apparently it's been quite effective."

Ohana held out his hand. "Listen to me, Mr. Flynn, that Glock has a hair-trigger. Please be careful."

Goldhammer glared at Ohana, his voice rising with anger. "Shayetet 13 is supposed to be the best of the best. The most dangerous and effective special ops team in the world. Yet you let this psycho get the better of you. Not once, but how many times? I should fire you,

Ohana!" He pointed at the other Black Star operator. "You too! Both of you! All of you!" He turned his furious gaze at Flynn. "What is wrong with you?"

"Don't agitate him," Ohana pleaded.

Chloe rose and slowly approached Flynn; her voice gentle as she gestured for him to lower the gun. "James, please. Put down the gun. I'm really okay. Honestly."

Tyler tried to calm him down as well. "James, look at me. Listen to me. We worked it out. We're all good."

Flynn kept the weapon on Ohana, but turned his gaze to Goldhammer. "The merger is just the beginning, isn't it? Chloe got in the way of something much larger, didn't she? What's the plan, Goldfelcher? What exactly do you intend to do?"

Goldhammer's face turned a light shade of pink. "What did you call me?"

"Goldfelcher. Isn't that your real name?" Flynn prodded his adversary, hoping that he might reveal something in anger.

Goldhammer's eyes blazed. "It's Goldhammer!"

"I know who you are. I know exactly who you are. A psychopath who twists the truth to create his own reality. You don't fool me, Goldfelcher."

Goldhammer jumped to his feet, his face red, his eyes blazing. "Stop calling me that!"

With Flynn's attention diverted, Ohana dove for his SIG. But Flynn shot it away before the ex-special op could get his hands on it. Focused as he was on Ohana, Flynn didn't see the beautiful woman's left foot until it was too late. She caught his wrist with a spinning hook kick, slapping the Glock right out of his hand. It spun away into the dark as she followed up with a roundhouse and a flurry of punches. Flynn tried to defend himself and managed to block a few kicks and punches. He also caught quite a few in the face before a side kick in the ribs sent him splashing into the infinity pool.

Flynn swam for the side, gasping and choking, until he finally got his hand on the edge. That was when he saw an angry Ohana and the black barrel of his SIG-Sauer.

CHAPTER SEVENTEEN

Flynn found himself in the back seat of the black Mercedes GL feeling foolish and furious. He couldn't believe he let that woman get the drop on him. Ohana's men changed the slashed tire and trussed Flynn up in plastic handcuffs, binding both his hands and feet, the hard plastic painful and tight. His head throbbed and he tasted blood from one of the tall, attractive woman's many kicks and punches. Breathing too deeply caused a sharp stab of pain, and he wondered if she broke or bruised one of his ribs. Like Bambi and Thumper who he tangled with in Las Vegas so many years ago, she was as dangerous as she was beautiful. Still soaking wet from his fall in the pool, he watched through the window as Chloe and Tyler climbed into another vehicle with Ohana. A sleek Jaguar. Probably one of Goldhammer's cars.

Chloe and Tyler bought so easily into Goldhammer's lies. Couldn't they see what a sociopath he was? Or did Chloe have an alternate strategy? Perhaps she intended to gain Goldhammer's trust and go undercover to reveal his ultimate plan. If so, she could be putting herself in great danger.

Flynn would have to save her. But first, he would have to save himself.

The two Black Star operatives returned to the Mercedes. Without a word, they started up the SUV and pulled out onto Pacific Coast Highway. Flynn sat directly behind the driver and tried to catch his eye in the rear-view mirror, but the man kept his focus on the road.

"I hope you know Goldhammer will never get away with this," Flynn said, his voice firm and full of confidence. The driver glanced at the passenger riding shotgun and they exchanged a smirk. "His plan is preposterous and he's mad as a hatter."

"Shut up," the driver said. Like Ohana, he had an Israeli accent.

"Black Star will be implicated. At the very least, you'll be charged as accessories after the fact."

"What did he just say to you?" the passenger cautioned.

"Killing me won't save you. I'm just one of many Double-0s. Kill me and another will come. That you can count on."

"No one's killing anybody," the driver said.

"Where do you plan to bury my body? The Santa Monica Mountains?"

"Are you not listening to me? We're taking you back to the loony bin."

"City of Roses," the passenger added.

The driver glared at Flynn in the rearview mirror. "So do me a favor. Shut the hell up."

The Mercedes hugged the road as they took the tight turns high on the bluffs above Malibu Beach. Flynn knew it was now or never and since he never said never, it had to be now. He partly stood, lunging forward, and clamped his teeth down on the right ear of the driver. The man screamed and tried to hit him with his elbow, but the angle was awkward and Flynn just bit down harder. He tasted blood and Axe body wash. The passenger punched him in the head and tried to pull him off the driver's ear.

The Mercedes swerved as the driver fought to free himself. The panicky passenger pulled his gun and put the barrel to Flynn's head. "Let him go! *Let him go!*"

But Flynn knew he couldn't. He was dead either way and this way he still had a chance.

The tires squealed as the GL swerved left and nearly hit a truck head on. The blinding lights disappeared as the car swerved right.

"Shoot him! *Shoot him!*" the driver shouted.

Before the passenger could squeeze the trigger and launch a bullet into Flynn's brain, the Mercedes GL hit something. Flynn didn't know what. Whatever the car hit was huge and solid and immovable because the airbags exploded and Flynn, being the only one in the SUV not wearing a seatbelt, flew from the back seat and through the front windshield like a missile.

There wasn't pain, but he did remember an incredible cacophony followed by complete silence, cold air, and the smell of the sea. Flynn fell for what seemed like an eternity before he plunged into the ocean and everything went black.

• • •

Chloe sat in the back seat of the Jag next to Tyler. Ohana drove while another Black Star Op rode shotgun. Sixty minutes previously, Goldhammer agreed to give her everything she ever wanted. So why didn't she feel victorious? Instead, she felt nauseous. She often daydreamed about success, but this wasn't how she pictured it. She knew she might have to compromise, but she never imagined she would have to sell her soul. And for what? Fame? Fortune? A TV show?

Tyler patted her on the hand. "You okay?"

Chloe leaned in close to Tyler's ear and whispered, "What did I just do?"

"What you had to," he whispered in return.

"Really?"

"Yeah, he needs to pay for what he did to you."

"Paying would mean going to prison."

She glanced up at Ohana driving and caught his eye in the rear-view mirror. "What are you two whispering about?" Ohana asked.

"Nothing. Just brother and sister shit," Tyler said.

After a few minutes of silence, Chloe whispered to Tyler again. "It just doesn't feel right."

"Success probably always feels like that. Everyone has to sell themselves out a little bit."

"Seriously?"

"You won. Stop beating yourself up for once and declare victory."

Chloe leaned in close and whispered even quieter. "How is this a victory? We don't have what Goldhammer wants. Why the hell did you tell him I had that recording? It's bullshit."

"He doesn't know that."

"Eventually, he's going to want it and then what?"

"Then it'll be too late. You'll be on TV and the world will have fallen in love with you."

"Stop whispering," Ohana ordered.

Chloe did just that. She closed her mouth, leaned back, and looked out the window at the hillside lights of Pacific Palisades. Her stomach in a knot, she tried to keep her anxiety in check by taking deep breaths through her nose. But one of the ops wore a sickly-sweet body spray that just made her queasy. The few seconds of silence shattered when Ohana's phone rang.

He answered. "Ohana."

Marta's voice boomed through the blue tooth speaker. "I have some instructions for Ms. Jablonski for tomorrow."

"She can hear you," Ohana said.

"Mr. Goldhammer will send a car to your apartment for a 9:00 a.m. pick up. We will be flying to Las Vegas on his private jet. Make sure to pack clothing appropriate for semi-formal parties and a press tour. Mr. Goldhammer will be introducing you to the public tomorrow. Get a good night's sleep. You need to look your best. We will see you in the morning. Have a good night." Marta clicked off, breaking the connection.

CHAPTER EIGHTEEN

Over the years, Alessandra found countless things washed up on the beach, but this was the first time she found a man. He looked dead. A pale, wet corpse covered in sand and kelp, his wrists and ankles bound with plastic handcuffs. He wore an expensive suit that fit him well. The label identified it as a Zegna. She once met Angelo Zegna in Paris during fashion week. He pursued her with great ardor, but at the time she was involved with Jean-Paul Belmondo. It was the late sixties and she was at the peak of her stardom.

She put her head against his chest and heard a heartbeat; felt his chest rise as his lungs filled with air. She touched his bruised and scratched face, avoiding the shallow cut on his forehead. He was strikingly attractive. Movie star handsome. He looked to be in his late thirties or early forties. If he were an actor of any renown, she would recognize him. She stayed current with all the latest films. As a member of the Screen Actors Guild, she received screeners for every movie and TV show that was up for an award.

Alessandra awoke every morning at 5:30 a.m. sharp. A habit ingrained since her days as an actress. She'd arrive on set before the sun so she'd be ready for the first shot of the day. Fifty years later, she still liked watching the sun rise over the Malibu hills.

Every morning, after working in her garden, watering plants and pruning roses, she took Peanut, her Pomeranian, for a walk on the beach. She considered it her morning constitutional. Physical fitness had always been important to her and, at age seventy-eight, she still took some pride in her appearance. Time and too many years in the sun had weathered her skin with lines and wrinkles and varicose veins, though sometimes she still turned the occasional head. Until they got a good look at her face. That look of surprise sometimes stung, but only for a moment. She was glad not to have all that attention anymore. Back when she reigned as a sex symbol, no one ever saw her for who she really was. Just the outer wrapping and image designed by the studio and their publicity department. It was a relief not to be instantly recognized anymore.

Alessandra considered calling an ambulance and even pulled out her phone, but she had no bars. Cell reception on Malibu Beach was terrible.

Peanut sniffed the man's face and began licking his chin. "Peanut, stop that. Peanut!"

The man opened his eyes, surprised to find an adorable Pomeranian licking his face. Instead of jumping up in a panic, he slowly looked around and then at Alessandra. He saw the phone in her hand. "Who are you calling?" he asked her.

"I was going to call the police, but I can't get a damn signal."

"No reason for that. I'm fine." The man tried to get up, but the plastic handcuffs on his arms and legs made that difficult. He rolled over onto his hands and knees and then pushed himself to his feet. He looked shaky. Weak. Dizzy.

She grabbed his elbow to steady him. "You don't look fine."

He peeled some kelp off the front of his suit. "I just need to get my bearings."

"Why are your legs and arms bound? Did someone want to do you harm?"

"That was my impression."

"Did they throw you overboard?"

"Something like that." Alessandra pulled a pruning knife from her sweater pocket and cut the plastic handcuffs off his wrists and ankles.

The man massaged his skin where the plastic rubbed it raw. "Thank you."

"You're very welcome." She folded up her knife and put it back in her pocket. He took a step, teetered, and nearly fell, so she grabbed him by the arm and steadied him. "Come with me to my place so you can sit and rest for a little while."

"I appreciate the offer, but perhaps you shouldn't invite perfect strangers into your home."

"Perhaps not, but I'm an excellent judge of character and you don't seem like a psycho."

"Is that an Italian accent I detect?"

"Yes. Very good. You're not from around here either, are you?"

"Not originally, no."

"English, right?"

"Indeed."

"I once dated Michael Caine. Of course, that was many years ago. After Bianca Jagger and before he met Shakira. Lovely woman."

"I thought you looked familiar. Are you an actress?"

"Was. I'm retired now." Peanut did her business on the sand. "That's a good girl! Such a big poop for such a little girl!" Alessandra used a plastic bag to pick up the poop. She glanced up at the man, who wavered. "Are you sure you can walk?"

"I'm good. I promise."

"Okay then. Come with me."

The man seemed dizzy, so Alessandra took him by the elbow to steady him.

• • •

Flynn's head swam. He felt off balance, but the woman held him firmly by the elbow. He must have injured his left knee. A sharp pain accompanied every step, and he walked with a noticeable limp.

"I'm James, by the way. James Flynn."

"Alessandra. Good to meet you James."

"Alessandra. Beautiful name."

"It was my grandmother's."

"What part of Italy are you from?"

"Roma."

"Incredible city."

"Indeed, it is."

Flynn's head ached and a dull pain throbbed in his side. He must have bruised a rib. The last thing Flynn remembered after exploding through the windshield was the smell of the sea. He didn't recall falling, though he did remember the darkness. And then nothing until that tiny little dog licked his chin.

Chloe needed him. She was in danger, whether she knew it or not. Goldhammer bought her off with promises of fame and fortune. He was sure Chloe felt she had no choice but to give into him. Who knew what Goldhammer had in mind for her?

Clearly, he had some ultimate plan. A plan that Chloe nearly exposed. To save her, Flynn would have to foil Goldhammer's scheme. Whatever it might be.

Flynn faltered, but Alessandra kept him upright and moving forward. She wore faded blue jeans, a black turtleneck, and a long blue cardigan sweater. Her shoulder length silver hair was tied back in a bun with some loose strands blowing free. She was clearly once a great beauty and still had the cheekbones to prove it.

He wondered how long he'd been unconscious. The sun was up and by the way the light fell Flynn could tell it was still early morning. His head throbbed, and when he touched his forehead he felt blood. Scratches from the windshield, most likely. He wondered if he had a concussion. It wouldn't be surprising considering how hard he hit that windshield.

Alessandra led Flynn towards a beach house much more modest and twice as inviting as Goldhammer's. A white washed wooden gate led to a patio and lagoon-style pool area with lush landscaping and a wide wooden deck. The house itself had a steep slate roof, white washed shingle siding, and many multi-paned windows that let in a lot of light and offered an impressive ocean view.

Inside, Flynn found a house with white beamed ceilings, white walls, and cozy shabby-chic furniture. The only other splashes of color were the bright, cheerful plein air paintings on the walls. Alessandra helped Flynn to one of her living room couches where he half-fell/half-sat and tried to catch his breath. He felt something wet on his forehead and looked at his fingers to see blood. Then he noticed he was bleeding on her pristine white couch. "Oh, my goodness. I apologize." Flynn struggled to stand and felt the world fade as the floor came up and hit him in the face.

• • •

When Flynn opened his eyes again he was horizontal on the couch. Alessandra sat on the coffee table and tended to his cuts and scratches with antibiotic ointment and bandages.

"I'm terribly sorry," Flynn said.

"I played a nurse in 'Call to Arms' and learned quite a bit from one of our advisers. She was a former combat nurse."

Flynn tried to sit up, but she gently pushed him back down.

"I really should call you an ambulance."

"Please don't."

"Why not? I can pay for it. My late husband left me quite a lot of money."

"Again, perhaps you shouldn't be so forthcoming with a complete stranger."

"Perhaps, but it's not like you're going to overpower me. You're weak as a kitten."

"You live here alone?"

"Ever since Philip passed away. Unlike my first four husbands, he was a very good man. In my younger days I wasn't such a great judge of character."

"Calling an ambulance might draw… undo attention."

"Are you in trouble with the authorities?"

"I am the authorities," Flynn replied.

"You're a policeman?"

"Something like that."

"Something like what?"

"I work for Her Majesty's Secret Service."

She looked delighted. "You're a spy?"

"The official title would be intelligence officer."

"Who's after you?"

"It's probably better if you don't know."

Alessandra couldn't help but grin. "How exciting."

"It's not like in the movies."

"Of course not. Though I have played spies in more than a few pictures. My very first film, the one that brought me my initial fame, was about an international super spy. I was the love interest. Tatiana."

"I once knew a Tatiana. A very spirited, beautiful woman. Much like yourself."

"Please. I'm an old lady now."

"Still beautiful."

"Stop it."

"It's true."

"And I think you must be suffering from a head injury."

Flynn smiled at that. "I'm fine. Truly. I appreciate your help, but I really must go. To stay any longer would put you in danger."

"You can barely stand. You're in no condition to go anywhere."

"There's someone who needs my help. A young woman. An aspiring actress."

"Is she in danger too?"

"A powerful man has taken advantage of her. Used her. Abused her."

"There are many men like that in Hollywood. I have suffered at the hands of more than a few. That's partly why I left that filthy business behind."

"So you understand?"

"Of course I do. And I want to help you *and* that poor young actress. That men like that still exist is… is unconscionable."

"I appreciate your willingness to help, but—"

"Don't condescend to me, young man. You are in no shape to do anything but lie there and bleed. If I can help you, let me help you. What else do I have to do?"

"Alessandra—"

"Call me Alessa."

"Alessa, listen—"

"No, *you* listen. I lost the love of my life three years ago and since then I've been alone. Most of my contemporaries are dead or gone or moved away. My world has grown smaller and so has my life."

"Don't you have children?"

"Two and neither one want anything to do with me. I don't blame them. I was a terrible mother. Too young. Too selfish, immature, and foolish. I tried to make it up to them, but what's done is done. I live a quiet life now. Away from the spotlight. That's what I wanted after all the attention. All the paparazzi. But you know how the saying goes, be careful what you wish for."

"So you're bored?"

"Life has become something of a chore. At this point, it's just me and Peanut."

"I'm not sure that's a good reason to want to risk your life."

"It's as good a reason as any. Someone once said if you have nothing to die for, you have nothing to live for."

"Who said that?"

"Martin Luther King. I marched with him on Washington in 1963. Burt Lancaster was there. Lena Horne. Marlon Brando. Sidney Poitier. Paul Newman. I heard the 'I Have A Dream' speech first hand. The world, the future, everything seemed so much more promising back then. So much more hopeful."

A wave of exhaustion swept over Flynn. Suddenly, he could hardly keep his eyes open. "Maybe I should rest for a bit."

"Close your eyes. Take a nap. And when you awaken, I'll make you some breakfast. Do you like pancakes? I make amazing blueberry buttermilk pancakes."

CHAPTER NINETEEN

Chloe slept the sleep of the dead. She was exhausted after their escape from the Biltmore and her fitful few hours of slumber in their stolen Grand Caravan. She couldn't believe Jenna betrayed them the way she did. Jenna blamed the betrayal on her editor, but she was the one who lured them to the Huntington. That was all on her. Goddamn Goldhammer. He had "friends" everywhere and terrified everyone. No one wanted to cross him. She couldn't believe she had to sit across from him again and stare into that fat face and those self-satisfied eyes. So damn arrogant. He didn't show one iota of remorse. So positive he could buy her off.

Tyler just went for it and dragged her along for the ride. Giving into him like that made her sick, but what else could she do? The asshole would have ended her career before it even started.

Black Star totally trashed their apartment. It took her and Tyler almost two hours to straighten up. She didn't climb into bed until midnight and fell asleep instantly, so grateful to lay her head on her own pillow.

She awoke at 5:30 am filled with anxiety and couldn't fall back asleep. Chloe kept replaying the disappointed look on Flynn's face when she refused to pick up Ohana's gun and point it at Goldhammer. By now, he probably was back at City of Roses. She thought about calling him, but what would be the point?

She took a shower, did her hair and makeup, packed for a weekend in Vegas, and waited for Tyler to get his ass out of bed.

At eight she finally decided to wake him. Tyler always took forever to get ready. He was still packing when Ohana rang them up. Chloe looked through the window and saw him parked out front.

"I can't believe I'm doing this," she mumbled to herself.

"It is what it is." Tyler rolled his suitcase into the living room.

"I hate that."

"What?"

"*It is what it is?* What does that even mean?"

"You know what it means."

"It's like *no worries* or *it's all good.* There are always worries and it's never all good."

"It's not the same at all."

"You say *It Is What It Is* when you want someone to shut up. When you don't want an argument."

"Are you kidding me?"

"It's conceding defeat. It's saying change can't happen. That it's something we have to live with."

"Sometimes it is."

"What if I can't?"

"Can't what?"

"Live with it."

"Look, I know that asshole makes your skin crawl. I get it. But if we can go to Vegas and get this done, you'll get everything you ever wanted."

"Will I?"

"Do you want that asshole out of your life? This is how you do it. Give him a victory and he will go away."

"What if he doesn't?"

"He will. He'll get bored and move on."

"To the next poor girl."

"Karma will catch up with him. Maybe not today. Maybe not tomorrow. But eventually it will. It catches up with everyone."

"Does it? I don't know about that."

• • •

Flynn sighed as the hot water pounded his back. Every muscle loosened and relaxed. His last shower was two days ago at the

Biltmore. It felt good to wash away the sweat and grime. Like the rest of Alessandra's house, the master bath was entirely white.

The spacious shower stall easily accommodated Flynn, and he appreciated the three powerful shower heads. Steam filled the stall, fogging the glass doors. A patch of cloudless blue brightened the skylight above. He also noticed marks he hadn't seen before. On his legs, his chest, his arms, and his abdomen. He winced as he ran the washcloth over his bruised rib. Before he left the shower, he turned the hot water to icy cold and let it invigorate him and tighten his pores.

The white Turkish towels were more rough than plush; just how he liked them. He dried himself off, padded into the guest bedroom, and did his morning routine; twenty toe touches, twenty slow press-ups, and enough leg lifts to make his stomach muscles scream. His injuries made his usual exercises a bit difficult. When his head began to swim, he sat on the edge of the bed.

Alessandra told him that right after Philip died, she couldn't bear to part with his clothes, so she hung them in the guest bedroom's walk-in closet. As Flynn's Zegna suit was ruined, she invited him to wear whatever he wanted.

Flynn and her late husband apparently had similar taste. He found some well-worn chinos and a navy-blue polo shirt. Her husband's shoes were a little big, but he found a pair of light blue canvas espadrilles that fit him well enough. He wandered from room to room, looking for Alessandra, and found himself in some sort of library or study that doubled as a media room. Movie posters featuring a young Alessandra covered the walls. Some of the titles seemed familiar.

What's New Pussycat? starred Peter Sellers, Peter O'Toole, Woody Allen, and a number of glamour girls of the era. Flynn remembered the song by Tom Jones, but couldn't remember if he ever saw the film. He saw a poster for an Elvis Presley movie, *Fun in Acapulco.* A Matt Helm picture starring Dean Martin. A western with Sammy Davis Jr. and Frank Sinatra. There were also posters for a 1960s spy thriller, an Italian biblical epic, and a Hammer horror film. A dusty Golden Globe Award for Most Promising Newcomer sat on a shelf as a bookend. Flynn ran his finger over the name engraved in gold—*Alessandra Bianchi.*

"I won that in '63."

Flynn turned. Alessandra stood in the doorway.

"I was so excited. So many amazing actresses won it before me. Lois Maxwell, Shirley MacLaine, Kim Novak, Natalie Wood, Ann-Margret, Jane Fonda." She crossed the room and touched the tarnished award as if it were a talisman. "I was so hopeful. And so naïve."

"Hollywood wasn't what you thought it would be?"

"I worked with some good people, I worked with some bad people, and I worked with some truly evil people." She approached a poster for one of the Westerns. "I loved the Westerns the best. Out on location in such beautiful places. Riding those magnificent horses. Though, there weren't many parts in westerns for a girl with an Italian accent."

"You like to ride?"

"My late husband and I owned a ranch in Ojai. I loved it, but after he passed it broke my heart to be there. So I gave it to our niece. We had another house in the Holmby Hills, but I was tired of paying the property taxes, so I sold it. This house was mine before we married. We kept it and we would stay here occasionally, but Phillip wasn't very beachy."

"Was your late husband in the movie business as well?"

She smiled and shook her head. "He hated show business. Thought it was ridiculous. He made his fortune in real estate. One of the richest men in Los Angeles. But unlike most ambitious men, he wasn't a *stronzino*. He was kind. Caring. A good person. Very different than most of my ex's. Are you hungry?"

"Famished."

"Come."

She led him to the kitchen and Flynn sat at a butcher block table next to some French doors. Alessa poured him coffee and put a plate of blueberry buttermilk pancakes in front of him.

Flynn drizzled a bit of real maple syrup on the plate, cut a piece, and took a bite. "Delicious."

"I told you."

The coffee was as good as the pancakes and Flynn ate with relish. Alessandra sat across from him and seemed to enjoy watching him eat.

"You're not having any."

"Oh, no, I don't eat pancakes. Too many carbs. But my husband used to love them."

"You said he was very different from your other ex's."

"Yes, he wasn't a jerk. For whatever reason, I was always attracted to bad boys. Bastards. I found them exciting. Dangerous. Sexy. Men like Jean-Paul Belmondo. James Dean. Warren Beatty. Robert Mitchum. Steve McQueen. You."

Flynn smiled at that. "Me?"

"I told you. I'm an excellent judge of character. And you have a wild streak. I can see it in your eyes."

"So, what are you saying? I'm not really your type?"

"After enough men broke my heart, I went into therapy. I had to learn to love myself before I could accept that someone decent and kind could love me." Her eyes grew shiny and she rose from the table. "This young girl you need to save. Do you have a number for her?"

Flynn shook his head. "No."

"Do you have any idea where she might be?"

Flynn nodded. "Las Vegas. Caesars Palace."

"Vegas? My late husband and I traveled there often. I haven't been there since I lost him. In 1994 we saw Frank Sinatra there. His last concert ever. The MGM Grand. Gregory Peck was in the audience, his wife Veronique, Robert Wagner, Jill St. John, Roger Moore and his wife, Luisa." She pointed to his plate. "Would you like some more?"

"They were delicious, but I couldn't eat another bite."

"When do we need to leave for Vegas?"

"We?"

"I told you I would help you."

"And you have. But this man I'm dealing with—he's dangerous."

"You think I haven't dealt with dangerous men? Harry Cohn, Jack Warner, Louis B. Mayer. Each one was a sexual predator. I know how these men operate and I know the damage they can do."

"Alessa, please—"

"Besides, you're in no shape to drive. If you want to leave today, then I'm doing the driving."

"All the way to Las Vegas?"

"Why not?"

"Fine. As long as you promise not to put yourself in harm's way."

"I promise. Now go pack some clothes. You'll find my husband's luggage in his walk-in closet. Borrow whatever you want."

Her husband's suits were a little dated, but that didn't bother Flynn. He preferred classic, vintage clothing. He found two bespoke Savile Row suits. One in black, the other in a dark blue tropical worsted. Both fit a little tight, but not uncomfortably so. He also selected an Armani tuxedo, a pair of black oxfords, a pair of brown suede chukka boots, and the blue espadrilles. More casual clothes like chinos and polo shirts and a vintage leather jacket rounded out his wardrobe for Sin City. He also borrowed a vintage Rolex Submariner watch which reminded him of one he once owned.

He found Alessa in the three-car garage with a huge suitcase and a garment bag. She had three sets of keys.

"Which do you prefer? The Jaguar? The Range Rover? Or the Aston Martin?"

"The Aston Martin, of course."

CHAPTER TWENTY

Eighty acres of walnut and peach orchards in the San Fernando Valley were cleared to make room for Metropolitan Airport. It was built in 1928 by a consortium of Los Angeles businessmen, twenty-five years after the Wright Brothers' first flight and one year before the first building went up at Los Angeles International. When the stock market crashed a year later, the airport remained open, but the business changed. Bootlegged booze from Mexico brought in most of the money. The attack on Pearl Harbor changed all that when the army took over the airport and it became the home of the 428th Fighter Squadron. A curly-haired redhead named Norma Jean Dougherty worked on the assembly line at the airport's military factory when she was photographed for a story for Yank magazine. Later, she reinvented herself as Marilyn Monroe just as the Metropolitan reinvented itself as Van Nuys Airport.

The drive to Van Nuys Airport from Burbank took twenty minutes. Chloe and Tyler didn't say a word as they sat in the back of the black Lincoln Navigator and cruised across the valley with Ohana at the wheel. His fellow operative sat in the passenger seat like a statue. His massive shoulders motionless. His huge square head pointed straight ahead.

Ohana pulled the black SUV through the gates and navigated the private airport. A jet roared overhead before touching down on a nearby runway. They passed multiple hangars and rows of prop planes before pulling up in front of Goldhammer's private hangar. It had the golden logo of his company across the top and seemed sleeker and newer and more luxurious than most of the other hangars. His Gulfstream G700 sat parked inside.

"Wait here," Ohana said. "I'll let you know when we're ready to board." He and the larger, refrigerator-shaped agent climbed from the Navigator and slammed the door.

Chloe glanced at Tyler. He didn't look as confident as he did back at their apartment.

He reached over and squeezed her hand. "I know this is hard for you."

"You always act like you're so damn sure of yourself."

"I'm not."

"I know."

He smiled. "I know you know."

They sat silently, holding hands. "Promise me something," Chloe said.

"Anything."

"You cannot leave me alone with him. Not for a second."

"I won't."

"If we're doing this, we have to do it together."

Tyler nodded. "We will. We are."

"Promise?"

"I promise."

Ohana opened Chloe's door. "Time to go."

The other agent opened Tyler's door.

The siblings climbed out and followed Ohana into the hangar. Chloe watched their luggage being loaded into the cargo hold.

Marta stepped from the Gulfstream and stood at the top of the airstair. "Come! Make yourself comfortable. Mr. Goldhammer's on his way. He'll be joining us shortly."

Chloe and Tyler followed Marta inside. She led them to plush seats, brought them refreshments, and there they sat. Goldhammer's voice bellowed outside the plane. He was furious about something, and his untethered anger filled Chloe with dread.

"I don't understand! How could that happen?"

"He thought they were going to kill him," Ohana said.

"Why would he think such a thing?"

"Because he's out of his mind."

Chloe's blood ran cold as Goldhammer continued to lose his shit. "He went through the windshield?"

"Apparently, he wasn't wearing a seatbelt."

"Whose fault was that?"

"That was our fault."

"Unbelievable."

"The tide was going out, so it likely carried him out to sea."

"Likely?"

"He may wash ashore at some point. He may not. His legs and wrists were bound, so it's unlikely he survived."

Marta moved to the passenger door and urgently whispered something down the airstairs. Goldhammer and Ohana instantly lowered their voices. Their conversation continued though Chloe could no longer make out any of the words.

Tears sprang to Chloe's eyes as she looked back at her brother. *Were they talking about Flynn? Could this be true? Jesus Christ. What did that lunatic do?*

• • •

Alessandra had done the drive to Vegas many times. Once past San Bernardino County, the journey became a desolate ride through the Mojave desert. Interstate 15 traversed Victorville and Barstow, eventually passing Zzyzx Road before reaching the halfway point of Baker, California.

The world's biggest thermometer towered over the shuttered Bun Boy restaurant. It stood 134 feet tall to commemorate the hottest day ever recorded in Baker. 134 degrees Fahrenheit. A couple of gas stations and fast-food establishments were still open, even if most of the rest of the town was not. Buildings were abandoned and boarded up, including the iconic Bun Boy motel across the street.

Alessa once spent a night in Baker with Robert Mitchum. They were too tired to make it all the way to L.A. and found a room at Arne's Royal Hawaiian Motel. That, too, was now shuttered and abandoned.

The decay and desolation didn't depress Alessa the way it might have at one time. At seventy-eight she was much more philosophical. Anything that lived had to die. True of Robert Mitchum. True of Steve McQueen. True of sad, declining tourist towns like Baker.

They bought burgers and drinks to go at the Dairy Queen Chill and Grill and hit the road. Flynn seemed to be enjoying himself as he watched the desert rush by. He wore her late husband's Armani tux and ate carefully so as not to get any burger grease on it.

After Alessa accelerated to ninety to pass a truck on a blind curve, Flynn smiled at her. "You drive like a man."

"What's that supposed to mean?"

"You're aggressive. Fast. Decisive. Skillful."

"Can't a woman be all those things?"

"Yes, but it's unusual."

She shook her head. "I would think a man your age would be more enlightened."

"I just look at the world the way it is."

"You are an anachronism. What they used to call a male chauvinist pig. You would have fit right in with the Rat Pack."

"I was complimenting you."

"Maybe I drive like a woman who knows how to drive."

"A woman of many talents."

"Are you flirting with me, Mr. Flynn?"

"What if I am?"

"I'm old enough to be your grandmother."

"There's something to be said for a woman with experience."

Peanut put her paws up on Flynn's arm and barked. She was belted into a car harness to keep her safe in the backseat.

"Looks like Peanut agrees."

"She just wants you for your meat," Alessa said.

Flynn fed her a bit of burger.

"See! She's training you."

"As all women do," Flynn said.

Alessa smiled at that and hit the gas, throwing Flynn against his seat as she rocketed up the road.

• • •

Tyler and Chloe couldn't believe the size of their suite at Caesars Palace. Apparently, Goldhammer was trying to impress her, but all he managed to do was gross her out.

The place was ridiculous.

The Marc Antony Villa had to be at least 5000 square feet. There was an indoor fountain, a full bar, a state-of-the-art media room, an outdoor whirlpool, and a huge private patio with a panoramic view of the Las Vegas strip."

"This place is crazy," Tyler said.

Marta smiled her robotic smile. "Mr. Goldhammer wanted to make sure you both were comfortable."

Chloe looked out the window at the incredible view. "Thank you, Marta, but I think we can take it from here."

"Mr. Goldhammer would like to invite you out this evening."

"I think that's doable," Tyler said.

"Actually, the invitation is only for your sister."

The hair rose on the back of Chloe's neck. "Wherever I go, Tyler goes."

"But Tyler isn't invited."

"Then I guess I won't be joining him."

Marta's only reaction was a slight pause. "Let me ask Mr. Goldhammer if he would also like to invite your brother."

"You do that."

Marta nodded, turned, and left.

Chloe locked the deadbolt and put the swing bar in place. Tyler put his arms around her and hugged her tight. "We can go home right now if you want to."

"Can we? And what about Flynn?"

"We don't know for sure it was him in that car accident."

"And we don't know it wasn't either."

"So call City of Roses. See if he made it back."

Chloe found a hotel phone and called directory assistance. They connected her directly.

"City of Roses Psychiatric Institute."

"Hi, could I please speak to Mr. Sancho Perez? He's an orderly there."

"Sancho Perez? Can I tell him who's calling?"

"Tell him it's Chloe Jablonski."

"Hold on please."

She looked at Tyler, but he couldn't bear to meet her gaze. She held the phone to her head, stared out the window, and watched as the sun set over the strip. The lights of Las Vegas slowly blinked on.

"Sancho Perez."

"Sancho, hi, it's Chloe."

"Chloe? Jesus! Are you okay?"

"I'm fine. I'm calling about Flynn."

"What about him?"

"I just wanted to make sure he got back to the hospital okay."

"He's not here yet, but if he shows up, I'll let you know. Can I get your number?"

"I'm at Caesars Palace in Las Vegas. Just ask for my room."

"Caesars Palace? Nice. Have fun!"

Chloe hung up. Her voice caught as she started to cry. "Oh, my God…"

The phone immediately rang.

She stared at it.

It rang again.

Chloe picked up. "Hello?"

"It's Marta. I talked to Mr. Goldhammer about your request and he'd be more than happy to host Tyler as well. He explained that he's playing in a private high-stakes poker game this evening. One of the players is the CEO of Xumo. They are the network producing Bombshells and he would like to introduce you."

"Tonight?"

"Yes, at 8:00 p.m."

"Was Mr. Flynn in a car accident?"

"Excuse me?"

"Mr. Flynn. Was he in a car accident?"

"Why would you ask that?"

"Because he hasn't arrived back at the hospital yet," Chloe replied.

"You called City of Roses?"

"They said he never got there."

"Perhaps they took him to a different facility."

"Where?"

"I couldn't say, but would you like me to try and find out?"

"Yes, that would be great."

"Good. I'll come by to pick you and your brother up at 7:45. Sharp."

Marta hung up. Chloe slammed down the receiver. "Different facility my ass."

CHAPTER TWENTY-ONE

The first time Evel Knievel saw the fountains at Caesars Palace, he knew he had to jump them. It took a while to convince the casino's CEO, but once he did, a date was set. December 31, 1967. Knievel was twenty-nine. He tried to cajole The Wide World of Sports *to air the jump live, but they declined. So he hired John Derek to produce a low budget film of the stunt. Derek's then wife, Linda Evans, filmed the famous landing. Right before the jump, Evel stopped in the casino and bet his last hundred dollars on a blackjack hand — and lost. He downed a shot of Wild Turkey and headed outside where two showgirls escorted him to his bike. It would have been the longest motorcycle jump of his career, 141 feet. But he never made it to the other side. The crash was spectacular and he suffered a concussion, a crushed pelvis, fractures to his hip, wrist, and both ankles. Some say he was in a coma for 29 days. Others refute that. What isn't refuted is that seven years later he jumped the Snake River Canyon in Twin Falls, Idaho and survived with just a few scrapes and cuts.*

Alessandra's late husband bought the Aston Martin Vanquish in 2016. He loved sports cars. He loved driving fast. He loved the history and romance of Aston Martins. She knew he saw himself as boring and stodgy and hoped some of that steel and gasoline-fueled glamour would rub off on him. He worried that one day Alessandra would grow weary of his dreary personality and leave him.

But by the time Alessandra married Phil, she was tired of the turmoil and chaos bad boys brought to the party. She knew Phil would never break her heart the way the others had. He treated her with respect and showered her with affection. So what if she didn't feel that thrill of lascivious danger?

She felt protected.

Cared for.

Loved.

In her younger days, Flynn would have easily swept her off her feet. He was just her type. Handsome, but not pretty. Tall and lean with a coiled energy that created a constant sense of excitement. Charming, but slightly distant and mysterious. She knew he had secrets and some deep inner pain that he kept under wraps. Occasionally, she'd catch a glimpse, but he quickly covered any hint of vulnerability with a well-placed bon mot.

If she was forty years younger, she might have been tempted. But she was an old woman now. Most people, especially younger people, didn't recognize her. She was invisible in the way old women often were. It was somewhat of a relief, but also disappointing as she was no longer special. Just another anonymous senior citizen. Because of that, she hid out in her Malibu retreat and didn't venture out into the world all that often.

This road trip to Vegas might be her last hurrah. To that end, she brought some of her favorite outfits along. Clothes she hadn't worn in years. Helen Mirren was a few years younger than her. They were friendly in the late seventies and early eighties, though Helen was more the serious actress and Alessa was more the sex symbol. She always admired Helen's sense of style and in the '90s decided to borrow her look. For the ride to Vegas Alessa wore a black cocktail dress from Dolce & Gabbana. Elegant yet still sexy. Shorter than a woman her age would normally wear. She also wore high heels for the first time in a long time. As painful as they were to wear, they raised her derriere, lengthened her legs, and showed off her calves, which were still quite good, even though she had a few varicose veins.

The bellhops all hopped to when she pulled up in front of Caesars Palace in her late husband's Aston Martin. Flynn emerged wearing his tux and Alessa climbed out showing lots of leg and looking much like the glamorous movie star she once pretended to be. One of the older doormen even recognized her. She could see acknowledgment and surprise and then delight in his eyes. She felt a flash of pride. Maybe she hadn't lost it yet.

After the bellhops unloaded their luggage, Alessa led the way as they crossed the hotel lobby. When they passed the towering statue of Caesar Augustus, Alessa rubbed Caesar's left index finger for luck, as was the tradition. She approached the VIP check-in desk and the smiling gray-haired man behind the counter greeted her by her married name.

"So good to have you back again, Mrs. Zimmel."

She smiled her movie star smile as she read the name on his tag. "Thank you, Edward. It's good to be back."

"I was very sorry to hear of Mr. Zimmel's passing."

"Thank you, Edward. Phil was very fond of you."

"With the TCA Press conference happening this weekend, we're very booked up as you can imagine. I know you requested the Titus Villa, but I'm afraid it was unavailable. I hope I'm not being presumptuous, but I thought you might be comfortable in one of our private suites at the Laurel Collection."

"How kind of you."

"I booked you into the Agrippina. It's in the Octavius Tower. Right across from the Garden of the Gods. Gratis, of course." Edward smiled at Flynn. "Is this your son? Mr. Zimmer spoke of him often."

"No, this is not Edward's son. This is Mr. Flynn. He is my escort on this... excursion."

Alessa watched as Edward struggled to keep his eyes from going wide with surprise. "Oh. Of course."

"Good to meet you, Edward," Flynn said.

"Good to meet you too, sir."

"We're here at the invitation of Mr. Goldhammer. We understand he's staying here."

"Of course, yes. His was the party who booked the Titus Villa. Would you like to give him a call?" Edward pointed to a phone on the counter. "I can connect you with his suite if you like?"

"No, I think we'd rather surprise him," Flynn said.

"Of course. I'll have the bellman show you to your room." Edward handed them each a keycard. "Thank you for joining us again, Mrs. Zimmer. Enjoy your stay."

• • •

After freshening up in the Agrippina Suite, they headed four floors up to the Titus Villa and rang the bell.

A butler in a tux answered the door. "Good evening."

Behind him, Flynn noticed two hulking security operatives in dark suits. He stepped just out of view as Alessa addressed the butler.

"Good evening. We're here to see Mr. Goldhammer."

"He isn't here at present," the butler said.

Alessa looked put out. "That's strange. He called and left a message for me."

"He said he wanted us to come by," Flynn added.

"Here?"

"He didn't specify."

"Perhaps he meant for you to join him in the Sky-High Limit Room," the butler offered. "He's hosting a high stakes charity poker tournament and—"

"Of course!" Alessa smiled. She looked abashed. Flynn decided she was a better actress than most gave her credit for. "The Tournament. How silly of me."

CHAPTER TWENTY-TWO

Chloe wasn't sure how much more of this shit she could put up with. Per Goldhammer's instructions, she dolled herself up. Not just for him, but for Andy Dempsy, the CEO of Xumo, the network producing and streaming *Bombshells*. Once again, she had to trade on her looks and sexuality simply to find work as an actress. The very idea made her both furious and nauseous.

Goldhammer sent her shopping with Marta and they hit all the high-end shops in the Forum. Fendi, Jimmy Choo, and Kate Spade to name a few.

When she arrived at the Sky-High Room, every man there turned to watch her walk in. She wore a sheer black lace minidress that left nothing to the imagination. Andy Dempsy smiled with delight when he met her, though he didn't look her in the eye. He just held her hand with his sweaty paw and gawked shamelessly at her cleavage. The skinny little dweeb skeeved her out, but she did her best to pretend to be charmed. Balding with a creepy smile and half-lidded eyes, he wouldn't let go of her hand. Damn gatekeepers. Entitled assholes all. Would Andy Dempsy want something from her too? What was *that* slimy douchebag's price? She finally pulled her hand from his sweaty palm and nonchalantly wiped it on Tyler's shoulder.

Once she established herself, she hoped the power would tilt in her direction, but for now she knew there wasn't much she could do. They held all the cards. Well, not *all* the cards. Goldhammer believed she had that recording. Maybe Tyler was right about having something to hold over him. Or at least the perception of something. If he messed with her, she would mess with him. Mutually assured destruction.

This charity poker tournament was just another opportunity for these rich dipsticks to compare the size of their tiny little dicks. So insecure. Every single one of them. Which is probably why they wouldn't let her play poker. They were too busy living out their power fantasies, dressed to the teeth in elegant tuxes. Their arm candy hovered behind them, trying not to look too bored in their two thousand dollar dresses.

Chloe figured she could beat every one of their smug asses if given half a chance. Her parents frowned on gambling, but her Uncle Dave, the black sheep of the family, taught her how to play no limit Texas Hold'em when she was ten. She was a natural and could bluff anyone. After all, bluffing was just acting. Uncle Dave would stake her and she would take out much older players, much to her uncle's delight. When her parents discovered what Uncle Dave was doing, they forbid her from ever seeing him again. That broke her heart. She loved her Uncle Dave. He believed in her. He made her laugh. He knew how to have fun.

When she was twenty, Dave died from cirrhosis of the liver. Though her mother didn't tell her until six months after he passed away. They were ashamed of him, so no one from the family went to his funeral. However, the lessons Dave taught her never left her. She played online poker in college and won enough to pay part of her tuition and most of her room and board.

She wished she could face Goldhammer across the table and put that arrogant butt plug in his place. But the tournament had a minimum million dollar buy-in. She'd need to find $999,987.47 before she could take a chair.

Tyler sat at the bar, flirting with a bartender. He was just Tyler's type. Tall and slender and Aryan-looking. At least *he* was having a good time.

The floor-to-ceiling windows offered a spectacular view of the strip. The setting sun lit up the sky with crimson clouds. Chloe sipped on a gimlet and tried to feel optimistic. Tried to imagine the promise of a bright future and fabulous career. But try as she might, she couldn't shake the cold dread or the nagging despair.

She also couldn't stop thinking about Flynn. Where was he? Was it him in that car accident? If something happened to him, she'd never forgive herself. Yes, he was a complete wackadoodle, but he was so damn charming. His only intention was to protect her. Unlike Goldhammer, who only wanted to use her.

She stood just behind the douche as he sat at the poker table and stared at the back of his pudgy head. His red-tipped ears. That mole on his neck with the hair growing out of it. He kept a constant stream of patter going as he played. Boasting. Bragging. Puffing himself up with stories meant to intimidate and psych out his opponents. "I haven't played serious poker since I won the WPT in Barcelona back in 2012. For a brief moment I even considered going pro, but of course, I have a company to run. I do enjoy the action though. Pitting myself against the best of the best. It's the ultimate mind game, isn't it? Even more so than chess." Chloe hated his arrogant, high-pitched, adenoidal voice. She battled a powerful compulsion to pour her gimlet over his fat head and storm right out of there.

And then everything changed.

Flynn walked in.

James Fucking Flynn.

He wore a tuxedo that fit him perfectly, and caught her eye from across the room, smiling, confident, charming. Just as Chloe caught every male eye on her entrance, Flynn caught every female eye as he made his way towards Goldhammer's poker table.

Tyler noticed his grand entrance and nearly fell off his stool. He looked at Chloe and mouthed the words, "What the hell?"

The woman who walked into the room with Flynn also looked familiar. Tall and elegant, slender, and surprisingly attractive for a woman her age. Was she in her sixties? Seventies? Chloe couldn't tell. Though her skin had some wrinkles and sun damage, her cheekbones could cut glass and her eyes were unbelievably blue. Her white hair was shoulder length and chic and perfectly coifed. Who the hell was she?

Play at the poker table came to a screeching halt as Goldhammer looked positively gobsmacked. He stared at Flynn in stunned silence, as did Ohana and Marta and the rest of his security team. Ohana moved for him, but Goldhammer raised a hand that froze him in his tracks. The poker table was packed with other rich and famous jerk-offs and there were journalists and gossipmongers everywhere. She figured the last thing Goldhammer wanted was a scene.

The oldest and crankiest man at Goldhammer's table, a casino owner in his early eighties, noticed Flynn's companion and broke out in a huge tobacco-stained grin.

"Alessandra!" the man shouted in delight.

"Hey Rudy," Alessandra replied, flashing him a dazzling smile.

"I was so sorry to hear about Phil."

She nodded. "Thank you."

"Do you know Gary Goldhammer?"

"Only by reputation."

"Gary, this is Alessandra Bianchi," Rudy motioned to her proudly. "I'm sure you've seen her in the movies. She starred in *Fun in Acapulco* with Elvis Presley. *Death and Diamonds! Assignment in Vienna!*"

"That was all a very long time ago." Alessa offered a subdued smile to Goldhammer.

"Of course I recognize Miss Bianchi," Goldhammer replied as he shifted his gaze to Flynn. "How do you know Mr. Flynn?"

"We're old friends," Alessa said.

"I assume you know who and what he is?"

"Of course I do, and more importantly, I know who and what you are."

Goldhammer's head moved as if on a swivel as he turned his attention back to Alessa. "And what would that be?"

"A powerful and influential man."

Tears filled Chloe's eyes as she smiled at Flynn. "We were worried about you."

"Well, I'm here now, Chloe. No reason to worry."

"So *this* is the famous Chloe?" Alessa said with a grin.

Flynn nodded. "Indeed. Chloe, meet Alessandra Bianchi."

"It's an honor." Chloe dipped her head.

Marta looked serene and gave nothing away. Ohana, on the other hand, looked ready to jump out of his skin.

While Goldhammer's pale face remained impassive, his eyes were anything but. "It's good to see you again, Mr. Flynn, but as you can see, we're in the midst of a charity poker tournament. Perhaps you and I can visit another time."

Flynn rested his hand on the last open chair at the table. "Actually, I was hoping to buy in."

"Buy in?" Goldhammer nearly smiled. "You do realize it's a one million dollar minimum."

Flynn's eyes widened with surprise. "One million dollars?"

"No limit Texas Hold'em. Winner takes all. Of course, ten percent does go to charity. The Make-A-Wish Foundation."

"One million?" Alessa pulled a checkbook out of her purse. "I can cover that. After all, it's for such a good cause."

Rudy, the old casino owner and Alessandra fan, pointed to the open chair next to him. "Have a seat, Mr. Flynn. Welcome!"

Chloe could only see the back of Goldhammer's noggin, but from the set of his head and his glacial stillness, she assumed he was furious.

Flynn took the seat and the dealer pushed his chips to him. Multiple stacks of various colors. Black hundred-dollar chips, orange thousand-dollar chips, and gold one hundred thousand-dollar chips. Flynn seemed cool and confident as he arranged them in elegant piles.

Tyler hopped off his stool and moved closer to follow the play as the dealer dealt the hole cards.

Chloe watched as Flynn picked them up in a way that let everyone see what he had. Horrified, she motioned for him to keep them hidden, but Flynn seemed oblivious as he waved to a waitress. "Can I get a vodka martini, please? Three measures of Gordons, one of Grey Goose, a half measure of Lillet Blanc. Shake it until it's ice cold and add a thin slice of lemon peel."

"Shaken, not stirred?" Rudy said with a grin.

"Of course," Flynn replied.

Alessa leaned down and whispered something in Flynn's ear and he immediately pulled his hole cards closer to his chest.

Still, he played erratically, stupidly, but with such confidence and capriciousness, no one knew how to counter him. He made wild, ridiculous bets and rarely ever folded. Being so unpredictable and

125

impulsive, his opponents couldn't read him and much to Chloe's surprise, Flynn began to win.

Watching him play made her jumpy as hell. She could barely contain her rising anxiety. Chloe tried to calm her breathing and center herself, but Flynn was an out-of-control train on a collision course with a gasoline tanker truck. Each time he made a stupid play, her blood pressure rose. Still, he seemed so cool and collected, so self-assured and charming. She knew it was all a facade and that beneath that veil of confidence was someone completely disconnected from reality. Even so, she had to admire his batshit crazy bravado.

How did Flynn know Alessandra Bianchi? What was that about? And what did he think he was doing here?

Somehow, she had to get Flynn alone and convince him to go back to the hospital. Maybe she should call Sancho. At the moment, she couldn't do anything but watch Flynn play cards like a complete lunatic.

An hour later, Flynn had eliminated most of the other players. Rudy, the casino magnate, busted first. Next came the cowboy guy who owned that trucking company. And then Andy Dempsy, the CEO of Xumo. Followed by the old Chinese man and the very tan white-haired hedge fund owner. Second to last was the former senator who sat on the board of some bank.

When the dust cleared, only Goldhammer remained.

It was mano-a-mano.

Both had huge stacks of chips. At least five million each. Flynn sipped his third martini and didn't seem the slightest bit snockered. Chloe studied the side of Goldhammer's face as he turned to reach for his drink. He looked tired and irritated; his pale skin covered with a thin, greasy sheen of perspiration.

"Perhaps we should take a short break," Goldhammer said.

"If you're getting tired, by all means," Flynn replied.

"Did I say I was tired?"

"No, but you do look a little fatigued."

"I'm fine."

"Good! Let's keep at it then. Unless you'd like a breather?"

"I'm *fine*."

"Excellent." Flynn waved to the waitress. "Can I get another martini, please? What about you, Mr. Goldfelcher? Would you like a fresh drink?"

"What did you call me?"

"Pardon me. Goldfelcher was your grandfather's name, wasn't it?"

"My name is Goldhammer."

"It is now. But that's what America is all about, isn't it? Reinventing oneself?"

"Can we please play?"

"Isn't that what we're doing? Personally, I find the American penchant for reinvention inspiring. This country loves to replace the old with the new. Start over. Start fresh. In the UK, it's not like that. The class system there keeps everyone in their place. Not like here. In America Archibald Leach could become Cary Grant. Norma Jean Mortenson could become Marilyn Monroe. Gary Goldfelcher could become Gary Goldhammer."

"Stop it! *Stop it!* That was never my name! I've always been Goldhammer! That's who I am! You are the one pretending to be *something he is not!*"

The room went dead quiet at the end of Goldhammer's rant. No one knew what to say and instead just exchanged freighted glances.

The dealer dealt the hole cards.

Flynn picked his up so carelessly Tyler could see his hand. Chloe caught Tyler's eye and raised an eyebrow as if to say, "Well?"

Tyler frowned and made a face indicating that Flynn had a shit hand.

Goldhammer lifted his cards off the green baize just high enough to see what he had. Chloe managed to see them too.

A queen of diamonds and a queen of clubs.

Chloe could see Tyler's surprise when Flynn didn't fold. Instead, Flynn bet a hundred grand. A big opening bid for such a shit hand. Goldhammer betrayed no emotion when he met Flynn's bet, but didn't raise it. He clearly didn't want to scare Flynn off. As if that was possible. As if Flynn played poker like someone with a plan or any skill or instincts at all.

The dealer dealt the flop and revealed the three cards.

A queen of hearts. A jack of hearts. And a seven of clubs.

Goldhammer already had three of a kind. Queens high. When she glanced across at Tyler she saw him looking at Flynn's hand with alarm. Clearly, he still had a shit hand.

Yet, Flynn bet another hundred grand. Goldhammer's bulbous head stayed very still. Then he raised Flynn. Flynn raised the bet again and it went back and forth a few times before the dealer dealt the turn card.

A seven of hearts.

Goldhammer now had a full house. Queens over sevens. Shit.

Flynn seemed so confident as he bet again, a tiny smile playing at the corners of his mouth. Tyler looked terrified. Chloe hoped Goldhammer didn't see the look on her brother's face. Not that it mattered as Goldhammer raised Flynn, and Flynn raised him back and soon almost all their chips were on the table.

Every eye in the room watched what happened next. The silence was palpable as they were going for all the marbles.

At least seven million dollars.

The dealer dealt the fifth and final card.

The queen of spades. Goldhammer now had four of a kind.

Tyler looked apoplectic as Flynn pushed all the rest of his chips into the center of the table. "I'm all in."

Rivulets of sweat ran down the back of Goldhammer's neck. He peeked at his hole cards. He stared at the community cards. He fingered the last of his chips. She could almost hear the gears turning in Goldhammer's head. He was so far in now. How could he not go all the way? He had four of a kind. Four queens. How could Flynn possibly win? Only a few hands could beat him. She knew the odds against Flynn were astronomical. Sweat continued to roll down Goldhammer's face as he tried to calculate the risk.

By the look on Tyler's face, Chloe was sure Flynn didn't have a winning hand. Still, Flynn sat there so confidently, staring coolly into Goldhammer's eyes.

No one made a sound as Goldhammer searched Flynn's inscrutable face for some clue.

"You must be bluffing. You have to be bluffing," Goldhammer stammered, wiping the sweat off his face with the crook of his elbow.

"There's one way to find out, isn't there?" Flynn grinned. "Call me."

Goldhammer looked at the last of his chips and nearly pushed them all in, but hesitated and made a guttural roar before throwing down his cards and folding.

Flynn grinned, reached his arms out, and scooped up over seven million dollars in chips. Goldhammer lunged across the table and snatched up Flynn's cards.

A terrible breach of poker etiquette.

His face turned bright red and his eyes nearly bugged from his head when he saw what Flynn had. Shaking with fury, he threw the cards down on the table. A two of clubs and a seven of spades. Flynn had a pair of sevens.

Goldhammer would have crushed him. But he gave up.

He folded.

Goldhammer abruptly stood, knocking over his chair, and shouted across the table at Flynn. "Why are you doing this to me?"

"You know exactly why."

"Is this about the girl?"

"No, it's about you. What you've done and what you're planning to do. And know this. You won't get away with it. Any of it. I will stop you. One way or another. I will do *whatever* is necessary."

"Are you threatening me?"

"I don't make threats. I make promises."

With the press and all the celebrities watching in stunned silence, Goldhammer stormed from the room, furious at his humiliation at the hands of a lunatic.

Chloe looked across the table. Flynn smiled at her. "Would you and Tyler care to join Alessa and I for dinner? I'm buying."

CHAPTER TWENTY-THREE

When Jay Sarno and Stanley Mallin conceived of Caesars Palace, they imagined a resort and casino where every guest would feel like Caesar. That's why there's no apostrophe. It isn't possessive, but plural. They held the grand opening on August 5, 1966, and spent one million dollars on the event. The cost included the largest order of Ukrainian caviar ever placed by a private organization. Cocktail waitresses in tiny togas greeted guests by saying, "Welcome to Caesars Palace, I am your slave." In the Bacchanal Room, guests were fed grapes by those same toga-clad waitresses who performed neck massages on male diners as they drank from silver-lined chalices.

Alessandra gazed at the Eiffel Tower from their table at Restaurant Guy Savoy. It was the ersatz Eiffel Tower at Paris Las Vegas across the street from Caesars and stood half the height of the actual one. Still, it lit up the night.

The original Restaurant Guy Savoy was in Paris. Alessa and her late husband dined there many times, but not as many times as they had at the Vegas location. Sitting there with Flynn, Chloe, and Tyler felt celebratory but also a little melancholy. She missed Phil desperately. Never more so than when she visited places that held so many memories.

Guy Savoy served classic French cuisine, and Flynn ordered with panache, clearly in his element. The sommelier complimented him effusively when he requested a bottle of Krug Clos du Mesnil Champagne. At twenty-seven hundred dollars a bottle it barely made a dent in Flynn's winnings.

Alessa enjoyed watching Flynn humiliate Goldhammer. She'd dealt with *bastardi* like him many times. Men who weren't used to hearing the word "no". To see him storm out of there gave her great satisfaction. She could see Chloe was relieved that Flynn was still alive, but also irritated with him. Irritated that he would challenge Goldhammer the way he did. She worried that Chloe didn't understand she was dealing with the devil.

Alessa caught Chloe's eye and held it. "This arrangement you have with Goldhammer. You will live to regret it."

"What do you know about it?" Chloe went on the defensive.

"I've been where you are, and I know where that path leads. You don't need someone like Goldhammer. Not when you have someone like me. I still know more than a few casting directors, producers, and studio executives."

"I appreciate your concern, I really do, but I have it handled." Chloe drained her glass of champagne.

"Do you?"

"We do." Tyler sipped his champagne as well. "Damn, this is good. But twenty-seven hundred dollars a bottle good? That's like, what? Three hundred and fifty dollars a glass? What is that per sip?"

Alessa continued to hold Chloe's gaze. "If you're as talented as you are beautiful, you don't need him."

"Maybe so, but I *do* need him to pay for what he did to me."

"But he's not paying, is he? He's simply using you in another way. Putting you under his control. That's what men like him want. Control."

"She's taking back control." Tyler put his drink down a little too hard. "Taking back her power. Getting a chance at a career. Does that make up for what he did to her? No. No way. But it's something. And something is better than nothing."

Alessa shook her head. "I've dealt with men like him before. They always want more."

Chloe poured herself another glass of champagne. "Can we please talk about something else?"

Alessa sighed. "Certainly."

But no one brought up another topic or even said another word until Tyler could no longer stand the awkward silence. "I got a question," Tyler pointed at Flynn. "How'd you meet our friend here?"

"In Malibu. Washed up on the beach."

"Did he tell you he was in a car accident?"

"He said someone was trying to kill him."

"Did he also tell you he worked for the British Secret Service?"

"He did."

"And that didn't strike you as weird?"

"A little, but he went into great detail about it and seemed quite sure of himself and by the end…"

"You believed him?" Chloe asked.

"I did. I do."

"I know, right? He can be very convincing. But here's the thing. He's out of his mind. He's a mental patient. That's where we met. A mental hospital." Chloe guzzled her champagne.

Alessa glanced at Flynn, who laughed at that. "I don't think she'll buy our cover story now, Chloe. The cat's out of the bag. I already told Alessa the truth."

"The truth is you're delusional." Chloe grabbed the Clos du Mesnil out of the wine bucket and poured herself another glass. "You mean well. You really do. But you're not all there."

Alessa gave Flynn a sideways glance. "What is she talking about?"

"The cover story headquarters concocted for me."

"James is a good guy," Tyler explained. "And I know he's trying to help, but he is totally off his nut."

The food arrived and the conversation awkwardly paused once again while everyone dug into ice poached oysters, beluga caviar on ice, artichoke soup with black truffle, oven baked John Dory and foie gras with aged wagyu steak.

As they ate, Alessa tried to make sense of Chloe and Tyler's crazy explanation for Flynn's behavior. Could he really be a mental patient? He seemed so competent and self-assured and grounded in reality. But maybe that was the giveaway. He exhibited no doubt whatsoever. Not the slightest hesitation or hint of insecurity. That abnormal level of confidence wasn't natural or even logical. She'd met overly confident men like that before, and each of them suffered from that same narcissistic personality disorder. One of them was even elected President of the United States.

Alessa reached across the table and rested her hand on Chloe's arm. "Putting Mr. Flynn's motivations and mental state aside, his concern for you is real."

Chloe removed Alessa's hand. "And I appreciate that. I really do. But I don't need his help."

Flynn poured himself the last of the Clos du Mesnil. "You know, it's not just about you. Goldhammer's machinations will have worldwide repercussions. He's an ambitious man, hungry for power, and will do whatever is necessary to get what he wants. It's imperative we uncover and foil whatever evil plan he's plotting before it's too late. The very fate of the planet could be at stake."

Chloe gave Alessa a long meaningful look as if to say, *See? Batshit crazy.*

• • •

The food at Guy Savoy kicked ass, but not being used to food that rich, Chloe felt a little queasy. Or maybe it was all that pricey champagne. She pushed back her chair to stand and wavered unsteadily. "Look, it's late. I'm tired, and I'm going to bed."

"Me too." Tyler drained the last of his champagne, took one last bite of steak and stood.

"You're right," Flynn agreed. "It's been a long night. I'll see you tomorrow."

"Sure," Chloe said.

"Just not too bright and early," Tyler added.

Chloe and Tyler left the restaurant and took the elevator up to the Marc Antony Villa. As soon as they walked inside, Chloe bolted the door.

"You okay?" Tyler asked her.

She shook her head. "Not really."

"When Flynn walked in with that old movie star on his arm, I thought I was going to shit a brick," Tyler said.

"No kidding."

"I'm glad he's okay, but Jesus Christ, he really screwed things up. You think Goldhammer's gonna renege on your deal?"

"I don't know."

"We have to get Flynn out of here before he messes things up even more."

Chloe nodded and crossed to the minibar, which wasn't very mini, and found a split of champagne. She popped the cork and poured herself a flute. "Do you want some?"

"I could do with a nightcap."

She handed him a glass of bubbly, and he took a sip. "Tastes just like that twenty-seven hundred dollar a bottle champagne." He downed the rest of the flute. "How old do you think Alessandra is?"

"No idea."

"Did you remember ever seeing her in a movie?"

"Not really."

"Elvis didn't make a movie after 1969. If she was in *Fun in Acapulco*, she's gotta be at least eighty, right?"

"Maybe."

Tyler considered that as Chloe poured more champagne. "You think he's doing her?"

"No way."

"She's still pretty hot even if she *is* eighty."

"Seriously?"

"Maybe Flynn's a granny banger."

Chloe sat heavily on the bed. "I'm going to call Sancho. Let him know that Flynn's alive and well and right here in Las Vegas."

"Sancho?"

"At City of Roses. He's an orderly. Works nights."

"Good idea. Maybe they'll come get him before he gets his crazy ass in more trouble."

Chloe picked up the room phone and placed a call to City of Roses. She sat on hold for ten minutes until they located Sancho.

"Sancho Perez."

"Hey Sancho, it's Chloe again. I found Flynn."

"Found him where?"

"Las Vegas."

"*Las Vegas?*"

"It's a long story."

"So he's okay?"

"Physically. Not mentally."

"How'd he end up in Vegas?"

"I'll explain later, but right now I'm worried he's going to do something crazy."

"No doubt about it."

"Can the hospital send someone for him? He's staying at Caesars Palace."

"Caesars Palace? How the hell can he afford that?"

"He's staying with someone who can."

"Who?"

"Alessandra Bianchi."

"*Who*?"

"Like I said… it's a long story. Can you come here and get him?"

"Come to Vegas?"

"Why not? It's like a five-hour drive. He likes you. He might listen to you."

"I don't know, Chloe. He hardly ever listens to me."

"Look, I'm worried about him. Worried what he might do. Worried what might happen to him."

Sancho sighed.

The silence stretched for ten seconds. "Sancho, are you still there?"

"I got six more hours left on my shift. Let me think about it." After another pause. "I'll get back to you."

CHAPTER TWENTY-FOUR

Flynn believed that Chloe still suffered from PTSD. After the torture and brainwashing she underwent in that enemy prison camp, she clearly couldn't see reality or think properly. This disorder made her especially susceptible to the lies and manipulation of someone like Goldhammer.

If Chloe wouldn't listen to reason, he'd have to take her by force and return her to headquarters. Of course, first he would have to deal with Goldhammer.

Discover his plot.

Foil his plan.

Flynn considered all this as he let the hot jets in the Jacuzzi pummel his still aching muscles. He brought an additional bottle of Clos du Mesnil up to their luxurious villa and put it on ice. There it sat, chilling at the perfect temperature in a bucket on the floor of the Agrippina Suite's palatial bathroom.

As he sipped some champagne, he wondered what was going on with Alessandra. She started acting oddly soon after Chloe and Tyler excused themselves. She kept her distance and grew strangely silent. Perhaps something Chloe said disturbed her. Or perhaps she was coming off the rush of that poker tournament and feeling the stress of real-life danger. She played a secret agent in the movies, but this was different. The cold, gritty reality had none of the glamour and all the peril. It was all fun and games until one's life was on the line.

The bathroom door opened a crack and Alessa poked her head in. "So, this hospital you and Chloe we're in. What's it called?"

"City of Roses Psychiatric. Of course, it's all a front."

"A front?"

"A cover. It's not a real hospital."

"What is it?"

"It's the California field office for Her Majesty's Secret Service. They have similar such satellite offices all over the world."

Alessa's eyes grew shiny. Was she crying?

"Are you all right?"

"I'm fine. I'm tired. It's way past my bedtime."

She cinched her robe tighter and started to close the door before poking her head in again. "I just wanted to thank you."

"For what?"

"For helping me to step outside my comfort zone. After Philip died, my world grew so small. I never wanted to venture out. It was nice to step out into the world again and remember who I used to be."

"Who you still are."

She smiled at that and left the bathroom.

Flynn climbed from the tub, dried himself off, and wrapped the large Turkish towel around his waist. He pulled the Clos du Mesnil out of the ice bucket, grabbed his champagne flute, and headed into his bedroom. Alessa insisted on separate rooms. Flynn figured she was just old-fashioned that way. He slipped off the towel and slid into bed between the cool sheets. Turning off the light, he closed his eyes.

• • •

Flynn awakened in the dark with a silencer pressed against his head. "Rise and shine, Mr. Flynn." Ohana. "And let's not do anything stupid. We wouldn't want Miss Bianchi caught in the crossfire."

"Where is she?"

"In her room. In her bed. We injected her with something to keep her asleep. She'll wake up with a headache, but she'll be just fine."

"What do you want?"

"I want you to put your clothes on and come with us."

"Where?"

"You'll see."

"And if I refuse?"

"Why make things more difficult than they have to be?"

• • •

Flynn once again rode in the back of a black Lincoln Navigator, only this time Ohana wasn't taking any chances. This time, he handcuffed Flynn's hands behind him. He wore the same Armani tuxedo he wore earlier in the evening and lay on his side in the rear cargo area, his ankles trussed together with duct tape. They tethered him to a metal cargo anchor to keep him from moving about, and tossed a heavy blanket over him.

"Where are you taking me?" Flynn was more curious than cowed.

"Away from here. Away from Vegas. You need to disappear, Mr. Flynn. Mr. Goldhammer is tired of your constant interference."

"With his plans?"

"Yes."

"For world domination?"

Ohana laughed at that. "He does like to dominate, but I don't think he wants to be in charge of everything. Just a few things. Mainly, he wants his merger to go through."

"So he can control the world?"

"He is a bit of control freak. I will give you that. He doesn't like to lose, and you beat him badly. Publicly humiliated him."

"And now he wants me dead."

"He does. I wanted to take you back to that mental hospital, but he believes you're too much of a threat. A lunatic convinced he has a license to kill? He worries you may try to murder him. Not an unreasonable fear. What if you were to escape again? God knows what you would do to him."

"You'll never get away with this."

"Actually, I will and I have before. For whatever nonsensical reason, you have decided that Mr. Goldhammer is your enemy. Well, congratulations. You have made that delusion a reality. He *is* your enemy now, and he wants you to disappear. Permanently."

"What do you get out of this?"

"Part of your poker winnings. Half of which you already donated to the *Make-A-Wish-Foundation*."

"So it's a win-win for everyone."

"Except for you, of course."

"Do you plan to bury me in some anonymous hole in the desert?"

"No, your abrupt disappearance would raise uncomfortable questions. Instead, we will leave clues to make it look like you jumped to your death."

"From where?"

"The Pat Tillman Memorial Bridge at Hoover Dam."

"M would never believe that."

"Who?"

"The operational head of Her Majesty's Secret Service."

Ohana chuckled. "You were quite the challenge, Mr. Flynn. Completely unpredictable because nothing you did was logical. But now, the game is over and as sorry as I am to see you go... I'm afraid it's time to say goodbye."

A needle pricked his leg as Ohana injected something into Flynn's blood stream. The drowsiness was almost immediate as the narcotic moved through his circulatory system with great rapidity. He tried to stay conscious, but lost the fight. An empty darkness swallowed him.

• • •

Sancho charged into the new head psychiatrist's office soon after he arrived at work. He blew right by Ms. Honeywell and found Dr. Michaels working at his desk. When he replaced Nickelson as head honcho at City of Roses, he brought a very different style to the job. Where Nickelson was open and welcoming, Michaels was dismissive and intimidating. He had hard, gray eyes behind his stainless steel glasses and didn't exude the slightest bit of compassion or warmth. His bald, almond-shaped head only added to his hard-driving, no-nonsense demeanor. Michaels didn't look up and continued to work on some paperwork. Sancho stood there, staring, waiting, wondering if he should clear his throat or make some other sort of sound to alert Michaels of his presence. Finally, after a few painful seconds of feeling ignored and yes, intimidated, he said, "Sir, do you have a minute?"

Michaels raised his gaze and didn't smile or greet Sancho. He just glowered. "I'm afraid not, Perez. I'm already late for my first appointment."

Honeywell stood in the doorway and she did not look happy. "What do you think you're doing, Perez?"

"I got a call about Flynn."

Honeywell narrowed her eyes. "From who?"

"Chloe Jablonski. She says he's in trouble."

"What kind of trouble?" Honeywell placed a fist on her hip.

"She wouldn't say."

Michaels sighed. "Who's Chloe Jablonski?"

"She used to be a patient here," Sancho said. "It's the woman Flynn escaped with."

Michaels nodded. "Oh, yes, Ms. Jablonski. Did she say where she was?"

"Vegas. Flynn's there too. And she says he's in danger."

"Mr. Flynn's in Las Vegas?"

"He's staying at Caesars Palace."

Honeywell's eyes went wide. "Caesars Palace?"

"I thought maybe you could call him. Talk to him. Tell him to come home," Sancho said.

"Mr. Flynn and I haven't really had time to establish a relationship yet. Perhaps you should call him instead."

"Even though he doesn't know you well, he sees you as an authority figure. I think he might listen to you more than me."

Michaels closed his eyes and sighed with irritation. "Do you have a room number?"

"No, but he's staying with Alessandra Bianchi."

"Who?"

"She used to be a movie star."

"Alessandra Bianchi?" Honeywell looked nonplussed.

"That's what Chloe said."

Another heavy sigh from Michaels as he looked at Honeywell. "Would you please get me Caesars Palace?" Honeywell returned to her desk, found the number, made the call, and beeped Dr. Michael's intercom. "Caesars Palace on line one."

Michaels picked up. "Alessandra Bianchi's room, please."

The reception connected him, but the call must have immediately gone to voice mail as Michaels left a message. "Miss Bianchi, my name is Dr. David Michaels and I'm the Senior Psychiatrist at the City of Roses Psychiatric Institute in Pasadena. I understand one of our patients is staying with you. His name is James Flynn and I would like to talk to him. He's non-violent for the most part, but he is suffering from a severe delusional disorder. Please have him call me as soon as possible. I'm at 626-555-1520. If he refuses to call me and/or exhibits any erratic, aggressive, or violent behavior, please call the local police department. Once he's in custody, you can give the police my number. Again, this is Dr. David Michaels at the City Roses Psychiatric Institute." Michaels hung up and looked at a worried Sancho. "Anything else?"

"Do you think I should drive to Vegas?"

"Neither I nor the hospital can authorize that."

"There must be something we can do."

"Mr. Flynn is a voluntary commitment. A legal guardian administers a trust that pays for him to stay here. We can't force him to return against his will. I can try to apply for a 5150 hold, but I'm not sure an order in California would be valid in Nevada."

"If the police pick him up there, they'll throw him in jail. He could end up in a state hospital."

"That's true. But perhaps then his legal guardian can have him transported back to City of Roses. I'm not sure there's much more we can do."

"Sir, you need to get to your meeting," Honeywell said.

Michaels nodded. "Sorry Perez, I know you have a personal relationship with Flynn, but that's even more of a reason why you shouldn't go. Hopefully, Mr. Flynn will call me and I can convince him to return voluntarily. Once he returns, *if* he returns, you will no longer be working with him on a one-to-one basis. There needs to be a certain professional distance between our staff and our patients and I'm afraid you and Mr. Flynn have crossed that line more than once."

Michaels grabbed a file off his desk and hurried out the door.

Honeywell grabbed Sancho by the arm and ushered him out of Michael's office. "Blow by me like that again and I will put my foot so far up your ass you'll have toes for teeth. Is that understood?"

"Yes, ma'am."

• • • •

While everyone else headed for work, Sancho drove his tired ass home. His Aston Martin DB 9 Volante burned a lot of gas and he had to fill it up twice a week. He bought a thirty-two-ounce Kiwi-Strawberry Slurpee in the mini-mart because the forty-four-ounce size wouldn't fit in his cupholder. Climbing back in his car, he turned the key, and the twelve cylinder, five hundred horsepower engine rumbled to life. He burned a little rubber pulling out and instead of heading for the Boyle Heights bungalow he shared with his mamá, abuela, and tata, he had a change of heart. He merged onto the I5 and headed for Las Vegas.

Sancho fingered the puckered scar under his shirt. The bullet didn't damage any major organs. It missed his heart and lungs, but fractured his collarbone. He was in the hospital for weeks before they sent him to rehab. He often had nightmares and awoke in a cold sweat. Mendoza, the man who shot him, sat in the Twin Towers County Jail in downtown Los Angeles. He hadn't intended to shoot Sancho. His target was James Flynn.

Over the years, Flynn had roped him into one dangerous adventure after another. Sancho nearly died more than once and this last time, Sancho didn't escape unscathed. But Flynn believed in him and taught him to believe in himself. He gave him the Aston Martin and enough money to pay off his bills and buy his tata a new truck. Sancho even had enough left over for a down payment so finally his family could own their own home. He couldn't just abandon Flynn. He didn't want to see him roughed up and tossed into some general lock up before being thrown into a state mental hospital.

Flynn didn't deserve that.

No one did.

CHAPTER TWENTY-FIVE

The Mike O'Callaghan-Pat Tillman Memorial Bridge is 1,905 feet long and soars 900 feet above the Colorado River, making it the longest single-span concrete arch bridge in the Western Hemisphere. It's named after "Mike" O'Callaghan, a Korean War veteran and two-term Nevada governor and Pat Tillman, the former professional football star who gave up his career to fight in Afghanistan only to perish in a "friendly fire" incident. There's a walking path on one side of the bridge that offers spectacular views of Hoover Dam. Since the bridge first opened, seven people have killed themselves by jumping to their death. An additional hundred or so people have leaped from the dam itself. Though, it's not the number one suicide bridge in the country. That honor goes to The Golden Gate Bridge in San Francisco.

Flynn felt numb. His every limb weighted with lethargy. He fought to rouse himself from the paralyzing stupor. What exactly did they shoot him up with? He snaked his head out from under the heavy blanket and saw the brightly lit sign of a casino pass by overhead.

The sky turned from black to dark blue as the sun rose in the east. He knew he needed to shake off this torpor if he ever hoped to see tomorrow. That thought brought words and a tune to mind. He quietly began to sing to get the blood flowing to his brain.

"There's a man who lives a life of danger. For everyone he meets, he stays a stranger. With every move he makes, another chance he takes. Odds are he won't live to see tomorrow."

"What the hell are you singing?" Ohana asked him.

Flynn continued with his impromptu song. "Secret agent man, secret agent man. They've given you a number and taken away your name."

The vehicle made a hard turn and Flynn's head banged into the hard-plastic side of the cargo area. An abrupt stop caused him to slide forward and bang his head again. Moments later, the lift door opened and two of the operatives unfastened Flynn from the metal cargo anchors and dragged him out. He hit the ground hard, his face bouncing off the asphalt as someone cut the duct tape that bound his legs.

The world blurred when they pulled him to his feet. As they dragged him across the parking lot, he glimpsed another operative climbing out of what looked like Alessa's late husband's Aston Martin.

They made their way up a winding path. Flynn didn't see another soul. Early as it was, the tourists weren't out and about yet. Most were still hungover and asleep after a long night of gambling and drinking and losing.

They arrived at the edge of the bridge, and a harsh, cold wind whipped their faces. Ohana led the way as two burly Black Star operatives half-carried, half-dragged Flynn down the path. Traffic on the bridge was light at this early hour of the morning. The odd sixteen-wheeler occasionally screamed by, but otherwise the only sound was the wind.

"No one will believe this," Flynn slurred.

"Shut up, Mr. Flynn."

"I stole Alessa's car and drove it here so I could throw myself off the bridge? Is that the story you're trying to sell?"

"It's a sad story, but not so uncommon. Many lost and distraught people have thrown themselves off this very bridge."

"I'm guessing your man wore gloves?"

"Of course."

"So the only fingerprints they'll find on the steering wheel—"

"Will be yours."

"Sorry to burst your bubble, but I never drove it. Alessandra wouldn't let me."

"What are you talking about?"

"She didn't think I was in any condition to drive."

"Nice try, Mr. Flynn."

"Fine. Don't believe me. You'll find out soon enough."

They dragged Flynn a third of the way over the walkway and held Flynn against the railing. As the sun rose in the east, the shadow of the bridge slowly traveled over Black Canyon and the Colorado River below. Flynn blinked and focused on the jagged outcroppings of red granite 900 feet down. He tried to struggle, but he had no strength or control as they lifted him into the air.

"Hold it," Ohana barked before huffing and grunting like an angry bear. "Back to the car!"

Flynn's feet touched back down. The Black Star operatives dragged him back across the bridge; back up the windy path, and back to the parking lot.

Ohana pointed at the Aston Martin Vanquish. "Open it!" The operative who drove it pulled out the key and opened the door. "Now get his hands on the wheel."

Flynn fought them. They struggled to get him into the car. One choked him out as the other twisted his arm. Flynn banged his head as they shoved him inside and into the front seat. One ran around to the passenger side, opened the door, and climbed in to grab Flynn by his other arm. Flynn made his hands into fists and refused to grab the wheel. Each man pulled back his fingers, bending them hard, threatening to break them until finally he acquiesced.

"You win! You *win!*" Flynn insisted. "Let go! Let go and I'll do it."

"Let him go," Ohana said.

They did and Flynn reached for the steering wheel with both hands, balled his hands into fists, and backhanded each operative in the face.

They fought to grab his arms as Flynn flailed around like a lunatic. He got his hands into the pocket of the operative who drove the Vanquish, found the fob, and pulled the Desert Eagle from the other op's shoulder holster.

Ohana drew his own Desert Eagle, but not before Flynn shot one operative in the knee and the other through the hand as he tried to grab the gun. The op with the injured hand fell screaming out of the car. Flynn started the Vanquish and jammed it into reverse.

Ohana raised his weapon as the car roared backwards, burning rubber and skidding sideways. He leaped back to avoid getting hit as

Flynn shifted into first, put the pedal to the metal, and squealed out of there.

Ohana stood dumbfounded as one operative lay bleeding on the asphalt with a shattered kneecap and the other stared in horror at the hole in his hand.

Flynn glanced into the rear mirror. Ohana ran for the black SUV.

As Flynn cut right, he began to hear the music. Whenever he faced great danger, whenever enemies pursued him or death stalked him, Flynn would hear that fuzzy electric guitar with its rhythmical, rousing, exhilarating beat. The music always galvanized him. The adrenaline it provided overwhelmed the drugs in Flynn's system and bolstered him with steely determination.

He saw the road ahead and Hoover Dam in the distance. First, he would have to get past the security station. A guard stepped from the kiosk as Flynn propelled the Vanquish forward. He smiled at Flynn, holding a hand up, offering a greeting, but also letting him know he needed to slow down.

Flynn sped up.

The guard, decked out in a blue uniform and an orange safety vest, held up both his hands, his smile gone, his face grim. He shouted something Flynn couldn't hear over the sound of the screaming engine.

Another officer stepped from the kiosk and drew his weapon. Flynn didn't want to kill him. They were innocent first responders, protecting a national treasure that was likely a target for terrorists.

They fired their weapons. Flynn veered left, careful not to hit them as bullets shattered the windscreen. He tried to flip up the armrest so he could access Q's gadgets, but there was no armrest and he quickly realized this wasn't his DB5, but Alessa's late husband's Vanquish. He had none of Q Branch's ingenious contraptions. No front battering ram or rear bullet shield or front-mounted machine guns.

Flynn crashed through the drop-down boom barrier-gate with only his front bumper and ducked down as bullets shattered the car's rear window.

Flynn glanced in the side-view mirror. Ohana's black Navigator wasn't far behind.

Both police officers dove for safety as the Navigator roared between them. Ohana didn't swerve one whit to avoid hitting them.

Flynn flattened the gas and shifted into fifth. Q's oil slick and smokescreen would have come in handy, but the only accessories this Aston Martin had were a sunroof and cigarette lighter. There wasn't even a cupholder. He rocketed around the curves that led to the dam, tires squealing as he skidded on the sharp turns. He noticed the Navigator in his rear-view mirror and blinked, struggling to focus his bleary eyes. Still wankered from the drugs, the world shot by in a smeary blur. Distant gunshots echoed. Bullets shattered glass and tore into the Aston Martin's interior.

A muzzle flash appeared from inside of what looked like a cement pillbox up ahead. Flynn knew they built defenses into the dam prior to World War II as it seemed a likely target of German or Japanese agents. Apparently, they still had a sharpshooter inside there to handle any suicidal jihadi driving a car bomb.

Now they fired on the Navigator. Ohana swerved, but didn't slow. Flynn guessed Ohana didn't want him falling into the hands of the rangers. But he had no intention of being waylaid by the local constabulary. He bypassed a parking area and continued on the two-lane highway that used to be the main byway into Arizona before they built the Mike O'Callaghan-Pat Tillman Bridge.

Far in the distance, Flynn tracked two Park Ranger patrol cars blocking the way to the Arizona side. Officers climbed out, guns in hand as they positioned themselves behind the open car doors.

Flynn squealed to a stop and leaped from the Vanquish as the Navigator slammed into it from behind. The SUV's airbags deployed with an explosive pop. He glanced back to see Ohana covered in white powder and fighting to free himself from the flaccid bag.

Flynn leaped over a low wall and raced across the concrete bridge connecting the water intake towers to the top of the dam. The massive cylindrical structures contained huge pumps that took the water from Lake Mead and pushed it into the electrical turbines deep inside the dam's power plant. Looking back, he saw Ohana jumping from the Navigator. Flynn fired and the Israeli took cover behind the SUV, crouching down next to the man whose hand Flynn put a hole through.

Ohana fired back. Though he missed, the bullets ricocheted off the cement and sprayed Flynn's face with concrete shards.

Flynn spotted a door in one of the intake towers and hoped against hope it was open.

It wasn't.

"Dammit!" Flynn shouted as he continued across the solid cement bridge to the next cylindrical intake tower. He glanced back to see that Ohana and his man were moving on him.

An icy wind buffeted Flynn, nearly sweeping him off the edge of the walkway. But he steadied himself and made his way forward. He yanked on the steel door of the second intake tower. Locked tight.

"Bloody Hell!"

The operative with the injured hand tackled Flynn and grabbed for his gun. Flynn fought back as they struggled for control. They grappled. They grunted. They battled for domination and fumbled for the gun.

As Ohana came running around the corner, the gun boomed. A bullet ricocheted off the ground and pinged a concrete wall before hitting Ohana in the arm.

Ohana shouted an expletive as he dropped his Desert Eagle. It fired when it hit the cement, putting a bullet in the one-handed man's arse. Flynn kneed the stunned commando in the knackers and, as the guy doubled over, grabbed him by the hair and slammed his head on the concrete ledge.

Ohana tried to pick up his gun, but Flynn kicked it away and aimed a tiny can of Binaca Blast at his face. Flynn registered the confusion in Ohana's eyes as he blasted him. The Israeli shrieked and held his palms over his burning peepers.

"Goldhammer's plan! What is it?" Flynn demanded.

Flynn kicked Ohana's legs out from under him and the Israeli fell to his knees, blinded by pain and confusion. Ohana said something in Hebrew that sounded like a question as he took his hands off his face and looked up at Flynn with teary, bloodshot eyes.

Flynn sprayed him again, and Ohana shrieked again. "This is Q's truth spray, so don't bother lying to me!"

Hands back covering his eyes, Ohana screamed, "What the fuck is wrong with you?"

"Goldhammer's plan! Tell me!"

Flynn heard running footsteps and saw park rangers taking cover behind the cement intake towers.

One ranger yelled to Flynn. "Put down your weapon and get on the ground!"

Flynn looked down at the water below.

"Don't even think about it," the ranger shouted.

So Flynn didn't.

He just jumped.

He executed what he thought would be a perfect swan dive, but instead landed flat on his belly. The smacking sound was incredibly loud and the pain, excruciating, but Flynn quickly recovered and dove deeper.

For a moment, a euphoric sense of freedom filled his soul, but that brief flash of positivity changed to fear when the current began dragging him back towards the intake tower. He swam against it, but the strength of the backflow was hard to fight as the turbine sucked him towards certain death. Just then, it occurred to Flynn that diving off one of the world's largest dams and plunging into the drink right next to a water intake tower might not have been the best move.

If the turbine sucked him inside, he'd be ground up like a rump roast in a meat grinder. An ironic way to die, considering all the other gruesome deaths he avoided over the years. His enemies had tried to feed him to sharks, throw him under trains, and cut him in half with industrial lasers. No matter the method, Flynn always found some way to escape. How ridiculous that this time he would be the architect of his own foolish demise.

That thought gave him extra impetus as he swam and kicked harder to break free of the deadly current. He still fought the effects of the sedative, but the proximity to certain death helped to power him forward. The farther away he swam, the weaker the pull. Finally, he broke free and kicked his way to the surface.

Flynn gulped down air as the ice-cold water chilled him to the bone. He swam and kicked and splashed his way to the edge of Lake Mead. Flynn reached the craggy shore and scrambled up the red granite rock. He expected bullets to rain down around him, but when he looked back at the dam, the police had their hands full with Ohana. As far as they knew, he and Flynn were working together.

The road to the Arizona side was blocked, so the handful of rangers still pursuing him were on foot and a good distance away. Powered by pure epinephrine, Flynn clambered up the cliffs to a sparsely populated parking area on the Kingman Wash Access Road.

An elderly couple taking pictures of the dam caught sight of him as he approached. Soaked to the skin and wearing an Armani tuxedo, he knew he made for an incongruous sight. The couple looked more startled than scared as he straightened his jacket and stepped closer. "Hell of a bachelor party last night," Flynn said with a smile.

The elderly man smiled back. "Must be a heck of a story."

Flynn detected a Minnesota accent. "I'd be glad to tell you all about it if you can give me a ride to Caesars Palace." The wife seemed uncertain, so Flynn turned on the charm. "The name is Flynn. James Flynn. And this lovely lady must be the missis. You sir, are a lucky man."

The wife immediately grinned. "I'm Heidi. This is Dan. We're the Olafsons."

"Heidi. What a charming name." Flynn kissed Heidi's hand and she nearly swooned. "Us meeting like this is serendipitous."

"Why's that?" Dan asked.

"My wedding begins in less than thirty minutes. So if you can give me a ride, I can make it more than worth your while."

"Well, to be honest, sir, we just came through Vegas and are on our way to Zion National Park."

"I know it's an inconvenience, but here, perhaps this will help..."

Flynn reached into his inner jacket pocket and pulled out a thick bundle of hundred-dollar bills. He offered the soaking wet wad with a smile. Dan stared at it wide-eyed, but hesitated. Heidi had no such hesitation. She snatched the stack of drenched and dripping hundreds and jammed it in her purse.

"Come on, Dan. Let's get this young man to Vegas. Don't want him late for his own wedding!"

They led Flynn to a large RV. A Minnie Winnie Winnebago. Dan drove, Heidi rode shotgun, and Flynn sat on the couch across from the kitchenette. As they exited the parking lot, Flynn saw the two park rangers still a short distance away. They didn't look twice at the Minnie Winnie or the elderly couple piloting it. The RV was just one of many. Flynn was home free.

CHAPTER TWENTY-SIX

Visitors to the 1939 World's Fair in Toronto were stunned to see moving pictures and sound on a tiny black-and-white screen built into a huge wooden box. Radio with pictures would soon be in living rooms all across America. The President of RCA, David Sarnoff, announced that, "This new art and industry will provide entertainment and information to millions, shining like a torch of hope for a troubled world." Some of the shows created for just that purpose include Manimal, My Mother the Car, The Mystery of Al Capone's Vault, and Here Comes Honey Boo Boo.

The Television Critics Association Annual Show started at 9:00 a.m. each morning. Different networks took the stage at different times throughout the day to announce their new shows.

Goldhammer always made sure his lineup made the biggest splash and garnered the lion's share of media time and attention. Most moguls at his level didn't get into the trenches like he did, but Goldhammer reveled in the glitz and glamour and sheer showmanship. His fame was part of his brand and, in some ways, he was as well-known as the TV and movie stars who headlined his shows.

Tyler pondered all this as he sat among entertainment journalists, TV critics, and celebrity broadcasters in the Augustus Ballroom. As he waited for the show to start, he wondered if this was what Chloe really wanted. He worried he may have pushed her into something she wasn't completely comfortable with. But he also knew that men like Goldhammer only understood one thing. Power. Chloe needed leverage if she ever hoped to protect herself. Once she reached a certain level of celebrity, Goldhammer wouldn't be able to hurt her.

At least, that was his hope.

Marta stood to the side of the raised stage, watching the crowd. Looking past her, Tyler saw a male TV star he had a massive crush on when he was a teenager. Neil Patrick Harris played *Doogie Howser* and later womanizer Barney Stinson on *How I Met Your Mother*. Being out and proud encouraged Tyler to do the same. Though, he didn't have the nerve to pull the trigger until he was out of college, living on his own, and working as a bartender at Kenosha's most notorious gay bar. His parents didn't take it very well, but luckily Chloe was always there for him. He just wanted to be there for her.

The lights went dark and after a pregnant pause, a single spotlight illuminated John Fogerty as he launched into the Creedence Clearwater Revival hit "Run Through the Jungle." Stage lights lit up the entire band and Fogerty's seventy-something face filled big screens on both sides of the stage.

As the song finished and the music faded, an announcer's booming voice echoed through the hall. "Bombshells! A private, elite force of female special ops who fight for justice and bring help to the hopeless! Athena! Lotus! Jinx! Domino!"

One by one, the stars of Goldhammer's new TV show danced onto the stage, dressed in tiny cargo shorts, skimpy tank tops, and combat boots. First out was Selena Gomez, then Nina Dobrev, then Emma Roberts, and finally, Chloe strutted out on stage, smiling a big phony smile. Tyler knew she loved performing and dancing and always fed on the energy of an audience, but he caught a certain hesitation in her eyes. Reluctance. Uncertainty. Whatever it was, it worried him.

The announcer's voice continued to boom. "Together they are known as the E-Team! E for Estrogen! A female force for right who fight for the innocent and protect those who need protecting!"

Tyler realized that the concept was very similar to the TV pilot Uma Thurman's character in Pulp Fiction told John Travolta about. *Fox Force Five*. A wonderfully cheesy female empowerment fantasy cooked up by middle-aged white men.

The lights went out on John Fogerty and came up on Gary Goldhammer as he stepped through a curtain at the rear of the stage. He pointed and winked at the Bombshells and then smiled at the audience. Tyler marveled at how Goldhammer could turn on the charm when necessary. Like many psychopaths, Goldhammer knew how to believably model human emotions. Wired with a mike, his imperious, adenoidal voice filled the convention hall.

"Meet the stars of this year's newest ratings juggernaut! Selena Gomez! Nina Dobrev! Emma Roberts! And my newest discovery! A wonderful young actress who I believe is destined for greatness! Chloe Diamond!"

Diamond? Did Goldhammer decide to change her name from Jablonski to Diamond? *Diamond? Seriously?* Chloe looked as confused as he felt. Then Goldhammer put his chubby arm around her, pulled her close, and kissed the top of her head. Chloe struggled not to flinch or grimace or pull away. She just kept that phony smile plastered to her face.

• • •

Alessandra opened her eyes to find Flynn gently slapping her face to prod her awake. "Alessa? Are you awake?"

"I am now." She blinked and tried to clear her head. A dull pain throbbed behind her eyes. Exhaustion weighed her down. How could she be so hungover? She only had two glasses of champagne. What time was it? Flynn pulled back the blackout curtains and bright desert sunlight filled the Agrippina Suite. She squinted against the light, covering her eyes with her hand. Her stomach felt queasy and she had to pee. Flynn loomed over the bed, wearing what looked like a wet tuxedo.

"Why are you all wet?"

"I was at Hoover Dam."

"What?"

"I dove into Lake Mead."

Alessandra tried to make sense of what Flynn was saying, but had difficulty parsing the words. "Lake Mead?"

"Black Star broke in here last night. They injected you with something. Drugged you. That's why you can't wake up. It's almost eleven."

"Black Star?"

"Former operatives for Mossad. Israeli Intelligence. They work for Goldhammer and they took me last night. Tried to kill me. Tried to push me off Hoover Dam."

"Hoover Dam?"

"They wanted it to look like a suicide."

Apparently, Chloe wasn't kidding. Flynn wasn't in his right mind. Clearly, he was suffering some sort of paranoid delusion. Alessa felt foolish for believing his cockamamie story about him being in Her Majesty's Secret Service. But then again, why was he wearing a wet tuxedo?

"I need to pee," Alessa mumbled. God, her mouth felt like the inside of a sneaker. She struggled to throw the covers off and put her feet on the floor. "Can you wait in the sitting area for me?"

"Of course." Flynn turned to go and stopped at the door. "I don't want to rush you, but I'm afraid we're not safe here."

"Maybe you should change out of your wet things."

Flynn nodded and left. Alessandra padded into the luxurious bathroom. After a quick pee, she stared at herself in the mirror over the marble sink. Her tired eyes had dark circles under them and she saw every one of her seventy-eight years reflected back. The cheekbones were still impressive, but her neck sagged and her jaw looked jowly. The careful plastic surgery she had in her fifties was beginning to fray and she no longer looked like that young actress who won the Golden Globe's Most Promising Newcomer Award. Instead, she looked like her late mother.

Alessa tried to figure out how to handle Flynn as she pulled on a robe. She decided to humor him. For now. Later she could call the hospital Chloe said he escaped from.

She walked out and found two other people standing with Flynn in the large, elegant seating area. They were about her age, but considerably plumper, grayer, and wrinklier. Middle class, midwestern snowbirds dressed in polyester and plaid. Both looked thunderstruck when Alessa entered the room. The man seemed stupefied. The woman beamed.

Flynn introduced them. "Alessa, I'd like you to meet Dan and Heidi Olafson. They're visiting from Fridley, Minnesota."

Alessa smiled a stunned smile. "Well, hi."

"They were kind enough to drive me back from the dam. When I told them I was here with you they asked if they could get autographs."

"I'm a big, big fan," Dan said.

"That's true. Dan has always loved you," Heidi added.

"I think I first saw you in that Elvis Presley Movie. *Fun in Acapulco!*"

"Didn't you and Elvis date?" Heidi asked.

Alessa smiled. "We went out once or twice."

"You are still so beautiful and congratulations!"

"For what?"

"For your coming nuptials!"

Alessa retrieved some headshots from her suitcase. She always brought a few with her for just this reason. The older folks who remembered her weren't into selfies. She signed the pictures "to Dan and Heidi". Dan couldn't help but stare in stunned wonderment. She always had that reaction on men of a certain age. They fantasized about her all during puberty. To see her in the flesh was almost too much. She thanked them for bringing Flynn back to Caesars and ushered them out the door. Alessa shook Heidi's hand and gave Dan a quick peck on the cheek. He turned red and touched his face with reverence.

"Come on now." Heidi grabbed Dan by the arm. "Let's go before you really embarrass yourself."

Alessa closed the door and turned to Flynn, but he was already in the other room, changing out of his wet clothes.

"I'm sorry about your car," he shouted.

"Sorry for what?"

"It sustained quite a lot of damage. It's still back at the dam."

The Olafsons were evidence that Flynn did, in fact, go to the dam. So that part of the story wasn't fabricated. However, she still didn't believe that Israeli agents tried to throw him to his death. "So, you drove the Aston Martin out to the dam?"

"No, I told you. I was kidnapped and held prisoner. The operatives from Black Star brought it with them as part of the plan. They wanted it to look like I drove out there on my own and threw myself off the dam."

"But you *did* throw yourself off the dam."

"Only to escape." Flynn poked his head out of the bedroom. He was naked save for a towel wrapped around his waist. "You need to pack and get yourself out of here. Check into the Flamingo across the street and don't use your real name. Use an alias. And don't use a credit card. Only cash. You need to remain untraceable. You'll also need to remove the sim card on your cell phone."

"Aren't you coming with me?"

"I have some other things to do, but I'll catch up with you. What name are you going to use?"

"Um…. Scarlett O'Hara?"

"Perfect."

"Now, go pack. Please. You're in danger."

Alessa showered while Flynn threw his clothes into a suitcase. She then packed herself up, checked out, found a cab, and ferried her luggage across the street to the Flamingo. She didn't bother checking in under an assumed name because she assumed Flynn was off his nut. But she did tell the desk clerk that if someone called asking for Scarlett O'Hara, they should send the call to her.

Once in her room, Alessa put a call into the Las Vegas police and reported her Aston Martin stolen. They checked the license number and told her that a vehicle with that plate was damaged in an accident at Hoover Dam and towed to a local police impound lot. If she wanted to claim it, she had to do so within the next thirty days. She thanked them, hung up and immediately called the City of Roses Psychiatric Institute in Pasadena, California.

CHAPTER TWENTY-SEVEN

The well-guarded entrance to the Octavius Tower required a special keycard for entry. As the Agrippina Suite resided in that same sequestered tower, Flynn didn't have to worry about hotel security. He and Alessa visited the Titus Villa earlier that day, so Flynn knew exactly how to find it.

If the rangers at Hoover Dam had Ohana in custody, the operatives here would have no clue that Flynn was still alive. Of course, if Ohana did escape and report back, then Black Star would be waiting for him.

Each villa had a team of butlers and valets that saw to each guest's every whim. Since they used a separate entrance, Flynn decided that might be the best way in. He headed into the staff only area. The back of the house at Caesars Palace sprawled in all directions, a massive city under the city. Dressed in one of Alessa's husband's Savile Row suits, Flynn exuded such a forceful take-charge attitude, the workers all stayed out of his way.

After locating the butler and valet locker room area, he waited until a butler approximately his size and weight arrived. He grabbed the man from behind, dragged him into a maintenance closet, and held his forearm against the man's carotid until he fell into unconsciousness. Gently, he set him on the floor, stripped him naked, took off his Savile Row suit, and replaced it with the butler's outfit.

He then grabbed a room service cart in the kitchen and headed down a hallway. The back of the house looked like what you'd see behind the scenes in a large, enclosed shopping mall. Linoleum floors and industrial carpeting, plain white walls with high ceilings and fluorescent lighting. He passed large, framed pictures showing blueprints, concept art, and construction photos dating back to the

1960s. There was a ribbon-cutting picture in black and white and pictures of celebrities like George Burns and Frank Sinatra at the Bacchanal, posing with waitresses with big bouffants and tiny togas.

Flynn passed through a set of ugly gray metal security doors and made his way to the private valet and butler elevators. He passed two security guards who didn't give him a second look. Signs on the walls pointed out the locations of various private elevators and soon Flynn found the right one. His stolen keycard allowed him to call down the lift. The doors opened and Flynn wheeled the cart in, pushing the button for the Titus Villa.

As the elevator rose, Flynn checked his stolen Desert Eagle and flicked off the safety. He held it loosely at his side as the elevator finally came to a stop and the doors opened. A Black Star operative sitting in a folding chair glanced at the room service cart and then saw Flynn and the weapon he held in his hand.

Flynn kept his voice low. "Hands up. On your feet."

The man complied.

"Now turn around."

He did and Flynn pulled the op's pistol from the concealed carry holster before cracking him on the back of the head with the butt of his Desert Eagle.

The op staggered, but didn't fall, so Flynn hit him again.

"Ow!" the op said, but still remained standing.

Flynn had no choice but to hit him again. Even harder. This time the burly agent went down, crashed into the folding chair, and made quite a racket. Flynn stood stock still, listening and waiting in case the clatter caught anyone's attention.

A few silent seconds passed and Flynn heard approaching footsteps. Heavy footsteps. A monster of a man turned the corner and stopped when he saw the man Flynn knocked unconscious face down on the bent and broken folding chair.

Flynn raised his pistol and aimed it at the massive man's even more massive head. "Stay right where you are."

The immense Black Star operative had six inches on Flynn and probably outweighed him by a hundred pounds. His black suit barely contained his brawny physique. A pumpkin-sized head sat atop burly shoulders that stretched from one side of the corridor to the other.

The man didn't say a word or move a muscle. He just stared at Flynn through heavily lidded eyes.

Flynn motioned with the gun. "Hands up. Turn around."

The man didn't move. He just glared.

"Don't make me kill you," Flynn said, but the man didn't raise his hands. Instead, he started walking in Flynn's direction, not quickly, but with an even, measured pace.

"I won't ask you again," Flynn said with as much authority as he could muster.

But if the man heard Flynn's warning, he gave no sign.

Flynn shot him square in the chest and the man didn't flinch or wince or slow down. He sped up, charging down the hallway at a surprising clip for a man his size. Flynn aimed for his knee but missed, hitting him in the thigh. That didn't slow him down either. Before Flynn could decide where to shoot him next, the colossal operative slammed into him like a runaway freight train.

Flynn flew through the air and bounced off the wall, lost his weapon, and landed on his knees. A giant shoe came flying at his face and Flynn turned just in time, the steel-toed tip missing his chin by inches.

Flynn crawled past him and scrambled to his feet. A massive hand grabbed him by the collar. The op slammed Flynn into one side of the corridor and then the other before throwing him forward into some sort of sitting room.

Flynn bounced off an antique table before hitting the floor. Looking straight up he saw an extravagant crystal chandelier hovering above. Flynn tasted blood as he rolled over onto his knees and pushed himself to his feet. His assailant took his sweet time and moved towards him at the same steady pace, seemingly not at all bothered by the bullets Flynn put inside of him.

Flynn found that unsettling.

But it did give him time to think. His nemesis clearly wore a bulletproof vest. Otherwise, that shot to the heart would have slowed him down. But what about that bullet in the thigh? That had to hurt.

Flynn grabbed a bronze bust and threw it at the monster's head. The op slapped it away like a flying insect.

Flynn moved inside his reach, caught him in the chin with a left uppercut and drove his knee into the man's groin.

Nothing.

Like hitting a cement wall.

The gargantuan operative wrapped Flynn in a bearhug and held him tight, squeezing the life out of him. Garlic and sweat and some cloying aftershave only made the stranglehold more unpleasant. Arms trapped; Flynn used the only weapon he had left. His head. He reared back and head-butted him — again and again and again. Flynn decided the only person he was hurting was himself.

His strength ebbing, his consciousness slipping away, Flynn saw the monster look directly into his face. He knew what the beast wanted. To see the life leave his eyes. Certain sociopaths enjoyed that moment. Flynn wasn't about to give it to him.

He had one more weapon in his arsenal. His teeth. He clamped onto the monster's nose and bit down hard. The man bellowed, picked Flynn up, and threw him across the beautifully decorated room. He crashed into a settee, splintering the antique into multiple pieces. Flynn grabbed a side table and pulled himself to his feet. As the opponent approached, Flynn backed away. The angry monster stalked him, his fingers feeling for the bloody bite marks Flynn left on his nose. He looked at the blood on his fingertips and then looked at Flynn, his voice tight with outrage. "You bit me!"

"I'm normally not a biter. But you left me no choice."

"Ben-zona!" the monster bellowed.

Flynn looked around for a weapon, any weapon, and saw a beautiful crystal vase full of freshly cut flowers. Being the only thing in proximity, he picked it up and threw it at his assailant's massive head. The vase shattered against his forehead. Water splashed everywhere along with an assortment of peonies, daisies, hydrangea, and baby's-breath.

The beast roared, his eyes burning with liquid fertilizer as he lunged in Flynn's direction. He took one step before slipping on the spilled water, his feet dancing as he toppled backwards, banging his head on the edge of the grand piano. The lid came down and smacked him in the face. Flynn raced over, grabbed the lid, and slammed it down again.

The piano played a loud discordant chord each time Flynn brought it down on the man's massive noggin. This continued until the giant's face was bloody and his eyes rolled back in his head. He slithered to the floor. Flynn took the man's own zip tie handcuffs and bound his arms and legs to the piano. He then zip tied the man he knocked senseless by the servant's lift.

Flynn had hoped to find and confront Goldhammer, but apparently he wasn't there. The eleven thousand square foot villa was dead quiet. Well, not completely quiet. Flynn's noggin still rang from the futile attempt to head-butt that monster's concrete bonce. He assessed his injuries. Flynn had plenty of bruises, but no broken bones. He touched the beginning of a fat lip with his tongue and rubbed a tender knot at the top of his forehead.

He decided to search the place as thoroughly as he could. Perhaps he might find clues as to Goldhammer's ultimate plan.

The Titus Villa's decor seemed more English than Roman. The commodious rooms had crystal chandeliers dangling down from vaulted ceilings. The recreation room contained an extravagant bar with beveled Venetian mirrors. The dining area had a mahogany table that seated ten and a hand-painted mural of some bucolic scene that looked more like the Cotswolds than Tuscany.

A spacious media room contained a massive plasma TV and sumptuous leather recliners complete with cupholders. The library had a double-sided fireplace it shared with a billiard room that housed a colossal saltwater aquarium built into the wall. Flynn recognized the queen angelfish from his time scuba diving in the warm waters of Jamaica.

He discovered a guestbook on some sort of marble podium and glanced inside it. He found Goldhammer's signature, but also entries from Leonardo DiCaprio, Justin Bieber, and Bradley Cooper.

French doors led out to a private garden and pool area. The hot Las Vegas sun heated up the mid-day air. An enormous pool and Jacuzzi were decorated in exquisite tile. A firepit sat in the center of a travertine patio bedecked with lush potted plants more suited to the English countryside than the Nevada desert.

Flynn explored the bedrooms. Only two appeared to be occupied. From the clothes in the closet and the suitcases he located, he assumed that one room belonged to Goldhammer's rather formidable personal assistant/bodyguard—Marta.

Goldhammer's bedroom was twice as large and contained the master bath of all master baths. The walls and floors were inlaid marble. A pink onyx bathtub sat prominently in the middle. Empty suitcases filled Goldhammer's bedroom closet and a variety of formal and casual clothes neatly hung from hangers.

Flynn also found a rather large hotel room safe with a digital keypad. He knew such safes were famously unsafe. Having watched countless YouTube videos on the subject, he learned many techniques for cracking them.

All hotel safes had override codes, necessary in the event a guest locked something up and couldn't remember the code they created. He also knew that most hotels failed to change the standard factory override code on said safes. So, Flynn tried a few of the most common codes.

First, 000000.

Then, 111111.

Finally, 999999.

The safe stayed locked and Flynn decided perhaps Caesars was less lax than most hotels.

But recognizing the name brand of the safe, he realized this one had another backdoor. While taking the wallet of the monstrous bodyguard he dispatched, he also discovered a Swiss Army knife. He used it to unscrew the hex screws that fastened the nameplate to the front of the safe, revealing a tiny keyhole. He took a paper clip off some papers on the nightstand and straightened it. He then used it to pick the lock. He often practiced his lockpicking skills back at headquarters and could open any door in the place. Within seconds, he heard a click as the latch unlocked.

Inside, he found a few thousand dollars in poker plaques and pocketed them. He also found a thumb drive and a laptop computer which he assumed belonged to Goldhammer. After taking both, he made his exit.

He left the same way he came in and quietly headed back to the servant's lift. While passing through the music room, he found a tiny Hispanic maid standing over the unconscious monster.

Flynn feigned fear and surprise. "Who is that? What happened here? Should I call security?"

"I just did." The maid had a Mexican accent, stood under five feet tall, and didn't seem the slightest bit intimidated by Flynn. She pointed at his name tag. "You're not George Villanueva."

Flynn heard the front door fly open, followed by running footsteps. He decided that discretion was the better part of valor and hurried for the back elevator. The tied-up bodyguard by the elevator struggled on the floor in his plastic cuffs. Flynn pushed the down button on the lift and heard the tiny maid shout loudly from the other room.

"He went that way!"

The lift opened and Flynn jumped in with the laptop. He pushed the close button multiple times, but the doors didn't budge. Approaching footfalls grew louder as three hotel security guards rounded the corner with guns drawn. Flynn shot at their feet. They scrambled back around the corner long enough for the elevator doors to finally close.

Flynn figured security would be waiting for him at the bottom. They probably were stationed in the stairwells as well. He slapped a new magazine into his Desert Eagle and tried to come up with a way out of this.

He'd have to think fast.

CHAPTER TWENTY-EIGHT

Marta Karpenko stayed at Goldhammer's side as he moved through the TCA after-party. Jon Bon Jovi played to the assembled crowd of critics, actors, agents and producers as they drank and mingled and posed for pictures.

Marta watched as Goldhammer held court with a number of popular female celebrities. She spied Chloe across the room, standing by a bar, quietly if intensely conferring with her brother. She wondered if they were in contact with Flynn.

Ohana called her an hour earlier to tell her that Flynn had escaped. She had yet to tell Goldhammer. She knew he'd be furious. It was she who convinced Goldhammer that Flynn should die by "suicide." Returning him to the hospital would have been too dangerous. A maniac who saw Goldhammer as his arch enemy? A lunatic who believed he had a license to kill? What if he escaped the hospital again? Flynn was a threat to everyone. Marta couldn't believe that some in the press lionized him as a hero. But then the general public often glorified idiots, fools, and maniacs. At one time, the authorities would have locked Flynn up and thrown away the key.

Ohana had barely escaped the authorities himself. He managed to gather his two wounded men and make a getaway. If he'd been caught, all of Goldhammer's plans might have come to naught.

Flynn would have to be found. If Black Star wasn't up to it, she would find another organization with the requisite ruthlessness required.

Her phone buzzed. "Yes?"

"Miss Karpenko, it's Dan Simpson with Caesars' Security. I'm afraid there's been a break-in at the Titus Villa. We sent a team and the intruder is now trapped in the service elevator. If you want to meet me at my office, I can give you a status update."

"Have you called the Las Vegas Police?"

"Not yet, ma'am. Until we know what we're dealing with, we like to handle this kind of thing internally."

"Good. Thank you. I appreciate your discretion. Please do not call the police. I'm on my way."

She clicked off. It had to be Flynn. She didn't want him talking to the police. They probably wouldn't have believed him, but still, she wanted to keep the matter contained. If these problems with Flynn garnered any publicity, it could adversely affect the merger and Goldhammer would not be happy about that. She glanced across the room at Goldhammer. Now she had no choice. She had to tell him that Flynn still lived. But first she put a call in to Ohana.

Ohana couldn't let Flynn get away again. If he did, Goldhammer would terminate his contract and Black Star's reputation would take a major hit. In twenty years as an operator, he never encountered anyone like that loon. Flynn did things no one in their right mind would do. His actions were completely unpredictable, so Ohana could never construct a proper strategy to counter him. Whether intentional or not, Flynn used chaos and capriciousness to throw his opponents off balance. Ohana would have to think like a lunatic if he ever hoped to take him down.

The park rangers at Hoover Dam nearly caught him. His capture would have meant the end of Black Star. He and his two wounded men were lucky to have escaped at all. But this time, Flynn wouldn't get away. This time, he would end him. Marta was right. Flynn was too dangerous to let live.

Ohana followed the head of Caesars' security team. Dan Simpson was ex-FBI and so were many of his men. Ohana let Simpson run the show, but, in the end, he wanted to be the one who pulled the trigger on Flynn. He would force the *mashugana* into "suicide by cop". Enough was enough. The media loved him. Ohana knew he had to shut Flynn up before things spun completely out of control.

Security stopped the service elevator between floors and shut down the power, trapping Flynn inside. They arrived at the elevator doors one floor up. Simpson's men used a key to force the doors open. Ohana scanned the elevator car below. The trapdoor on top was still shut tight—Flynn had nowhere to go.

"He has a weapon," Ohana said. "A Desert Eagle."

Simpson and his security team suddenly seemed a tad less enthusiastic about storming the elevator.

"Maybe we should call the police after all," Simpson said.

"Mr. Goldhammer would prefer you didn't, but I understand your concern. Fortunately, this man knows me. I believe I may be able to talk him into giving up his gun."

"What if you can't?"

"Let's cross that bridge when we come to it."

Simpson nodded and took a step back. Ohana poked his head in the shaft and called out, "Mr. Flynn!" Flynn didn't answer, so Ohana tried again. "It's Agent Ohana, Mr. Flynn!" Still no answer. He glanced back at a skeptical Simpson before poking his head back into the shaft and shouting, "Mr. Flynn, there's no way out. Nowhere to go. No one has to get hurt here."

Silence.

"We were able to monitor him on video until he smashed the camera," Simpson said.

"Do you think he shot himself?" one of Simpson's men asked.

Ohana shook his head. "I don't think so. He has a pretty strong survival instinct. Who has the M84?" An agent handed Ohana the stun grenade. The Israeli glanced at a nearby maintenance man. "This elevator car? What's it made out of?"

"A steel framework, a steel structure, and steel sheeting," the man said.

"He can't shoot through that," Simpson said.

"Let's hope not," Ohana replied as he jumped down, lightly landing on top the elevator car. "Mr. Flynn!" He waited, but Flynn didn't answer. "I'm coming in."

Ohana opened the trapdoor. He tensed for gunfire. A bullet through an open trapdoor might ricochet and do some damage. Ohana immediately pulled the pin on the M84, dropped it in, and turned away. The explosion boomed in the enclosed space, flashing brightly.

Ohana dropped into the rising smoke, gun drawn, flashlight out, ready to fire.

But as the smoke cleared, Ohana saw no one inside the elevator. The tiny room was emptier than Hitler's heart. "You sure this is the right elevator?"

"Of course we're sure," Simpson shouted.

"Well, there's nobody in here!"

Simpson dropped down into the elevator, followed by three of his men, and they all stood in a tight circle, staring at each other in baffled wonderment.

• • •

When the elevator abruptly stopped and they cut the power, killing the lights, Flynn decided that staying put was not an option. He managed to get the top escape hatch open and climbed out. He jammed the laptop under his armpit and, finding foot and handholds, clambered up the shaft's metal framework, past the elevator doors one floor up, and kept climbing until he hovered twenty feet above the elevator car.

He braced himself and waited, knowing they would come.

Flynn heard them fumbling with a drop key before they forced the outer elevator doors open. He didn't expect to see Ohana, but there he was, poking his head into the shaft, calling down to Flynn, demanding his immediate surrender.

Flynn waited and watched as Ohana threw the flashbang into the elevator car and dropped in after it, weapon ready. Flynn grinned at Ohana's frustration as he called to others and told them Flynn had fled.

All but one of the men with Ohana piled in after him to see for themselves. That last guard was too large to fit through the trapdoor and peered down into the hole.

Flynn made his move.

As he descended like Batman, the laptop slipped out of his hands. It bounced off the head of the bruiser who remained. The man looked up as Flynn landed on top of him, slamming his head into one of the steel supports, knocking him cold. He then rolled his bulky body over the trapdoor.

Flynn picked up the cracked laptop and climbed through the open elevator doors to the muffled shouts of Ohana and the others trapped below. Still looking fairly official in his butler suit, Flynn made his way down the service stairwell and through the crowded, clattery kitchen. He knew they'd call for backup and Flynn wanted to be long gone before they did.

•   •   •

Sancho used Waze to find his way from Los Angeles to Las Vegas. He only had to stop for gas once along the way. A place called Baker, with a giant thermometer. He stopped at the casino in Primm to pee and couldn't believe how big it was. But the Primm Valley Resort and Casino looked like a Motel 6 compared to Caesars Palace.

Waze directed him into Caesars' vast circular driveway. He passed the famous fountains and pulled up in front, powering down the window of his Aston Martin. "Where's self-parking?"

"Back the way you came, sir."

"I didn't see the sign."

"You must have missed it then. This is valet only. Would you like to leave your car?"

Suddenly, Sancho's passenger door flew open and a breathless Flynn jumped in.

"Let's go!"

"Flynn?"

"We have to go! They're coming!"

"Who?"

"Them!"

"Where?"

"There!" Flynn pointed to a squad of serious-looking security guards charging through the double hydraulic doors.

"What did you do?"

"Go!" Flynn shouted. "*Go!*"

As the guards ran closer, Sancho slammed his car into drive, flattened the gas, and burned rubber as he roared around the hotel's circular driveway.

"Where to?" Sancho shouted over the thunderous roar of his V12 engine.

"The Flamingo."

"Across the street?"

"It's the last place they'll look for us!"

CHAPTER TWENTY-NINE

Benjamin "Bugsy" Siegel founded Murder Inc. with Meyer Lansky in the early 1920s. The handsome, charismatic, and much feared hitman also ran bootleg liquor and drugs for Lucky Luciano in New York. In the '30s he traveled to California to extend the reach of the east coast mob. He hobnobbed with Hollywood stars like George Raft, Clark Gable, and Cary Grant. That's also where he met aspiring actress Virginia Hill. Seigel nicknamed her "the flamingo" because of her long legs. That also became the name of the casino he built in Vegas. Costing six million in mob money, The Flamingo was the first luxury hotel and casino on the strip. Believing Siegel had skimmed money off the top, Luciano and Lansky gave the go-ahead to take Bugsy out. A wrecking ball leveled the original Flamingo in 1993, but the new Flamingo Las Vegas rose in its place, financed this time by the Caesars Entertainment Corporation.

Sancho drove his Aston Martin into the Flamingo's south driveway and found his way inside one of the garages. He parked his car, killed the engine, and tried to catch his breath.

Flynn looked at him with concern. "Are you all right?"

"Am *I* all right?"

"You look a little flushed."

"Dude, who were those guys?"

"Which guys?"

"The ones chasing you down!"

"Hotel security. Though some of them might be with Black Star."

"Who?"

"We'll need to catch you up on the particulars of this case. Did someone send you here?"

"I got a call from Chloe."

"I worry for that poor girl. Going undercover so soon after the trauma she's been through. I'm not sure her mind is right."

"Dr. Michaels wants to see you, dude."

"Who?"

"M. He wants you back at the hospital."

"You mean headquarters?"

"Yes!" Sancho exclaimed.

"When?"

"Today. Like now. Right now."

"But I'm just about to break this case wide open."

"He wants an update. What can I tell you? You know how he is."

"But the job is only half done."

"It's an order."

"I'm sure it is, but M needs to understand the situation here. It's very fluid. To leave now might jeopardize this entire operation."

Sancho pulled out his cellphone and dialed a number. He put it on speaker.

The first voice they heard belonged to Miss Honeywell. "Dr. Michaels' office."

"Miss Honeywell, it's Sancho Perez. I'm here with Mr. Flynn."

"And where is *here*?"

"Las Vegas."

"You went to Las Vegas?"

"Yes, ma'am, and Mr. Flynn is right here with me."

"Honeywell, it's so good to hear your voice," Flynn said.

"Are you okay, Mr. Flynn?"

"Right as rain. One of these days you and I will have to run off together to somewhere exotic. Have you ever been to Jamaica? The Blue Mountains are quite beautiful this time of year."

"Yeah, no, I don't think so. Hold on." She held the phone away from her face and shouted, "Dr. Michaels! I got Perez on the phone. He's in Vegas with Flynn."

A moment later, Michaels' stern voice emanated from the speaker. "Mr. Perez?"

"Hello, sir. I'm here with—"

"Yes, I know. You both need to return to City of Roses immediately."

"I think that would be a mistake, sir," Flynn piped in.

"Nevertheless, you are my responsibility and I'm afraid I must insist."

"Are you giving me an order?"

"I am indeed. Mr. Perez will drive you back. I expect to see you here by this evening. Is that clear?" When Flynn didn't answer, Michaels asked him again. "*Is that clear?*"

"Crystal, sir."

"Mr. Perez, I'm disappointed that you disobeyed me and went to Las Vegas against my wishes, but I do understand the close connection you have with Mr. Flynn."

"Thank you, sir."

"There will be consequences."

"I understand, sir."

"Back by this evening. Both of you."

Michaels hung up and Sancho pocketed his phone. He looked at Flynn. "If we're going to get there by tonight, we need to leave like right now."

"Right after I take care of one last thing."

"Dude, you heard the man. We gotta go."

"And we will."

· · ·

When Alessandra Bianchi opened the door, the sight of the former star left Sancho speechless. When Flynn said she accompanied him to Vegas, Sancho wondered if it was just another delusion, but there she stood in the flesh looking much like she did on the big screen. Even in her seventies, she was still breathtakingly beautiful. That smile. Those cheekbones. Her famous aquamarine eyes. He remembered her from some of his favorite movies. He'd watch them on TV after everyone went to bed. When the house was finally quiet, he'd sit there in the dark, disappearing into brighter, shinier, more exciting worlds.

Alessandra seemed both relieved and irritated to see Flynn. "Where have you been?"

"I told you. I had work to do."

"I called City of Roses. I talked to Dr. Michaels."

"So did we."

"Hi, I'm Sancho," Sancho said lamely.

"Sancho is a colleague of mine who came here to collect me."

"From City of Roses?" Alessa asked.

Sancho nodded, patting Flynn on the shoulder. "Yeah, and I want to thank you for keeping an eye on my friend here. We're going to gather up his stuff and hit the road if that's okay."

"That's great." Alessa waved them in and noticed the laptop Flynn clutched in his left hand. "Whose laptop is that?"

"I found it in Goldhammer's safe," Flynn said.

Sancho looked panicked. "You stole Goldhammer's laptop?"

"It's evidence."

"You gotta give it back."

"Not until we see what's on it." Flynn crossed to a desk and opened it up. The screen was badly cracked and it wouldn't boot up.

"Dude, what did you do to that laptop?"

"I had a slight mishap, but I'm sure any competent computer repair person can access the hard drive."

"You heard Michaels, man. We have to go back."

"But not until I uncover the secrets hidden on this device."

"I don't think you understand the situation."

"I'm not budging on this, my friend. The sooner we discover what's on this computer, the sooner we can go."

"Come on, man."

"No."

Flynn wouldn't back down, so to move things along Sancho reluctantly googled "computer repair" on his phone.

AA Computer Solutions sat at the top of the list.

Since Flynn had totaled her late husband's Aston Martin, Sancho invited Alessa to join them in his vehicle for the ride back to L.A. After packing them up, he crammed Flynn's single suitcase and Alessa's four suitcases into the rather tiny trunk.

As they headed for AA Computer Solutions, Sancho posed a question. "Why can't we just take it back to headquarters and let them hack it there?"

"Because time could be of the essence," Flynn warned. "We need to know what Goldhammer's ultimate plan is and we need to know now."

"What if he doesn't have a plan?"

"Of course he has a plan. Megalomaniacs with sociopathic tendencies always have a plan. Usually, it involves world domination. They need control, you see. They want to be king. They want to play God."

"Dude, he's just a movie producer."

"Yes, it's the perfect cover for a man like him. And what do movies do? Shape thought. Twist perception. Create alternate realities. What could be more dangerous?"

Sancho caught Alessandra's glance in the rearview mirror. She looked agitated and upset. Her eyes glistened. She rested her hand on Sancho's shoulder. "Can I ask a favor?"

"Of course."

"After we're through with this little errand, do you mind driving me to the airport? I'm not sure I'm up for a such a long drive."

"Not at all," Sancho said.

"Good idea. You're safer on your own," Flynn added.

Alessa nodded. "Once we're all back in Los Angeles, I'll come visit and see how you're doing."

Flynn turned to look at her directly. "I appreciate the gesture and I *have* enjoyed our time together, but I think it's best we go our separate ways. Getting involved with me would only put you in greater danger. You're an exceptional woman and you deserve someone who will be there for you each and every day. That's not me. For you see, I have a jealous mistress. Her Majesty's Secret Service. What I do is perilous and I refuse to put those I care about at risk." Flynn reached back to cradle her face. "But I'll always be there for you. If you ever need my help, you know where to find me."

Alessa held Flynn's hand against her face and squeezed it. "Thank you."

Sancho pulled into a shabby-looking strip mall just a few blocks off the strip. AA Computer Solutions sat between a nail salon and a Subway. Inside, they found a tiny and grimy storefront. Behind the counter, a sign on the wall said *Repair/Sell/Trade*.

The hairiest man Sancho had ever seen stood behind the counter. Balding, bespectacled, short and corpulent, he had a wide smile and a tightly cropped beard. His nametag read Aaftab Abboud and Sancho marveled at the immense thicket of black curly hair that erupted from the top of his plaid shirt. His sleeves were rolled up to his elbows, revealing equally hairy forearms.

"Welcome!" Aaftab held his arms wide. "How may I assist you?" Sancho detected some sort of vaguely Middle Eastern accent.

Flynn held up the laptop and set it on the counter. "I dropped my laptop and it seems to be malfunctioning. I wonder if there's a way to access the files on my hard drive?"

"Of course there is. I can't get to it today, unfortunately, but I can probably fit it in tomorrow. Once I diagnose the problem, I can call you with an estimate."

"Unfortunately, this is an emergency. I would be happy to pay you a premium if you could make this a priority."

"I wish I could, but that really wouldn't be fair to my other clients."

"Five thousand dollars on top of your usual fee if you can get to work on it immediately."

Sancho watched delight and surprise alight on Aaftab's furry face. "Of course, if it's that much of an emergency I wouldn't want to leave you in a lurch. Would you like to leave it? Or do you prefer to wait?"

"We'll wait," Flynn said.

· · · ·

Marta never saw Goldhammer so incensed. They were back in the Titus Villa, surveying the wreckage that Flynn had wrought. Ohana looked sheepish as hell. Flynn apparently trapped him in the service elevator along with the ex-FBI agent in charge of hotel security and his supposedly crack team of ex-federal agents.

Goldhammer's face turned pinker and pinker as he paced the room, his hands clenched into white-knuckled fists. Abruptly, he stopped inches from Ohana and hissed in his ear. "This is unacceptable."

"I know, sir."

"Not only is that maniac still alive, he stole my goddamn laptop."

"We will get it back."

"Do you know what's on that?"

"No, sir."

"Everything. *Everything! You let him take everything!*"

"We will find him and silence him and recover your laptop, sir. I promise you."

"Bullshit! *Bullshit!* I'm tired of your empty promises. That lunatic has gotten the best of you at every turn. *Every turn!*"

"We suspect he's coordinating with Chloe Jablonski and her brother. Which is probably why he's always one step ahead of us."

"I try to help that ungrateful bitch and her stupid, greedy, loser of a brother, and what do they do?" Goldhammer began pacing again. "That slut entraps me and tries to steal from me and now this?"

"Would you like me to find them, sir?"

"Find them and bring them to me. I need to interrogate them. And I want Flynn found! Otherwise, *what am I paying you for?*"

"I already talked to my superiors and we won't be charging you for any of this, sir."

"Damn right you won't. This is *your* screw up."

"I promise we will find him."

"Do you have any leads at all?"

"We do, sir. We install a proprietary LoJack-like system on all our client's laptops. We are already tracking yours down."

"Find him, Ohana! *Find him.* Do not fail me again."

CHAPTER THIRTY

Aaftab Abboud held up a tiny black memory stick. "The motherboard was fried along with the hard drive. It took some time, but I recovered most of your files and put them on this flash drive."

"What kind of files survived?" Flynn asked.

"Word files. Excel files. Some PowerPoint presentations. And quite a few videos and photos."

"Can you open the files?"

"I didn't want to open them without your approval."

"You have my approval. Let's see what survived."

Flynn, Alessa, and Sancho crowded behind Aaftab as he plugged the thumb drive into a large desktop computer. He clicked on one of the MP4s and a scene of extreme depravity filled the Ultra-Wide 32-inch QHD monitor.

Flynn had seen much bloodshed, horror, and suffering in his life, but nothing this heinous, twisted or debauched. He wanted to cover his eyes, but couldn't look away.

Somehow Goldhammer crammed his blubbery, milky-white body into a shiny black latex singlet that barely covered his huge naked ass. A black latex full face mask with eyeholes and a mouth hole and two strange purple pigtails couldn't hide who he was, even though it completely covered his large round head.

A crying woman wearing a ball gag, a latex bustier, and a choker with nipple clamps hung from chains bolted to a cement wall. Goldhammer repeatedly shocked her with a stun gun.

Sancho stared wide-eyed.

Alessa turned away.

Flynn said, "That's enough of that. What else do we have?"

All the movie files were either torture porn encounters with hapless young actresses or sexual assaults shot with an HD camera that Goldhammer hid somewhere in the room. Flynn recognized some of the actresses. They were well known. Others were simply anonymous, terrified women.

One of them was Chloe.

Flynn understood these videos were much like trophies taken by serial killers. Goldhammer needed these encounters memorialized so he could relive the crime again and again. This was clearly Goldhammer's personal collection or at least part of it. This was more than enough to bring him down and delay if not destroy his merger.

"What kind of monster are you dealing with here?" Alessa asked him.

"Someone deeply depraved and addicted to control," Flynn said.

Aaftab looked queasy. "Here. Take the mouse. I've seen enough."

"So have I. Let's take a look at that PowerPoint Presentation."

"Which one?"

Flynn pointed to a thumbnail on the monitor. "Operation Indoctrination."

Aaftab clicked on the PowerPoint presentation and the words "Operation Indoctrination" filled a black silhouette of a human head. "Should I play the slide show?"

"Please."

What followed was nothing less than a plan to take over the mind of every person in America. *Operation Indoctrination* was the most ambitious psyops program ever devised by private enterprise. By either buying or hijacking the data from multiple social media platforms, Goldhammer intended to obtain the personal information and browsing habits of millions of consumers. His plan was to use sophisticated algorithms to create detailed psychographic personality profiles, allowing him to segment these consumers by lifestyle, attitudes, beliefs, values, buying motives, and patterns.

This technology would foster the creation of shockingly effective hyper-targeted ads that would generate incredible click-through rates. Like Cambridge Analytica did in the run up to the 2016 U.S. election, they would use this behavioral advertising to play on fears and desires and everyday outrages. Truth didn't matter. All that mattered was that these messages reinforced deeply held beliefs, fostered divisions, and manipulated minds. With no clear truth, consumers would react emotionally. Soon, absolute truth would no longer exist.

The PowerPoint pointed out that unlike subliminal advertising, behavioral advertising was not illegal. And if used for political advertising, it could re-shape the political landscape; create a stark divide, accelerate divisions, split political antagonists into hundreds of different factions — balkanize the opposition until they had no unity, no power, and no solidarity. That way, Goldhammer could put his own people in power and eventually take over the entire government.

But that wasn't even Goldhammer's endgame.

Goldhammer's plans included a massive public policy institute and research organization designed to create and focus-test state-of-the-art behavioral advertising models. Refine the technology and research the psychology. Create advertising that couldn't be resisted. Bombard consumers with billions of microtargeted ads and generate sudden desires, desperate urges, and unfilled cravings that only Goldhammer's products could satisfy.

He would swallow up any and all competition, control markets, and tame any and all government regulation, including antitrust legislation.

It was an audacious plan. A slow-motion coup d'état of American democracy.

Flynn insisted that with this technology, Goldhammer would take over the government and brainwash every consumer in America and, later, the world.

Sancho seemed skeptical. "Isn't that just social media marketing? That's what everybody does now. Facebook. Google. Instagram."

"Not on this scale. Not with this level of sophistication."

"You really think he wants to take over the world?"

"Of course he does. They always do," Flynn replied. "Complete control. The ultimate goal of every power-mad megalomaniac."

Flynn noticed Aaftab staring wide-eyed in terror. This terror wasn't directed at his computer screen, however. He pointed through his storefront window at four men in black suits, all carrying assault weapons, all climbing from a black Lincoln Navigator.

"Is there a back door?" Flynn shouted.

Aaftab pointed towards the rear of the store.

"Follow me!" Flynn ordered.

Flynn dashed through the doorway into a back room filled with workbenches covered with the guts of countless computers. A red exit sign sat over another door. He glanced back to see that the rest of his team had yet to follow. The windows shattered in the front of the store and men with Israeli accents shouted, "Down! Down! On the ground!"

Rushing back in would only get Sancho and Alessa caught in the crossfire, so he burst out the back door into the alley behind the mini mall.

Ohana stood there waiting. Smiling. Flynn drew his weapon, but someone caught him from behind in a Krav Maga restraining hold, twisting his arm so hard he lost the Desert Eagle. He tried a countermove, but whoever held him had a grip of steel. And then Ohana stepped closer and brought the butt of his assault rifle down on Flynn's forehead.

• • •

When Goldhammer put his fat arm around her on that stage in front of all those people and planted his slimy lips on her forehead, Chloe nearly punched him in the balls. It took every ounce of self-control not to bring him to his knees.

She thought starring in his stupid TV show would make her a celebrity and give her more leverage. Instead, she had less. Much less. He owned her now, and the thought of that literally made her sick. She no longer had any desire to act or be on TV. She didn't want to be seen. She didn't want to be famous. She just wanted to disappear.

Flynn warned her, but Chloe didn't want to believe him. She didn't want to listen. She wanted what she wanted and she thought she could have it without selling out. Clearly not. Everything has a price and this price was more than she was willing to pay. She had to get away. She wouldn't tell Tyler because he wouldn't understand.

She stood in that ridiculously extravagant five thousand square foot Caesars Palace suite and decided to take what she had and go. She didn't have any of the money Goldhammer promised her, and would just have to get by. But that was fine with her.

She didn't want a penny from him.

Chloe packed a small suitcase on wheels and carefully, quietly wheeled herself out of there. As she passed the media room she could hear the TV. Tyler watched one of his silly reality TV shows. She lifted her suitcase off the floor to make her getaway even quieter. Leaving him like this broke her heart, but she couldn't face him. He'd try to talk her out of it, and what if he succeeded? What if she gave in and gave herself over to Goldhammer? That would be the end of her. Whatever spark of self-respect that still flickered inside of her would be extinguished. On the outside she'd be rich, famous, revered, but inside, she'd be dead.

Finally, she reached the front door of the suite and eased it open. Ohana stood there poised to knock. He grinned. Cold fear squeezed her heart. Two of his men stood just behind him.

"You going somewhere?"

"Get out of my way."

"Mr. Goldhammer wants to see you."

"Yeah, well, I don't want to see him." She tried to step around him, but Ohana blocked her way forward, matching her every move. "Get the hell out of my way!"

The smile left Ohana's face. "Where's your brother?"

She tried to shoulder past him. He pushed her back into the suite; she stumbled and nearly fell. Chloe took a swing at him. He grabbed her by the wrist, twisted her arm behind her, binding her with plastic handcuffs, pulling them so tight she cried out in pain.

"Find her brother," Ohana barked.

CHAPTER THIRTY-ONE

Aaftab knew that one day they would come for him—apparently, that day had arrived. Even though they weren't wearing the blue windbreakers or vests that identified them as U.S. Immigration and Customs Enforcement officers, he suspected they worked for ICE. He knew that ICE had many undercover agents who infiltrated and investigated and rooted out anyone who didn't have citizenship or a valid green card.

They flashed no identification.

Only guns.

In that moment, Aaftab entertained the notion that they might not work for ICE at all, but for the FBI Counterterrorism Division. They too had undercover agents. When they swept up suspects, they didn't have to follow the niceties of the U.S. Constitution. Not that he had the same rights being a non-citizen. They could drag him to some black site off-the-grid and hold him indefinitely. Waterboard him. Interrogate him.

His family would never know what happened to him.

He wondered who dropped the dime on him. The owner of Bits and Bytes? He accused Aaftab of stealing his customers more than once. Last year, during a small business networking event for local electronics retailers, the owner of Bits and Bytes drunkenly approached him and publicly accused him of poaching his customers. Big and fat with red hair and freckles, he poked Aaftab in the chest and asked him if he was a citizen. None of the other retailers came to his defense.

The men who came for him moved like soldiers. The customer with the English accent immediately took charge. He led the way out the back door, only to be brutally beaten down.

Aaftab tried to rush the other way, but the men grabbed him and pushed him down, slamming his face into the floor. Plastic handcuffs cut into his wrists. They pulled him to his feet and covered his head with a hood.

They might be FBI after all. Perhaps they assumed the others were part of his terrorist cell. After all, they took everyone prisoner. The Englishman, the Mexican, and the old woman with the European accent.

They shoved them all into their vehicle and drove off, speeding to some unknown destination. Trapped inside the hood, he nearly suffocated in a cloud of garlic. A plane roared overhead. Were they heading for the airport?

The vehicle squealed to a stop and they pulled him out. "Where are you taking me?" he demanded. But no one answered him.

Jet engines thundered as planes took off. Fuel and exhaust filled the air. The men in black ordered them to move and Aaftab stumbled forward. They spoke Hebrew—they were Israeli. Is that where they are taking them? To Israel? A black site in Israel?

They put them on a plane, but the flight lasted less than an hour. They kept the hood on him the entire time. Once they arrived, they loaded them into a van and drove for over an hour. When they opened the doors and let them out, the air seemed cooler. Aaftab detected the scent of... pine trees. Where had they taken them?

The Israelis led them forward, their shoes crunching on hard-packed snow. Aaftab tilted his head back to catch a glimpse of where they might be. He saw a shimmering lake and part of what appeared to be a massive stone mansion surrounded by towering evergreens and other shrubbery. Someone slapped him on the back of the head and pulled his hood back down.

When they finally removed his head covering, he found himself in a ten-by-ten-foot cell with the Englishman. The only light came from torch-like sconces on the rough stone walls. They flickered like flames but were LED bulbs. Wrought iron bars caged them in. Leather cuffs on chains were bolted to the walls. The cement floor slanted toward a drain in the center.

On the wall just outside the cell, various torture devices hung from wrought iron hooks: riding crops, whips, branding irons. Paddles made of wood, plastic, and metal. In the cell itself, Aaftab noticed a large pink tube labeled CGC Tush Ease Anal Gel with Benzocaine. A full bodysuit in black latex hung from a hanger on a hook.

What kind of black site was this? It looked like a damn dungeon.

Someone whispered from an adjacent cell. "Hello?"

"Hello!" Aaftab replied.

"Aaftab?" It was the Mexican man. "I'm locked up in a cell with Alessandra."

"Sancho?" a young woman asked, apparently in a cell on the other side.

"Chloe?" Sancho shouted. "Is that you?"

"My brother Tyler's here too," Chloe said. "Who the hell is Aaftab?"

"Me," Aaftab said.

"He's a computer guy we went to see," Sancho said. "Flynn stole Goldhammer's laptop."

"He stole his laptop?" Chloe sounded apoplectic.

"And dropped it and broke it and we needed someone to help us get inside of it."

"What was on it?" Tyler asked.

"All kinds of horrible shit."

"What happened to Flynn?" Chloe wanted to know.

"Is Flynn the tall Englishman?" Aaftab asked.

"Yes," Sancho answered.

Aaftab looked at Flynn. "He's here with me, but he's bleeding and he won't wake up."

"Is he breathing?" Chloe asked.

"I don't know."

"Can you get closer to him and see?"

"I'd rather not."

"What did they do to him?"

"They pistol-whipped him," Alessandra said.

"Oh, my God," Chloe cried.

"Please, Aaftab, Flynn's our friend," Sancho said. "Just crawl a little closer and put your ear on his chest. See if you can hear his heart beating."

Aaftab sighed. He didn't want to do what Sancho asked of him. But he felt somewhat responsible, seeing as they were swept up in a raid to catch *him*.

"Hold on." Aaftab slid closer to Flynn and leaned in, his head just above Flynn's chest. Nothing. He heard nothing. Resting his hand on the man's chest, he detected movement. Shallow breathing. His chest rose and fell, but just barely. "I think he's still breathing."

Chloe quietly began to cry. "Thank God."

"Ohana must have really whacked him hard," Tyler said.

"Why would they lock us up here like this?" Alessandra asked.

"It's my fault," Aaftab admitted.

"Your fault?"

"I'm not an American citizen and I have enemies who I believe ratted me. I am so sorry you were all swept up with me."

"It's not your fault," Flynn said. Aaftab jumped at Flynn's voice. The Englishman blinked and tried to sit up. "It's our fault for bringing this to your doorstep. I'm a Double-0 with Her Majesty's Secret Service and we have all been abducted by a man named Goldhammer."

"Not the government?"

"I'm afraid not."

"So when they know I'm not involved, will they let me go?"

"I suspect not. You saw what we saw and now you know too much."

"What about us?" Tyler asked from one cell over. "What did we do to deserve this?"

"You colluded with Mr. Flynn to help him obtain my laptop." Yet another voice that Aaftab didn't recognize.

Flynn called down the corridor. "Goldhammer! So good of you to join us."

CHAPTER THIRTY-TWO

Flynn wondered if he had a concussion. His head throbbed with a dull ache just behind the eyes. Head wounds often bleed profusely and Flynn had no way of knowing how much blood he'd lost. He felt a little dizzy, but his vision wasn't blurry. Those were all good signs that the concussion was a minor one. Considering their situation, he'd need his full mental faculties. Goldhammer might be insane, but he wasn't an idiot. And now that he had them, he would intimidate and torture them until he knew what they knew.

"Colluded with Flynn?" Tyler sounded aggrieved. "We did no such thing!"

"Shut up before I shut you up!" Ohana barked.

"This is all a mistake," Aaftab said. He held onto the bars and pleaded with his unseen jailer. "I don't know these people. They just came into my store. I have nothing to do with them. I don't know anything!"

Goldhammer appeared in front of Flynn and Aaftab's cell, along with Ohana and Marta. "You know enough," Goldhammer said.

"But I don't!"

Goldhammer rapped Aaftab across the hand with a riding crop. Aaftab stumbled back from the bars, howling, and holding his injured hand. Flynn glanced at Aaftab, held his finger to his lips and motioned for him to sit. Tears filled Aaftab's eyes as he bumped into the wall and slid to the floor.

Goldhammer turned his attention towards Flynn and tried to intimidate him with his flat, detached stare. "Mr. Flynn, I've amassed many enemies in my rise, but you have proven to be the most dogged and unrelenting opponent I have ever encountered. I'm guessing that's because your elevator does not go all the way to the top."

"I hope you know your mad plan will never succeed."

"What mad plan is that?"

"Using behavioral advertising to brainwash every man, woman and child on earth into believing your version of reality."

"Isn't that what all advertising does? Change people's perception of reality and steer them towards another point of view? This is not a new concept. Plato talked about this in his allegory of the cave. Knowledge gained through our senses is no more than conjecture. Opinion. Shadows on the wall. Truth is malleable and not absolute. It's what each of us decides it is."

"But in this case, you're deciding for everyone."

"Isn't that the *raison d'être* of every advertising campaign ever created? Every religion, too, for that matter. Up to this point, no one ideology or political philosophy has succeeded in coalescing everyone behind the same unified reality. But that is because they didn't have the technology. *I do.* This process has been messy. For the last hundred years, various governments, political factions, and religions have fought a pitched battle for people's hearts, minds, and souls. They used everything from conventional advertising and PR to social media, propaganda, books, movies, and TV. I will bring order to this chaos."

"And in return all you want is complete and utter control of every human being on Earth."

"Actually, I don't. I just want them to buy what I'm selling."

"By taking away their free will?"

"By helping them decide what it is they really want. People are stressed out by all the decisions they need to make. They want some guidance. Someone to tell them what to watch. What to wear. What to eat. What to do. Humanity craves order. Direction. Certainty. And I can help with that."

"People aren't that stupid," Chloe said.

Goldhammer laughed loud and long. "Surely you must be joking. Look who they elect to lead them? People will follow any fool who projects confidence and strength."

"Yes," Flynn agreed. "Frightened people can be misled."

"I've seen it firsthand," Alessa said. "I grew up in post-war Italy. I saw what happens when desperate people follow a leader who only wants power for power's sake. A leader who has no empathy. A leader who has no conscience or compassion or guiding philosophy."

"Indeed. The world doesn't need another sociopathic dictator," Flynn agreed.

"You disappoint me, Mr. Flynn. Even the founding fathers knew that unfettered democracy leads to anarchy. They understood that true democracy is the tyranny of the majority. That's why they formed a republic. Left to their own devices, the rabble would devolve into chaos. They need elite leadership."

"So, you think you're a philosopher king?" Flynn asked.

"I see myself more as a dream merchant. I give people what they want and in return, they give me what I want. Like Chloe here. Until you interfered, she was on the fast-track to stardom. Tyler's ambition was to be a director. I could have helped him with that. Just like I helped that journalist from the L.A Weekly. I optioned her screenplay and in return…"

"Jenna sold us out?" Tyler sounded both hurt and furious. "It wasn't her editor? It was her?"

"You see it as a betrayal, but in truth she was trying to help you. Offer you a hand. But you wouldn't take it. You slapped it away. Every day young women like your sister arrive in Los Angeles dreaming of fame and fortune. Each one is the prettiest girl from their little town. Each one believes they are special and destined for greatness. But they are nothing but chattel. Plunder. The spoils of war."

"I've known men like you my whole life," Alessa said. "Selfish, entitled narcissists."

"Says the sex goddess who sold herself to the highest bidder. You didn't marry a truck driver or a construction worker, did you? You married a billionaire."

"Who happened to be a good man."

"Good to you, maybe. But no one gets to where he did without ruining a few lives and making a few enemies."

"You have no idea who he was."

"He was someone who wanted to marry a movie star. A fabled beauty. An object of desire. But if he were still alive, he would have left you by now. He would have traded you in for a new and improved model. Age is cruel. Beauty fades. The bloom on the rose lasts only so long."

"You are such an asshole," Chloe said.

"Just a truth teller," Goldhammer said.

"Then tell us the truth. What do you want from us?" Tyler asked.

"I want to know who else you're working with. Who else has seen my private videos? Who else are you in cahoots with?"

"No one! We didn't tell anyone," Sancho said. "Ohana grabbed us before we could."

Goldhammer strolled back in front of Flynn's cell. "Is that true, Mr. Flynn?"

"I'm afraid not. Mr. Abboud here uploaded everything to a colleague who will send it to multiple media outlets if we do not check in with him."

"He's lying!" Aaftab shouted.

"Tell him the truth," Tyler pleaded.

"There's no point in prevaricating," Flynn replied, leveling his gaze at Goldhammer. "He's many things, but he's no fool." Flynn knew they needed a bargaining chip if they were to survive, and the only leverage they had was Goldhammer's fear of being exposed for who and what he was.

"Thank you for being frank with me, Mr. Flynn."

"Of course. But know this. If we aren't released in the next hour everything you've built for the last twenty years will be destroyed."

Goldhammer showed no emotion as he considered Flynn's threat. "It seems I have two different realities to sort through then. Perhaps a little of torture will help me find the truth."

"Do what you will, Goldhammer. I've been trained to withstand the most brutal interrogations and tortures ever devised."

"I have no intention of torturing you, Mr. Flynn. I'm going to torture Miss Bianchi and Miss Jablonski. I wanted to avoid this sort of unpleasantness, *but* you've left me no choice. I'll be back once I've made preparations. Often, the anticipation of pain is worse than the pain itself." Goldhammer smiled. "However, in this instance I doubt that will be the case."

Goldhammer left with Ohana. Their heavy footsteps slowly receding until the door at the end of the corridor slammed shut.

• • •

Aaftab Abboud stood over Flynn and castigated him. "Why would you do that? Why lie to him like that? Why not just tell him the truth?"

"Because if he knows the truth, he has no need to keep us alive."

"You think he wants to kill us?"

"Desperate men do desperate things," Flynn said.

The one they called Sancho joined the conversation. "Hey, James, I think this is getting out of hand, man. Goldhammer's no crime boss. If we can just reassure him that his shit is safe, he has no reason to retaliate. A cornered animal will always attack."

"He's not an animal. He's a monster." It was the younger woman. Chloe. "James, I'm sorry I didn't listen to you. You too Alessa. I thought I could make him pay for what he did to me, but you knew that wouldn't work. You tried to tell me, but I wouldn't listen. Monsters like him are never satisfied. Even if we give him what he wants, he'll just want more."

"I'm sorry too," the man named Tyler said. "I wanted to punish him. I wanted him to pay for what he did to you. So I pushed you into something I shouldn't have. I am so sorry."

Aaftab watched as Flynn picked up and examined the large tube of lube sitting on the floor of his cell. "Alright then, we're all in agreement. I've encountered power mad miscreants like Goldhammer before. Men like him believe they are Gods. They can't be bargained with and they can't be reasoned with. Luckily, I have another way out of this."

Aaftab watched as Flynn stripped off his ripped and ruined suit. "Why are you taking your clothes off?"

Flynn didn't answer, he just removed the black latex body suit off its hanger and put it on, one leg at a time.

"Hey James!" Sancho called out. "What are you up to?"

"You'll see."

"He's putting on a black rubber body suit," Aaftab said nervously.

It took some tugging to get the body suit over his muscular limbs and broad chest. It squeaked as he pushed his head into the black rubbery hood. There were eyeholes and a mouth hole with a zipper. A shiver of fear coursed through Aaftab. This man did not seem in his right mind.

"James, talk to me!" Sancho said.

"Patience, old friend," Flynn replied, his voice muffled by the latex mask.

"What's he doing now?" Tyler asked.

"I don't know!" Aaftab watched as Flynn unscrewed the cap off a giant pink tube of lube. "You're not planning to use that on me, are you?" Aaftab asked in a plaintive tone.

Flynn unzipped his mouth hole. "I can if you want me to. But being you're a bit bulkier, I thought I should try first."

"Try what?"

The bottle made a farting sound as Flynn squeezed out a handful of lube. He covered his latex body suit with it, slathering it over his legs, his torso, his arms, and even his rubbery head. He squeezed out handful after handful until he was covered from head to toe in glistening, strawberry-scented lube.

Flynn then turned and addressed Aaftab. "Take your clothes off."

"Why?" Aaftab asked.

"The slipperier you are, the easier it will be, which is why I decided to don this latex suit." He tossed Aaftab the Tush Ease Anal Gel.

"The easier what will be?"

"You'll see."

"I don't want to see!"

Flynn walked towards Aaftab and Aaftab backed away, bumping into the wall. He watched as Flynn approached the bars and tried to push his way through. The black latex squeaked as Flynn slithered in between the wrought iron. He managed to get his arm, shoulder and even his rubber hooded head through, but his torso proved too bulky to fit between the narrow bars. Flynn grimaced and pushed and grunted.

"James, what are you doing, man?" Sancho shouted.

Aaftab shouted back, "He's trying to squeeze through the bars."

Flynn shoved and strained and used every ounce of strength to slide his way forward, but even though he was slipperier than snot on a glass doorknob, he couldn't push through.

Flynn applied more anal gel until the tube was empty, but as slick as he was, the bars were too close together and he was too large. On Flynn's fourth try, the big door creaked open at the end of the corridor. Heavy footsteps echoed off the walls.

The two operators couldn't believe their eyes when they saw Flynn struggling to slide through the bars wearing a black latex body suit shiny with lube.

"Gotta give the guy points for originality," the larger of the two said.

The other operator pushed a baton through the bars to shove Flynn back. "Back away from the damn door!"

"Goldhammer wants you in with the girl," said the larger of the two. "He doesn't want you to miss a thing." He pulled his Glock. "Open it up, Ari. After we move Flynn we'll put her brother in here with the Arab."

Ari unlocked the door and entered, shoving Aaftab back with his baton and grabbing Flynn hard by the arm. Flynn didn't resist. He let himself be pulled along until they reached the cell door. At that point, he slid his slippery arm from Ari's grasp and kicked him hard in the ass, sending him flying into the guard with the gun.

Flynn grabbed a massive double-sided dildo as he stepped out of the cell. He whipped it down, slapping the gun out of the op's hand. Ari tried to tackle Flynn and slid right off of him, banging his head into the bars. The other op tried to grab his gun off the ground, but Flynn kicked it across the now slippery floor.

Both guards came at Flynn, determined to bring him down, but they couldn't hold on to him.

Couldn't get a grip.

And Flynn wielded the big pink dildo like a club. Slapping them across the face. Snapping them in the groin. Taking them out at the knees.

Ari lost his balance on the slippery floor and toppled back. Flynn used his downward momentum to slam him into the cement, knocking him cold.

The other op pulled a huge combat knife from a sheath on his ankle. Flynn tried to slap it out of his hand with the dildo, but the man sliced the sex toy right in half.

"Flynn!" Sancho slid the Glock across the floor. Flynn snatched it up.

"Drop it!" Flynn ordered.

The op hesitated, but finally complied by dropping his knife. "Now kick it towards me. Carefully."

The man did as Flynn asked. Flynn picked up the blade and ordered him into the cell where Aaftab cowered. "Inside! Let's go!"

The man backed his way into the cell.

"Against the wall. Hands high. Aaftab, put him in the restraints."

Aaftab didn't want to get in any more trouble, but he also didn't want to contradict a man waving a gun around. Especially one wearing a black latex body suit covered with anal gel.

Aaftab locked the guard in the restraints.

"Now the ball gag," Flynn said.

Aaftab fit a bright red ball gag into the man's mouth and strapped it to his head. Then, per Flynn's directions, dragged the other guard into the cell and handcuffed him to a metal ring screwed into the floor. He gagged him as well, using a combination blindfold harness and ball gag.

Flynn took the guard's keys and freed the others. Before leaving the room, Flynn grabbed a whip and a paddle and a tiny can of Binaca Blast sitting on a table with their other belongings. Aaftab grabbed his wallet as Flynn hurried off. Not having anywhere else to go, he reluctantly followed him and the others through the heavy wooden door at the end of the corridor.

• • •

Flynn knew the others were eager to escape, but first he needed to get his hands on the hard drive from Goldhammer's laptop, or at least a copy of what was on it. It held the maniac's trophies. Contained all his conquests. As sick and arrogant as Goldhammer was, Flynn knew he would never want to let them go.

They hurried through a maze of stone corridors lit with LED sconces designed to look like flickering torches, and finally found a staircase that led up to the house proper.

Decorated like a modern mountain lodge, the huge chalet had rustic wood paneling, rough stone fireplaces, hardwood floors, high ceilings, antique copper chandeliers and massive windows that overlooked snowy hills dotted with pine trees.

Flynn rounded a corner and nearly collided with one of Ohana's men. The op took in the gun in Flynn's hand, the head-to-toe black latex outfit, and immediately put up his hands. Flynn took the man's Glock from his shoulder holster and tossed it to a surprised Sancho, who fumbled and nearly dropped it. Flynn then dosed the Black Star operative with Q's truth spray. The man sputtered and spit and rubbed his burning eyes.

"Goldhammer? Where is he?" Flynn demanded.

The man pointed blindly down the hall and Flynn smacked him on the head with the butt of his pistol. He collapsed in a heap. Flynn hurried past him down the hall. The others followed and, as they approached a partly open door, they heard voices inside. Flynn stopped abruptly and looked back at his fellow escapees, bringing his finger to his unzipped lips. Sancho and the others quietly came to a stop.

Flynn listened at the door.

"You sure about this?" someone inside asked.

"Ohana was just here. Said he wants it melted down."

Flynn quietly pushed open the door to find two of Ohana's men standing around a metal wastebasket. One held a can of lighter fluid, the other a lit match. The floor creaked. They turned and saw Flynn holding his black Glock on them. So stunned were they by the sight of him, the one holding the burning match dropped it into the metal wastebasket.

Flames whooshed up. Flynn moved quickly, striking one man in the head, and kicking over the can. The second man bolted past Sancho and Chloe, Tyler and Alessa, and nearly knocked Aaftab on his ass as he raced off, his running footsteps echoing down the hall.

Flynn found the hard drive on the floor in flames. He fell on top of it like a soldier jumping on a hand grenade, smothering it with his latex suit. With the flame extinguished, he examined the hard drive closely. "A little melted, but none the worse for wear. Hopefully, the data will still be intact. Aaftab, what do you think?"

"It's possible."

Flynn grinned through his zippered mouth hole, got to his feet and turned to the others. "Shall we go?"

Flynn opened a pair of French doors that led out to a snowy patio. From the position of the sun in the sky, Flynn assumed it was midday. He slid over the railing and landed in a snowdrift. Alessa, Sancho, Chloe, Tyler, and finally Aaftab followed him over the railing into the snow.

Flynn crept around the building. One of Ohana's men stood by a ski shed. He wore black jeans and a black leather bomber jacket and smoked a cigarette. Flynn snuck closer. The man must have heard Flynn's latex boots crunching through the snow, because he turned and froze, stunned to see someone so tall in skintight black latex. Before he could draw his weapon, Flynn beaned him with the butt of his gun.

Inside the shed, they found racks with snowboards, skis and boots, and a large worktable.

"Who knows how to ski?" Flynn asked.

Chloe raised her hand.

"I can as well," Alessa said. "In my younger days I skied St. Moritz quite often."

Tyler said, "I can, but I'd rather snowboard."

"I tried it once, like five years ago," Sancho said.

Aaftab shook his head no.

"Well, it's a perfect time to learn," Flynn said.

Sancho looked at Flynn skeptically. "You know how to ski?"

"Of course, I do. I spent my younger days on the continent. Switzerland. My father taught me when I was five."

Sancho sighed. "Dude, I know you think you can do this, but look at me. You can't."

Flynn picked up a pair of ski boots. "Who wears a nine?"

CHAPTER THIRTY-THREE

While the allies were battling Hitler in North Africa, Olympic skier Wayne Paulsen and Harvard lawyer, Alex Cushing, began building the Squaw Valley Ski resort. It opened with fifty rooms, one chairlift, and two tow ropes in 1947. When Reno was in the running to host the 1960 Olympic Games, Cushing proposed Squaw Valley as the site of the Winter Games. Pushing the fact that Squaw Valley was a blank slate, he promised to turn it into the perfect Olympic venue. And that was exactly what he did, building roads and bridges, hotels and restaurants, event areas, toboggan tracks, ski runs, jumps, and everything else necessary for a modern Winter Olympics. Today, the resort offers access to 42 ski lifts, an aerial tramway, and 270 trails that attract more than half a million skiers and snowboarders every year. The Olympic Valley, as the area is known, is home to quite a few spectacular mansions and extravagant mountain lodges owned by millionaires, billionaires, and world-renowned celebrities.

Goldhammer and Marta sat in the chalet's formal dining room and enjoyed a salmon, asparagus, and couscous salad whipped up by his private chef. The picture window framed a spectacular view of the mountains. His home sat alone at the end of a quiet cul-de-sac, high above The Squaw Valley Lodge. He could see Alpine Meadows and High Camp at Squaw Peak. Though not an accomplished skier, Goldhammer enjoyed the atmosphere of ski lodges and resorts: the blazing fires, the brandy, the hot cocoa, the cool, pine-scented air, and the quality of the light. Not to mention the handsome and athletic young ski bums and ski bunnies who frequented the lodges *après-ski*.

Goldhammer felt excluded from that world as a teenager. Just like he suffered rejection from the surf bums and surf bunnies of Southern

California. Growing up in Huntington Beach as a pale, chubby, pimple-faced nerd. Not so much bullied as completely ignored by the surfers and volleyball players, and other denizens of the beach as well as the cheerleaders and football players at his high school. Even the girls in the marching band wanted nothing to do with him.

Now, they had no choice but to deal with him. Now, he couldn't be dismissed or ignored. Now, he had power. He could give them what they wanted: fame, fortune, stardom.

Before he made his first million, Gary knew he had to become a new person. Someone who couldn't be rejected, overlooked, or laughed at. He changed his name from Goldfelcher to Goldhammer because a hammer was a tool that could both build and destroy. A Goldhammer sounded powerful. A Goldhammer sounded dangerous. Unlike a Goldfelcher, a Goldhammer could build you up or break you down.

He worked with trainers and hired a private chef to create healthy meals that would help him lose weight. He didn't have the genetics or the physical discipline to turn himself into someone who looked like a movie star. But with help of dermabrasion, liposuction, a tummy tuck, a chin implant, hair transplantation, a buttocks lift, Botox injections, and other various plumping procedures, he turned himself into someone somewhat presentable. Inside, he felt like the same unattractive dweeb, but at least now his outer self better reflected who he wanted to be.

Not like Flynn. Given every genetic gift, that mental patient was movie star handsome, yet he took it completely for granted. Goldhammer found Flynn's easy confidence both confounding and infuriating, especially since it stemmed directly from his lunacy. He saw how women looked at Flynn; completely taken in by the outer package. If only they knew what he really was. *Who* he really was.

Goldhammer finished his salmon, asparagus, and couscous dish and wanted more. He had been eating 1500 calories a day for two months now. He dropped a few pounds when he first started the new diet, but not a single pound for three weeks. Obviously, he hit a plateau. He felt a flash of fury. He was tired of denying himself. Sick of the discipline. He wanted more. He needed more—to quell the hunger, to quench his desire. All his desires.

It infuriated him that he'd had to destroy his videos. His conquests. His recorded memories of total control and absolute supremacy. All gone. All because of Flynn. Once he finished this merger and initiated his plan, he would need to rebuild, create new conquests, produce new trophies, and enshrine those exquisite moments of ravishment and domination.

He glanced at Marta eating her salad. She ate so slowly. Not like him. He consumed his food like he consumed everything else.

Quickly.

Ravenously.

At least he had Flynn and the others. He would enjoy inflicting pain on them, seeing the fear dancing in their eyes. He needed them to surrender to the bite of his whip.

Ohana thought Flynn was bluffing about sending the videos to some mysterious colleague, but Goldhammer had to be sure. Once his plan was in place, his future would be secure, and no one would ever ignore him again.

He looked back at Marta. She stared out the window with alarm. Goldhammer followed her gaze and saw a tall man dressed head to toe in shiny black latex carrying a pair of skis on his shoulder. Others followed him in single file, all carrying their own skis and snowboards.

Was that Chloe Jablonski and her stupid brother?

Goldhammer leaped to his feet. "They're getting away," he whispered. "They're getting away," he shouted. "*They're getting away!*"

Much to his chagrin, Sancho found himself following Flynn once again. Only this time, Flynn didn't sport an Armani tux, but a black latex body suit slathered with strawberry-scented lube. The air was cold and fresh, and he had to hurry to keep up.

They all stole boots and skis from Goldhammer's ski hut. Sancho didn't even know how to put them on, but Tyler helped him while Chloe helped Aaftab. Flynn, of course, had no clue, though he pretended he did. Alessandra tried to show him, but he dismissed her assistance as unnecessary.

Flynn led the way down a paved driveway flanked on either side by three-foot-tall piles of snow. Chloe and Tyler followed close behind, accompanied by a determined Alessandra, who moved with strong and graceful strides, impressive for a lady close to eighty. Aaftab, already out of breath, struggled to keep up as his ill-fitting ski boots slipped and slid on the icy pavers.

Sancho glanced back to see if anyone was after them. Goldhammer's massive lodge sprawled into the trees and up the mountain, but apparently no one had raised the alarm. At least not yet. If he wasn't trying to escape from men intent on torturing him, he might have better appreciated the incredible beauty and quiet of Squaw Valley. The trees and hills behind the house sat dusted with a thick layer of snow. The only sound was the crunch of their footsteps.

The peace and calm ended abruptly as a snowmobile engine roared to life, followed by another and then another. The engine whine came from behind the house, and their harsh rumble echoed across the Olympic Valley. Sancho watched as three snowmobiles emerged from the trees. Men in black snowsuits and stocking caps rode down the slope, spitting rooster tails of snow as they picked up speed.

"Shit!" Sancho shouted.

"Follow me!" Flynn commanded as he climbed up and over the snow berm that bordered the driveway. He dropped his skis on the ground, snapped his boots into them, and… didn't move.

"Lean down the hill," Alessa urged, gently pushing Flynn forward.

Flynn did as instructed and took off so abruptly he nearly tumbled backwards, windmilling his arms to find his balance.

Tyler glided up next to him. "You okay, dude?"

"Of course I am."

"Maybe you should snowplow your way down."

"I know what I'm doing." Flynn fell on his side, making a body-shaped hole in the snow.

Aaftab fell as well and Sancho tried to help him up.

Alessa skied up behind them, kicking up snow as she stopped. She helped Sancho pull Aaftab to his feet. As soon as he was upright, he shot off down the hill.

Having skied twice before, Sancho half-remembered his beginner lessons. He relied mainly on the snowplow as he cut sideways across the hill and struggled to keep his ski tips from crossing.

Glancing back, he saw Flynn on his skis, arms flailing as he picked up speed. Flynn tried to turn to slow his momentum and crossed his ski tips, launching himself face first into the snow. Alessa helped him up again and he shrugged her off. Frustrated and furious, he aimed his skis straight down the mountain.

"Lean forward!" she shouted.

Flynn did and slid forward, faster and faster, barely staying upright, wobbling and windmilling like a drunk.

Tyler shot off down the hill after Flynn. The snowmobiles roared closer and Sancho decided his fear of Black Star trumped his fear of gravity. Abandoning the snowplow, he straightened his skis, held them parallel and picked up speed.

Chloe skied up next to him. "Careful! Not so fast!" Trees rushed by in a blur, the wind cold in his face. "Knees bent! Back straight! Lean forward!"

The snowmobiles sounded even louder now. Closer. Much closer.

Instead of cutting across the hill, Chloe turned her skis straight down and took off like a bullet. Sancho tried to follow and nearly lost his balance. He saw Alessa slaloming down the hill. Damn, she was good. Aaftab lay on his back, covered in snow, both his skis sliding down the hill without him.

Chloe shouted back to Sancho, her voice nearly lost in the wind. "Watch out for the moguls!"

"What?" he said before he flew into the air and caught a ski tip. Tumbling forward, he hit the hardpack and rolled. His legs bent at awkward angles as he lost both skis. Cold and covered in snow, Sancho glanced back to see a snowmobile roaring towards him. He tried to scramble out of the way as the snowmobile hit a mogul and flew right over him, the runners less than a foot from his stocking cap.

The other snowmobiles powered down the hill past him, the engines screaming and echoing across the canyon.

They didn't stop to apprehend him. They totally ignored him.

They were after Flynn.

• • •

As Flynn lay in the snow, he didn't understand why he couldn't stay upright. He hadn't skied for an awfully long time, but had many vivid memories of skiing in the past. He first put on skis at age five, and skied often with his parents in Zermatt and St. Moritz before he tragically lost them in that climbing accident in the Aiguilles Rouges near Chamonix. Flynn had escaped from his enemies on skis so many times. Why was he having such a problem? Skiing was like riding a bike. It wasn't something one forgot how to do. Perhaps the drugs Goldhammer used on him created a lingering effect. Perhaps these skis were defective. Whatever the reason, he had to find that muscle memory if he ever hoped to survive. The snowmobiles were almost upon him.

Using the last pole in his possession, Flynn pushed himself to his feet. Luckily, the latex body suit kept him warm and dry, though his heavy breathing pushed moist air through the eyeholes of his hood and fogged up his goggles. No time to clear them off. He aimed his skis down the hill and gravity tugged him along. Slowly at first, he soon picked up speed. A bracing injection of adrenaline rocketed through him as the familiar music played in his head — that driving guitar that always filled him with such energy and confidence.

He passed a sign marking this slope as a black diamond run. The grade seemed steeper. Flynn moved faster. *Now let's see those snowmobiles keep up with him.*

The rough terrain had ruts and moguls. Flynn's jaw rattled as he struggled to stay upright. The ground disappeared below him and he flailed through the air. A ski tip caught the top of a mogul and he flew ass over tea cup. His head dented a crust of ice as he somersaulted forward, losing both skis, but not his forward momentum. The lube-covered latex turned his entire body into a luge.

He shot down the steep, icy hill like a greased pig on a toboggan run.

He bounced hard from mogul to mogul and tried to see out his fogged-up eye holes. He caught sight of a surprised, middle-aged man moments before colliding with him. That impact changed his trajectory. Now, he zipped through a stand of trees.

Flynn miraculously slid between them, somehow avoiding a fatal collision. A booming explosion caught his attention as a burning snowmobile crashed into a tree. He didn't see the riders and assumed they fell off long before. Flynn's shoulder slammed into a low branch. He spun around into another tree and then another, banging into trunk after trunk, bouncing back and forth like a ball in a pinball machine.

And then, the sky opened above. Flynn was out of the trees, sliding straight down a snowy expanse. Up ahead he saw what looked like a ski class, all lined up in a row.

"Out of the way! *Out of the way!*" Flynn shouted through his zippered mouth hole.

They turned and stared like startled deer as Flynn knocked the stout man at the end of line off his feet. The rest fell like dominos. People standing in line at the lifts watched in wonder as Flynn shot by.

The angle of the slope was less steep now and Flynn struggled to slow himself down. People who saw him coming scattered in all directions as he slammed hard into a ski rack. Skis tumbled down on top of him. The surrounding crowd watched with worry and alarm as Flynn grabbed onto the rack and pulled himself to his feet.

Farther down the hill, Flynn saw Alessandra, Chloe, Tyler, and an exhausted-looking Sancho. Alessandra waved and Flynn started moving in her direction. Bruised and banged up, he walked with a limp as he pulled off his goggles and his black latex hood. The two remaining snowmobiles roared past him on either side and came to an abrupt stop, blocking his path forward.

Ohana and his compatriot climbed off their Ski-Doos and rested their hands on their holstered weapons. "Nice try," Ohana said. "But the race is over, Mr. Flynn. You have nowhere to run and nowhere to hide."

Chloe, Tyler, Alessandra, and Sancho slowly moved in Flynn's direction. He subtly raised his right hand to them, indicating that they should stay away. But they weren't about to abandon him, and Flynn couldn't help but feel grateful for that.

As they inched closer, Flynn conversed with Ohana. "I do hope you realize that your boss has completely lost his mind."

"You think he's the one that's crazy?"

"He's mad as a hatter. Completely crackers. The wheel is spinning, but the hamster is dead."

Ohana laughed at that as Alessa came up fast, her ski pole raised high over her head.

Ohana somehow sensed the impending attack and turned, grabbing the pole and wrenching it out of her hand. He slapped her across the face and she fell in the snow. Flynn moved for him and Ohana aimed the point of the ski pole at him. "I think I'm about done with you, Mr. Flynn."

Just then, three loud snowmobiles roared up and a trio of stolid young men dressed in bright red ski patrol jackets climbed off their rides, surrounding Ohana on three sides. The tallest of the trio seemed in charge. Broad shouldered with flowing blond hair and a full beard, he looked like a Viking in modern garb. He pointed at Ohana's snowmobile. "Sir, is that your Ski-Doo?"

Ohana nodded. "I work for Mr. Goldhammer."

"I don't care who you work for, sir. We have had multiples reports of you and your friends riding down a ski run. That is strictly prohibited. In fact, one of your party is currently being medevacked to a hospital because he crashed into a tree."

"I can explain."

"There is nothing to explain, sir. We'll be taking you and your friend into custody, impounding your vehicles, and calling the sheriff's department."

"I don't think so." Ohana snarled.

"Don't make this any more difficult than it has to be, sir."

"I could say the same to you." In one swift move, Ohana pulled his Glock and pointed it at the ski patrol ranger. Ohana's compatriot did the same.

The rangers all raised their hands. Surprise flashed across the young Viking's face. "Sir, please, you don't want to do this."

"And you need to stop acting like you're in charge here."

Flynn caught sight of Tyler out of the corner of his eye. Even without the Captain America outfit, he cut a heroic figure as he smacked Ohana's gun hand with his snowboard. The Glock boomed.

• • •

Sancho still suffered from PTSD due to the bullet he caught the last time someone tried to kill Flynn. He only recently recovered after a long period of convalescence. So, when the gunshot cracked, he froze.

Tyler didn't, however, and threw himself on Ohana's man, tackling him so hard he knocked the gun out of his hand. As they wrestled in the snow, Flynn made his play, disarming Ohana with a jiu-jitsu move.

Tyler was no match for the op he tackled, and the man quickly turned the tables on him with his Krav Maga skills, twisting Tyler's hand until something cracked. Tyler howled and fell back in the snow. The op snatched up his and Ohana's gun before Chloe could reach either one.

The op aimed both weapons at Flynn. "Ohana move! Let me shoot him."

"No, this meshugana's mine!" Ohana tied Flynn up in some kind of Krav Maga death grip as they wrestled in the snow. He held Flynn down and pummeled him, beating him bloody and breaking his nose.

"That's enough," Sancho shouted.

"I'm just getting started." Ohana grunted as he straddled Flynn and pounded his increasingly misshapen face.

"You're killing him!" Chloe shouted.

"Get off him!" Tyler screamed.

Ohana's compadre held the crowd back with his two guns, waving them around with a look of absolute fury. "Everyone back off. Give 'em room!"

. . .

Flynn couldn't fight back now. He couldn't even struggle. He just took punch after punch after punch.

And then Sancho heard screaming. A high-pitched terrified bellow that caused the crowd to part and scatter as a skier crashed right through the circle of spectators at high speed.

Aaftab, his mouth open in a now-silent scream, his eyes wide with terror, slammed into the op holding the dual Glocks and both he and his weapons went flying.

Alessandra caught one right out of the air and leveled the Glock at Ohana. After all the training she had for all the movies she'd starred in, she handled the weapon like a pro.

"Get off him!" she ordered.

"*Zine be-ayn!*" Ohana barked, driving his fist into Flynn's face.

"Shoot 'em!" shouted Chloe.

Ohana hit Flynn again and again. Sancho found the sound of meat pounding on meat sickening.

"*Get off him!*" Alessandra shouted.

Ohana turned and stared at Alessandra, eyes wild, splattered with blood. "Or what? What are you going to do? Shoot me?"

Sancho jumped at the sound of the Glock firing. Ohana seemed so surprised. He looked down at the bloody hole in his shirt. Shaky, he used Flynn's inert body to push himself to his feet. He wavered and fingered the hole and glowered at Alessandra. "What did you do?"

He took a step towards her and she shot him in the knee. He collapsed in an untidy heap and laid there on his side, more shocked than anything else.

"You shot me!" he said.

"Twice," she replied.

She aimed the Glock at the other operator, but the man lay motionless, unconscious in the snow under an exhausted Aaftab.

Sancho slowly approached Flynn. He put his ear against his chest. "I don't hear a heartbeat. I don't think he's breathing."

Chloe sobbed.

The ski patrol officer called for an ambulance and Sancho held his old friend's hand. "Don't you die on me, man. Don't you fucking die."

Flynn's eyes fluttered open and relief flooded Sancho's heart. Flynn whispered something no one could hear.

"He's trying to tell us something," Chloe said.

They all knelt around him and leaned in to listen. Flynn licked his bloody lips and marshalled every ounce of energy to whisper, "Drink."

"Water?" Chloe asked.

"Get him some water!" Sancho shouted.

"No," Flynn whispered. "Vodka. Martini. Shaken. Not stirred." A wry smiled curled the edge of his fat lip.

CHAPTER THIRTY-FOUR

The founder of gonzo journalism was born in Louisville, Kentucky in 1937. At age eighteen, Hunter S. Thompson was charged as an accessory in a robbery and spent thirty-one days in the Jefferson County Jail. One week after his release, he joined the air force, hoping to become a pilot. But instead of becoming an aviator, he became the sports editor of the camp newspaper. Enamored of the drug and hippie culture taking root in California, he moved to Berkeley after his discharge and started hanging with the Hells Angels. He wrote about them and sold some articles, and they showed their appreciation by savagely beating and stomping his ass. The resulting book put him on the map. He wrote about the 1968 presidential trail and was in Chicago for the police riot at the Democratic National Convention. Fear and Loathing in Las Vegas *followed. In 2005, he died of a self-inflicted gunshot. At his funeral, a cannon fired his ashes from the top of a hundred and fifty-three-foot tower shaped like a double-thumbed fist clutching a peyote button. Johnny Depp paid for the three-million-dollar funeral attended by the likes of Jack Nicholson, Ed Bradley, Charlie Rose, Lyle Lovett, Ralph Steadman, and Bill Murray.*

Along with Nellie Bly, Hunter S. Thompson was one of Bettina O'Toole Applebaum's journalistic heroes. Someone who didn't just report a story, but dove off the deep end to get his arms around it. Bettina did just that when she first reported on James Flynn. Going undercover in a mental hospital to find him, and then following him across the globe, helping him uncover an incredible plot to stop the engine of the world. She risked life and limb and reputation to reveal the truth and bring down a genius who had lost his mind.

After their time together, she wrote about her adventure and went on to fame and not much fortune. Flynn went back to the mental hospital he called home in Pasadena, California. She hadn't seen Flynn for over a year, so his call out of the blue surprised her.

Flynn claimed he had an incredible and important story for her. The fact that Flynn was officially delusional, of course, gave her pause, but she also had doubts the last time he brought her an unbelievable story—and that one turned out to be absolutely true.

Flynn told her he wasn't in any condition to travel and asked her if she'd mind coming to see him in Pasadena at the Southern California headquarters of Her Majesty's Secret Service. She had an interview scheduled in L.A. and took the opportunity to drop in on Flynn.

Bettina currently lived in Brooklyn and, like Hunter S. Thompson, worked as a staff writer for Rolling Stone. Unlike Thompson, she also wrote for the Village Voice, Wired, Elle, BuzzFeed, GQ, Vice, Salon, Mother Jones, and the Daily Dot.

On the appointed day, she packed a carry-on suitcase, took a Lyft to JFK International Airport, flew into LAX, rented a car and drove to the Hollywood Roosevelt Hotel. She met Patrisse Cullors, co-founder of Black Lives Matter, for an elegant dinner at Crossroads Kitchen on Melrose. Bettina was profiling her for Rolling Stone and discovered they had much in common. Like Patrice, she was queer and a vegan, and grew up feeling like an outsider. Bettina's father was the great-grandson of a slave and her mother was an Ashkenazi Jew. She was baptized as a baby, but later bat mitzvahed to mollify her mother's parents. Both Patrice and Bettina were in their late thirties and wildly ambitious. Bettina found her inspiring. They agreed to meet up again in a few days to continue the interview.

The very next morning, Bettina drove to the City of Roses Psychiatric Institute in Pasadena. Memories flooded her as she walked through the front doors, and she wondered if Nurse Durkin still ruled the ward with an iron fist. Her piece last year in Rolling Stone didn't portray Durkin in the best light, and Bettina wondered if she caught some flack because of that.

She looked forward to seeing Flynn and was surprised how much she missed him.

A nurse she didn't recognize led her through the ward. She remembered a few of the patients she saw in the rec room, watching TV or playing cards or talking to themselves as they wandered about. She smiled and waved at Ty, Q, and Rodney, and all three waved back. Mary Alice apparently still saw Bettina as a rival for Flynn's affections and glowered at her as she passed.

Nurse Durkin didn't seem all that happy to see her either. Bettina offered a little wave as she walked by. Durkin didn't reciprocate. Tall and bulky with broad-shoulders and a massive bust, Durkin's impassive face and ice-cold eyes still inspired fear.

Bettina followed the young nurse to a visiting area where she found Flynn sitting at a table with Sancho Perez. She couldn't believe how bad he looked. His face was swollen and bruised. He had a black eye and a fat lip and a huge bandage on his nose.

"Jesus," she said as she sat down.

"Looks worse than it is," Flynn said.

"You just can't stay out of trouble, can you?"

"Trouble can't stay away from me. But then that's my job, isn't it? Like Philip Marlowe, trouble is my business."

"Who?" Sancho asked.

"A fictional character created by Raymond Chandler. The private eye as a modern-day knight errant, righting wrongs and saving damsels from danger in a dark and cynical world."

"Sounds like someone else I know," Sancho said.

"With one significant difference. I'm not fictional."

"As your face perfectly illustrates." Bettina reached out to touch his bruised cheek. "What sort of trouble did you get yourself into this time? Another super villain with a plan for world domination?"

"There seems to be no end to them," Flynn replied with a smile. His split lip caused him to wince.

Even beaten to a bloody pulp, Flynn refused to dress like a hospital patient. He wore a black Brioni suit and a white cotton shirt. The only concession to his condition was that he didn't deign to wear a tie. He reached inside his jacket and retrieved a small thumb drive from his inner pocket. He slid it across the table towards Bettina.

"What's this?" she asked.

"Evidence."

"Of the plot?"

"And more. Goldhammer has been a very naughty boy."

"Gary Goldhammer? The media mogul?"

"Among other things."

"Sounds like quite a story." Bettina pulled a small digital recorder from her purse, set it on the table, and pushed the button for record.

"Where shall I begin?"

She slid the recorder closer to Flynn. "How about from the beginning?"

CHAPTER THIRTY-FIVE

Once all the women started coming forward, Gary Goldhammer's wife, Margot, filed for divorce. They spent very little time together anyway. She lived in Paris and he lived in Malibu, and she was well aware of his infidelities. How could she not be? He cheated with her on his first wife, Linda Romano of Encino. Margot was younger and prettier and posher than the first Mrs. Goldhammer. The former model starred in a few movies before starting her own health and lifestyle brand.

Without ever saying anything specific, Margot made it clear she could live with Goldhammer's perfidy as long as he didn't publicly humiliate her. She stood by him for a time when the first allegations hit the press. But when the videos came out and they arrested him for sexual assault, and perp-walked him in handcuffs in front of the whole world, she bolted along with all his supposed friends.

Goldhammer wasn't a fool. He knew none of his friends were actual friends. They were business associates. Famous acquaintances. Investors. Employees. The whole concept of friendship eluded him. Every relationship he made was built on a quid pro quo. Because if there was nothing in it for him... what was the point?

His board forced him from the company he founded. Every business partner and celebrity acquaintance ghosted him. Not even the actors he turned into stars wanted anything to do with him.

The scandal turned him into a pariah.

The FTC ruled against the merger with Globalcom right before his company kicked him to the curb. His plans for global domination were dashed. All his dreams destroyed. Much of his wealth was tied up in stock, and that too was in the toilet now.

All he had worked for. Everything he painstakingly built over thirty years.

Gone.

His marriage. His livelihood. Much of his fortune. All he had left was his freedom and that too was now on the chopping block.

His life as he knew it ended the day that story came out in Rolling Stone. The videos were everywhere and dozens of women came forward, claiming he had molested and assaulted them. He didn't understand why they turned the tables on him. Sure, he knew he could be sexually aggressive and cross the line at times, but those women took as much from him as he ever took from them.

It's Hollywood. Everyone did it.

Goldhammer sat in the steaming jacuzzi out by his infinity pool, sipping on a mojito, staring at the Pacific, waiting for his lawyer to arrive. Such a beautiful day. Such a beautiful view. Puffy clouds in a turquoise sky.

Yet everything was slipping away.

He only had two servants left. Juana and Rosa. Both under five feet tall. Sisters from Guatemala. They spoke little English and rarely looked him in the eye. Together they cooked for him and cleaned and washed his clothes and called him "mister." They seemed to treat him with deference and respect, but who could tell what they were really thinking.

Goldhammer fired those Black Star screw-ups after the disaster in Squaw Valley—not that he could afford them now. He heard Ohana spent six weeks in the hospital ward of the Placer County jail recovering from his gunshot wounds.

They didn't even charge the elderly movie star who shot him. She claimed self-defense and the police didn't bother arresting her. Not after what Ohana did to Flynn. He nearly killed him. Which is why Ohana and his men all faced charges of aggravated assault, reckless endangerment, and disorderly conduct. Goldhammer quietly covered their bail, hoping they would flee the country and save him the embarrassment of an investigation and a trial. Not to mention any criminal culpability.

214

At least he still had Marta. Loyal Marta. Loyal because he continued to pay her with what little money he had left. He actually had more than he let on. He had accounts hidden all over the world. Hidden because his wife, and her lawyers, and all those money-hungry attention whores wanted a piece of his fortune.

Marta didn't just serve as his personal secretary, but as his bodyguard. Her implacable toughness and skills as a fighter surpassed those of Ohana and all his men. Goldhammer received dozens of threats daily, promising him grievous bodily injury and death.

So he kept Marta close.

She was his Yojimbo.

He hired a personal PR firm to help manage the fallout, and they told him to hire a female attorney. So he did. Rachel Einbinder made her reputation as a women's rights attorney. For twenty years she fought on behalf of women battling sexual harassment, sexual assault, workplace discrimination, and wrongful termination. She went after high profile celebrities and politicians and fought tirelessly for a number of feminist causes. Some were shocked when she agreed to lead Goldhammer's legal team.

What they didn't know is that she wrote screenplays on the side and Goldhammer agreed to help her get one produced.

Goldhammer found her quite attractive for a raging radical feminist. Rachel dressed in a modest, yet still provocative manner, wore her long, red hair loose, and didn't shy away from makeup.

Perhaps he would invite her to a private dinner once this all was over.

Marta led Rachel out by the infinity pool and directed her to a seating area surrounding a firepit. As she took a seat and opened her briefcase, Goldhammer emerged from the hot tub bare ass naked but for the monitor that adorned his left ankle. He wondered if she would react to the fact that he was nude. The anticipation filled him with excitement. But she pretended to ignore his nakedness and busied herself with her briefcase.

Juana and Rosa helped Goldhammer on with a white, terry cloth robe which he tied loosely around his middle. During the gilded age, a man of his size would have been considered healthy and prosperous.

Weight went right along with status. Not like today, where repudiating one's appetites was considered virtuous. Goldhammer didn't agree. Not anymore. He was finished trying to live up to the expectations of others. Done with dieting and exercising and denying himself. If he ended up in prison, society would soon enough take everything he desired. Until then, he would satisfy his every craving and never delay gratification.

He sat himself down on a sofa across the firepit and didn't bother keeping his knees together. If Rachel didn't like it, she could look away. Goldhammer decided right then and there he wouldn't let the handwringers and social justice warriors and arbiters of political correctness dictate how he lived his life. He would win. He would triumph. He would take what he wanted and those who didn't like it would have to get out of his way.

Goldhammer eyeballed Rachel Einbinder and didn't bother smiling. He wasn't about to grovel or ingratiate himself. She worked for him. He didn't work for her. He could tell she expected him to greet her. Screw that. Screw her expectations. He just stared at her.

Finally, she nervously smiled. "How are you holding up?"

"Quite well, as you can see."

"I assume your ankle monitor is waterproof?"

"That's what I've been told."

"Good."

"Since I'm paying you $850.00 an hour, perhaps we could dispense with the pleasantries and get to business."

"Fine." She pulled a pile of papers from her briefcase. "The D.A. offered a plea deal."

"What did you tell them?"

"I told them I would talk to you. As your attorney, I'm obligated to present any deal they offer."

Marta stood just behind her and to her left. Goldhammer enjoyed the fact that Marta set Rachel on edge.

"What's the offer?" he asked.

"Ten years. But you'll probably be out in five if not sooner."

"Five years?"

"In a minimum-security facility."

Goldhammer glowered at her. "Five years?"

"They charged you with rape in the third degree and predatory sexual assault."

"It was consensual."

"I know you believe that, but we have no evidence or witnesses to prove that assertion. In fact, those videos prove quite the opposite."

"It was role playing."

"Not according to the women."

"Isn't it my word against theirs?"

"Yes, but you have 27 accusers with more arriving every day."

"Is there no way to get those videos thrown out? After all, they were acquired illegally."

"The police only saw them once they were part of the public record. As they weren't seized in an illegal search, we can't prove they are fruit of the poisonous tree."

"What if we pay the women off? Offer a settlement if they drop the charges?"

"It's gone too far for that now. As far as their attorneys are concerned, a criminal conviction will only bolster their civil suit."

Sweat beaded on Goldhammer's forehead. He wiped it off with the sleeve of his terry cloth robe. "I want to take it to court then. I want to fight it."

"That would be a mistake."

"I don't think so. I'm sorry the young ladies misunderstood our arrangement, but that's hardly my fault. Yes, I cheated on my wife, but since when is that a crime? Because of this 'me too' hysteria, thousands of men are now being accused of things they didn't do. There is no due process. They are tried and convicted in the court of public opinion. That is wrong and someone needs to take a stand."

"I'm not sure it should be you."

"If not me, then who?"

"You need to deal with what's in front of you, and right now what's in front you is a plea deal."

Goldhammer picked up the plea deal and threw it in the fire pit. He picked up a gold lighter next to an unlit cigar and set the pages aflame. "You have my answer."

A helicopter hovered above. Anger bubbled up inside of him. Ever since he'd been trapped in Malibu on house arrest, the cable news organizations had hounded him. Helicopters flew overhead with cameramen and paparazzi. The sound was constant. Often it would drive him inside, but not today. Today he wouldn't be intimidated. He stared at the helicopter overhead, his robe falling open as he stood over the burning plea deal and shouted over the roar of the propellers. *"As God is my witness, I will crush my enemies and see them driven before me, and revel in the cries and lamentations of their women!"*

CHAPTER THIRTY-SIX

In 1922 the owners of the Tam O'Shanter commissioned Ben Hur *art director, Larry Oliver, to design their new restaurant. Carpenters burned and burnished every piece of wood used in the structure so it would never have to be painted. The interior décor featured medieval weaponry, kilts, tartans, coats of arms, and family crests. Walt Disney and his team of animators would often lunch at the Tam and had a regular table. But they weren't the only celebrity diners. Over the years, stars like Rudolph Valentino, Fatty Arbuckle, Mary Pickford, and Douglas Fairbanks would enjoy traditional Scottish dishes like corned beef and cabbage, shepherd's pie, and toad in the hole.*

The Tam O'Shanter was packed and Chloe was slammed. She worked as a server there for two years before triumphantly quitting on the day she signed the contract for *Bombshells*. Once the scandal hit, the network canceled production. Chloe received a modest kill fee after the agents and lawyers and managers—that Goldhammer arranged for her—took their piece of the pie. Luckily, the assistant manager at the Tam took her back. She knew Ken had a crush on her, but as an equal opportunity harasser, he hit on every waitress there under forty. Then, of course, there was Raúl, the cook, who flirted relentlessly and would hold back the orders of waitresses who refused to flirt back. The customers also saw her as fair game. Young men. Old men. They all hit on her shamelessly.

"Hey doll!" A chubby fifty-something guy with a bad comb-over waved her over.

She pasted on a smile. "Can I get you something?"

"Another Heineken!"

His fourth. "Yes, sir."

"Wait. Hold it! Come here." He waved her closer and the three men eating lunch with him all traded smirks.

She sighed and stepped closer. "Do you need something else?"

"What's your name?"

She pointed at her nametag. "Chloe."

He grabbed her by the arm and pulled her close. "Didn't I see you on the Fappening?"

"Excuse me?"

"Your video. I saw your video online." Comb-over's dining companions all laughed at that. Chloe tried to extricate her arm, but he pulled her closer and then put his arm around her, resting his hand on her plaid-skirted bottom. "And I *liked* what I saw."

She removed his hand from her ass and glared at him. "I have other tables."

"Don't be like that! I just gave you a compliment."

"Sir—"

"Saw a comment on the video that said you worked here. That's why we came. Just to see you."

"Great." Her voice dripped with sarcasm.

"We're staying in Glendale. At the Embassy Suites. Maybe you'd like to meet up for a drink later."

"Are you kidding me?"

"No, doll." He grabbed her around the waist and tugged her closer, resting his hand on her ass again as his friends all laughed. "I'm dead serious."

"Dead for sure if you don't get your hand off my ass!"

"What did you say?"

She picked a mug of beer off the table and poured the full contents into his lap. He jumped to his feet, knocking his chair over, and stared stunned at his dripping crotch.

Ken, the assistant manager, came rushing over. "Is everything okay here?"

"No, everything is *not* okay!" shouted comb-over. "This bitch just poured a beer in my lap!"

Ken grabbed Chloe hard by the arm. "What the hell? What are you doing?"

Chloe grabbed another beer off the table and poured it over Ken's head. "Quitting."

. . .

Skinny old Superman had shuffled off this mortal coil, but fat Spiderman still walked *The Hollywood Walk of Fame*. So did shabby Batman and threadbare Elmo, tiny Darth Vader, and the not-so-incredible Hulk. They all congregated on Hollywood Boulevard, in front of the Chinese Theater, posing for pictures with tourists from all over the world.

Dressed like Captain America, Tyler Jablonski felt like himself for the first time in a long time. He wore black boots, red gauntlets, and a blue Spandex top emblazoned with a silver star. Even though he wasn't the tallest or buffest Captain America, Tyler stood there with confidence, smiling for the cameras.

An African American Wonder Woman approached him, wincing with every step. "Jesus, my feet are killing me."

"Maybe you should take a break."

"Ain't the same out here without old Superman."

"I miss him too."

Wonder Woman shook her head and limped away. "Maybe I'm getting too old for this bullshit."

Tyler felt a tug on his shield and looked down to see a little Asian boy gazing up at him. He didn't say a word and couldn't have been more than five. He just stood there, holding his mother's hand.

"Where's Elmo?" the boy asked.

Tyler looked around. "I don't see him here today."

"Who are you??"

"Captain America?"

"Are you a superhero?"

Tyler nodded. "I am."

"What's your superpower?"

"Well, I'm really, really strong," Tyler said.

"Stronger than the Hulk?" asked the boy.

"No, I'm not that strong."

"Stronger than Thor?"

"Probably not."

"Can you fly?"

"Nope."

"Are you bulletproof?"

"No, but my shield is," Tyler said.

The kid silently stared up at him. "So, you really don't have any super powers?"

"Not like superhuman superpowers. No."

"So, you're like Batman?"

"Kind of."

"Kind of sucks."

"I don't think so. I think it makes me more of a hero."

"Because you can't do anything?"

"Because I'm a regular human being, just like you. That means you can be a hero too. You don't have to get bitten by a radioactive spider or come from another planet. You just have to work out and learn how to fight and protect those who can't protect themselves. How brave do you have to be if you're bulletproof?"

"I wish I could fly," the boy said.

"So do I sometimes."

The mom looked up from her phone and smiled down at her son. Unlike her five-year-old son, she spoke English with a Korean accent. "Justin, do you want to take a picture with Superman?"

"He's Captain America."

"Well, pardon me," she said with a smile.

"Superman has superpowers. Captain America is just like a regular guy."

"Do you want to take a picture with him?"

"Okay."

Tyler took a knee so he would be on Justin's level. He held his shield in front of him, and Justin beamed along with Tyler as his mom snapped the shot.

• • •

Alessandra found her stay in Placer County Jail quite enlightening. She shared the general lock up with a woman arrested for a DUI, another woman arrested for possession with intent to sell, and a fifty-seven-year-old massage therapist arrested for solicitation. None of them recognized Alessandra, though they were all intrigued by her Italian accent.

However, the head sheriff of Placer County, sixty-six-year-old Darrel Bell, recognized her immediately. He proved to be a fan with a crush dating back to his teenage days. He even confessed to having Alessandra's famous late 1960s pinup poster on his bedroom wall.

Sheriff Bell listened to all sides of the story and interviewed thirteen witnesses, including the three ski patrols members Ohana assaulted. By the end, he believed Alessandra shot Ohana in self-defense. Alessa was released and Sheriff Bell confined Ohana to the County Jail's hospital wing. The judge set Ohana's bail at one million dollars. That same day, an anonymous person paid his bail. The Sheriff had no choice but to release him. Two weeks after that, Ohana and his men were gone. Alessandra assumed they fled the country.

She didn't regret shooting him, but was relieved she didn't kill him. She couldn't get the memory of it out of her mind. Nightmares woke her up several times a night and she had to eat THC-infused gummy bears to get herself back to sleep.

Alessandra usually awoke sometime after nine in the morning, still a little high from the edibles. After brewing herself a double espresso, she took a long walk on Malibu Beach with Peanut, her Pomeranian, hoping the cool, fresh, ocean air would clear her head. Some mornings were foggy. She enjoyed those most of all.

When Goldhammer was still under house arrest, sometimes helicopters would hover over his house, the *fwap-fwap-fwap* of the blades disturbing the peace of Malibu Beach. It irritated her, but also pleased her that the media mogul's rapacious and predatory life had fallen apart. He would no longer prey on the innocent and desperate. Instead, maybe he would pay for what he had done. Not for all of it. But hopefully some of it. It was more justice than she ever saw after what happened to her as a young starlet.

Bettina, the reporter from Rolling Stone, came to interview her twice. Alessandra told her the entire story, relieved to unburden herself. She enjoyed Bettina's company, but the resulting media storm the story engendered took her by surprise. Alessandra liked being out of the public eye. But now, for the first time in forty years, her face was plastered everywhere. Talk show producers and news reporters rang her day and night, hoping for an interview. But she already said everything she wanted to say to Bettina and was tired of the attention. She wanted to fade away. Go back to being anonymous.

She walked past a couple of surfers, smiled at Miley Cyrus walking her sheepdog, and said hello to Dyan Cannon, another star of her era. Dyan was once married to Cary Grant and Alessandra always admired her good humor and confidence. She owned two yappy Yorkshire Terriers who always wanted to visit with Peanut. After they said their hellos, Peanut pooped, Alessandra scooped, and they made their way back home.

She brewed herself another cup of espresso, decaf this time, and half-listened to MSNBC playing in the background. The mention of Gary Goldhammer's name caught her attention, and she carried her cup into the living room to see what Andrea Mitchell had to say. The jury already convicted him. Today was for sentencing and the judge threw the book at him.

Goldhammer could have gotten as little as five years, but the prosecutors in the case pushed for the longest maximum sentence. Something that would serve as a deterrence to other would-be predators.

The judge decided on seventeen years.

Alessandra watched as sheriff's deputies escorted Goldhammer from the courthouse. Looking old and pale, his shoulders hunched, the man slowly made his way down the stairs, supported on either side by his two attorneys. Reporters swarmed him, shouting questions, and an angry Goldhammer pushed past his lawyers to grab a microphone belonging to one of the female reporters. "I'll be honest, I don't understand any of this!"

"Do you feel any remorse?" shouted the reporter whose microphone he stole.

"Of course I feel remorse! I know I'm not a perfect person. I've made mistakes. I misinterpreted signals and occasionally crossed the line. Did I take liberties? Perhaps. But I always considered those relationships reciprocal! Consensual! Maybe I misread a signal now and then, but I never intended to hurt anyone. We each got what we wanted, and in the end, I loved them. All of them. They're great people and we had wonderful times together."

The reporter reached for her microphone, but Goldhammer's attorney, Rachel Einbinder, snatched it out of his hand so she too could address the crowd. She spoke forcefully with indignation and not a little outrage.

"Today was a travesty of justice. This sentence is beyond the pale. Especially for someone convicted of a first offense. My client was caught up in a witch hunt. This hysteria will end one day and when it does this decision and this sentence will be reversed on appeal."

Alessandra watched as Rachel Einbinder tossed the microphone back to the female reporter and led Goldhammer down the stairs, pushing past the cameras and the crowd clamoring for blood.

The courthouse doors opened again and out spilled Goldhammer's many victims, among them Chloe and her brother Tyler. Chloe did not look jubilant or victorious.

She looked exhausted and tearful.

Reporters converged and shouted questions.

"Do you feel vindicated?"

"Do you feel justice was done?"

"Are you happy with the sentence?"

Tyler tried to push them back but before he could, Chloe shouted into one of the microphones. "Happy? I'm not happy about any of this. What he did can't be undone. All I can do now is try to put this behind me and move on the best I can."

Another better-known actress stepped through the courthouse doors and the reporters immediately deserted Chloe to converge on her.

Alessandra picked up the remote, turned off the TV, and looked down at Peanut. "Who's ready for breakfast?"

CHAPTER THIRTY-SEVEN

Room 7021 at the Men's Central Jail is spacious compared to the jail's other accommodations. Painted eggshell white, it measures eight-by-ten feet. The door is solid steel with no slot, but there is a nine-by-nine inch Plexiglass window. The bed is bolted to the floor next to a stainless-steel sink and toilet. While the rest of the jail is an overcrowded madhouse, rated one of the ten worst prisons in the United States, room 7021 is reserved for prisoners that need to be kept in isolation. O.J. Simpson stayed there for a time. So did Robert Blake, Robert Downey Jr., Tommy Lee of Motley Crue, Richard Pryor, Night Stalker Richard Ramirez, and Hillside Strangler Kenneth Bianchi. The L.A. County Jail Protective Custody Unit is reserved for those who wouldn't be safe in gen pop, including famous and infamous celebrities and those whose crimes are so heinous even the worst of the worst would want to punish them.

The orange prison jump suit made Gary Goldhammer look fat. The unbreakable stainless-steel mirror over the sink distorted his face, making it twisted and misshapen, like Charles Laughton as Quasimodo in *The Hunchback of Notre Dame.*

Goldhammer sat on the skinny mattress on his bolted-down bed and contemplated his future.

They'd be sending him to a state penitentiary soon. It could be Folsom. It could be San Quentin. It could be anywhere. He gingerly touched his tender right eye. He licked his fat lip and cursed his fate. They moved him to room 7021 after an overzealous inmate who hated his remake of a classic crime drama gave him an on-the-spot review.

Goldhammer hoped the beating would convince the authorities to send him to a minimum-security prison. Maybe that place they sent

Michael Milken. Einbinder better get that appeal going soon, get this sentence reduced or at least get him released on bail. He would spend whatever he had, however long it took. It would cost money. It always cost money. Luckily, he had enough to pay his lawyers for the next twenty years. He had cash stashed all over the world.

Prison was not where he belonged. This was a just a blip in his ultimate destiny. He was fated for great things and would not spend the rest of his life rotting in a goddamn prison cell, looking fat in an orange jumpsuit.

And those who put him here? They would pay.

Dearly.

The lock on his cell door opened with a clank and two burly guards called to him. "Up and at 'em, Goldhammer. You got a visitor."

The guards led Goldhammer down an endless corridor to an elevator. They rode it down and the doors opened. After walking along another endless corridor, they arrived at an inmate visiting area.

A long line of green cubicles with Plexiglas windows stretched forever. A handset in each one allowed the inmate to speak to their visitor through the scratched Plexiglass. Goldhammer sat on a round green stool and waited to see his visitor.

He knew it wasn't his lawyer. He just saw her yesterday and told her to get a message to Marta. His wife wouldn't visit him. She wanted nothing to do with him. He had no friends. He was alone. All alone. But he was always alone. Even when surrounded by his employees and investors, board members and business associates. They all were opportunists. Leaches. Vultures. They used him and he used them. It's the way of the world. It was why capitalism worked. Enlightened self-interest—everyone wanted something. That was understood. And if you didn't understand that simple truth then you were worse than naïve. You were a fool.

He glimpsed Marta's long legs before he saw the rest of her as she sat down across him, separated by those few inches of Plexiglass. She didn't react to his pummeled face, but then Marta never reacted to much. She would smile when necessary and was quite beautiful when she did, but Goldhammer could never tell what was behind her eyes. He knew she had no affection for him. Their relationship was strictly transactional. And though he aggressively pushed himself on many women, he never made that attempt with Marta. In truth, she frightened him. He could point her towards a problem and she would deal with it. Fix it. End it. Kill it. Whatever he needed.

He picked up his receiver and held it to his head and she picked up hers.

"It's time," he said.

"That task we talked about?"

"Can you get it done?"

She nodded. "Do you care how or where?"

"I don't. But once it's done, you'll get what we agreed to. All the arrangements have been made."

"Then I likely won't be seeing you again."

"Not for a while."

"Is that it then?"

"That's it."

She nodded, hung up the phone, and stood. Her long legs were the last thing Goldhammer saw as she made her way out.

• • • •

"Mr. Flynn, you have a visitor."

Flynn stopped his karate kata mid-kick to turn and acknowledge Nurse Durkin. As usual, she was all business. The Pasadena-based field office for her Majesty's Secret Service masqueraded as a mental hospital and Durkin never broke cover. She never dropped the pretense of being the tough, irascible head nurse. Her unrelenting glower intimidated many, but not Flynn. He knew that beneath her tough-as-nails exterior beat the heart of a woman in need of affection. Perhaps she suffered some heartbreak or rejection as a young woman and developed a tough outer-shell to protect herself. Whatever the reason for her emotional armor, Flynn understood and didn't take her attitude personally.

"Thank you, Nurse Durkin. And I hope I'm not out of line by saying you look quite fetching today."

Durkin frowned, sighed, and left the activity room. Flynn picked up a towel, wiped the sweat off his forehead and upper torso, put on his black cotton front-zippered warm-up jacket and followed Durkin out the door. He continued down the corridor to the visiting area. The sight of Alessandra Bianchi delighted him.

She wore what she wore the day he met her on that beach in Malibu: faded blue jeans, a black turtleneck, and a cobalt blue cardigan sweater. Her shoulder-length silver hair was tied back into a ponytail. She smiled and nodded as Sancho whispered something into her ear. Her smile lines only made her more beautiful as they accentuated her cheekbones.

Sancho saw Flynn first. "Looks who's here!"

Flynn stepped closer, happy to see Alessandra more at ease, her famous hazel eyes less haunted. Shooting Ohana had been traumatic for her. After all, she wasn't a trained operative. She just played one in the movies.

"You look well," Flynn said.

"So do you." Alessandra gave him a smile. She took Flynn by the hand and led him to a faux leather couch.

"Catch you later, Alessa." Sancho pointed at Flynn. "You behave yourself, brother."

"Not an easy task around Alessandra Bianchi."

Flynn noticed Q conferring with an elderly and sad-looking woman on the other side of the visitor's room. Ty spent time with his mother, while big-boned, freckled-faced Mary Alice talked to a skinny little balding man who Flynn assumed was her husband. The redhead's loud raspy laugh turned into a hacking cough that continued until she choked down some water. When Flynn looked back at Alessandra, he caught a hint of melancholy.

"Are you all right?" Flynn asked.

"Are you?"

"Never better. Fit as can be and ready for my next mission."

She looked at him with concern. "Are you sure? Ohana really worked you over. A broken rib can take months to heal."

"Are you speaking from experience?"

"I am. I was in a car accident in Cannes with my second husband. I had two broken ribs. Six months later it still hurt to breathe."

"I'm fine. Truly." Flynn took her hand in his. "Any word on Ohana?"

Alessandra shook her head. "Only that he fled the country."

"You know you only did what you had to."

"I know." She tried to cover her sadness with a smile.

"You saved my life."

"I did, didn't I?"

"Don't let it go to your head."

She laughed. "I'm glad to see you're okay in here. Did you hear what happened to Goldhammer?"

"I did indeed. Chloe was brave to testify."

"The important thing is they put him away. In my day, there were no consequences for that kind of behavior. Men like him were untouchable."

Flynn nodded. "Of course, I saw nothing on the news about his plan for world domination. That they had to keep secret. Enslaving the minds of millions by reprogramming their brains? That dangerous technology is still out there and if we don't get a handle on it, others with ill intent will make the same attempt. There are many evil men plotting to destroy all that is good, and I can't stop them from behind a desk."

Alessandra reached out and took Flynn's hand. "It's not all on you, you know. It's all right to take some time to heal up and recharge. Let someone else save the world for a while."

Flynn caught something out of the corner of his eye that put him on alert. He wasn't sure exactly what raised his hackles, but the energy in the room changed.

The only new addition was a nurse pushing a wheelchair. He'd seen the man in the wheelchair before and assumed he was recovering from an injury he sustained in some far-flung mission. Flynn caught the nurse who pushed him in profile. Something about her seemed familiar. Her shiny jet-black hair was pulled back in a bun, held in place by a kanzashi. Flynn knew that the wives and daughters of samurai warriors used kanzashi as both a hairpin and a weapon.

Flynn registered this just as the woman turned to face him, pulling the kanzashi in one smooth motion, flinging it right at him. The blade sliced through the flesh on his right temple, just missing his eye and hit the wall behind him.

Flynn shoved Alessandra's head down before diving for the floor, somersaulting behind a table, and springing to his feet.

He met Marta's cold glare and caught the hint of a mirthless smile as shuriken appeared in both her hands an instant before flying through the air in Flynn's direction.

One razor-sharp ninja star caught him in the shoulder. The other stuck him in the chest. More ninja stars and sharpened darts flew across the room, sticking into walls and furniture as Flynn ran for cover.

Mary Alice looked down to see a ninja dart sticking out of her thigh. "What the hell?" she said with her raspy Arkansas accent.

Q reached up to touch a dart protruding from his forehead.

Flynn saw Sancho standing in the doorway, frozen in place, immobilized by fear, blocking any chance of an easy exit.

Flynn needed a weapon. Marta now wielded a double-edged butterfly knife. Where she hid that weapon under her nurse's uniform, Flynn had no idea. He pulled the shuriken sticking out of his shoulder and flung it back, missing Marta by at least two feet. He didn't miss Mary Alice though, as the ninja star buried itself in the flesh just above her belly button.

"What the shit!" Mary Alice shouted again.

Marta flipped and flicked, fanned, and twirled the butterfly knife in a deadly display designed to intimidate and demoralize.

Flynn came right at her, kicking a footstool across the floor. She easily side-stepped it and attacked fast, thrusting and slashing. He picked up a wooden chair, held its legs out, and used it to keep Marta at bay and far enough away so the butterfly knife couldn't slash him.

Marta leaped back and executed a perfect spin kick, her heel hitting the wooden chair so hard it splintered in Flynn's hands. He still held onto the chair back, however, and swung it like a club. She evaded his attack and slashed back, cutting his sweat shirt and slicing into his arm.

"A hand here, Sancho!" Flynn shouted.

But Sancho stayed where he stood, stuck in the doorway, frozen with terror.

Alessandra snatched up a table lamp and tried to take out Marta from behind, but somehow the assassin sensed the attack and executed another perfect spin kick. The lamp exploded in Alessa's hand as Marta followed with a second spin kick that caught the actress square in the jaw. Down she went like a marionette with its strings cut.

Flynn dove for the cord of the shattered lamp and somersaulted up, swinging it like a mace, the broken end just missing Marta's face. She circled Flynn, twirling the knife, lunging in close to cut him. But he avoided the blade and swung the broken base of the lamp. The cord wrapped itself around Marta's arm. Flynn pulled her off-balance and swept her legs out from under her. She toppled forward, hitting the floor hard, and Flynn kicked the knife out of her hand.

Furious, she spun around and scissored her legs together, catching Flynn's ankles. She brought him down and wrapped him in a Brazilian jujitsu hold that Flynn recognized as one of Royce Gracie's signature moves. A Star choke. The world faded as he tried to free himself. But Marta had a firm grip that Flynn couldn't break. He had to find some way to escape, because soon he would lose consciousness, and then his life.

• • •

Sancho couldn't breathe. Strange since he wasn't the one being choked out. He stood frozen in that doorway, watching as Marta cut off Flynn's air and blood supply. His old friend flailed and fought, but he had no leverage or strength left, and Marta seemed determined to end his life.

Sancho tried to move, but paralyzed by anxiety, his legs wouldn't work. His brain had no control of his body, but he couldn't just let Flynn die. He had to do something.

He had to do something.

Marta's eyes met his and her lips curled into a tiny smile. She enjoyed this. Enjoyed Sancho's helplessness. His hopelessness. His absolute impotence. And that's when he felt that first flicker of rage. That tiny flame grew into a blaze and then a conflagration as his fury overcame his fear. He found himself moving, grabbing the butterfly knife off the floor.

Sancho bellowed and slashed at Marta's head and she let Flynn go to block the blow. Somehow, she disarmed Sancho, taking back control of the blade, but before she could use it, Flynn slammed his head back as hard as he could, hitting Marta square in the nose.

She skittered away like a spider and rocked back with both her hands on the floor before kipping up and springing to her feet, ready to wreak bloody havoc on both of them.

Focused as she was on Flynn and Sancho, she never saw Mary Alice coming. The large lady from Arkansas held a heavy glass vase filled with glass marbles and brought it down hard on Marta's head. The vase exploded into shards and hundreds of glass marbles bounced off the floor.

The blow didn't even slow Marta down as she turned to confront her attacker, seemingly more angry than injured.

"Bitch has a hard head," Mary Alice said before Marta came at her with the knife.

She took one step and lost her footing, both her feet slipping and sliding on the marbles. Sancho watched as Marta ran backwards in place like a cartoon cat before her feet flew in the air and her head slammed into the floor.

Flynn took advantage of his attacker's dazed condition to flip her over and, with Sancho's help, hogtie her with the cord from the shattered lamp.

Alessandra sat on the floor, her back against the couch, bleeding from the blow she took to the jaw. "Are you okay, Alessa?" Sancho asked.

Alessandra held her chin with her right hand and worked her jaw. "I think so."

Sancho glanced at Q, sitting on a chair with a ninja dart protruding from his forehead. "Q?"

Q pulled the dart out, wincing. "Appears to be just a flesh wound."

Flynn looked at Sancho with gratitude and patted him on the back. "Appreciate the help, old friend."

"No worries, dude," Sancho said.

Mary Alice looked at Marta struggling on the floor, fighting to free herself from the broken lamp cord. "Guess the bitch's head wasn't that hard after all."

CHAPTER THIRTY-EIGHT

Once a vast orchard, the town of Toluca was dubbed "The Home of the Peach". To capitalize on the glamour afforded by the industry over the hill, the town council eventually changed the name to "North Hollywood". Suburban housing developments popped up, followed by strip malls and fast food joints on every other corner. Lankershim Boulevard became its own shopping district in the 1960s. Massive enclosed malls were built, retail business drifted away and the boulevard fell into decrepitude. Thirty years later, new investment revitalized the area. The NoHo Arts District sprang up and became home to restaurants, watering holes, and countless equity-waiver theaters.

Chloe never looked more beautiful as she stood center stage in the ninety-nine-seat black box theater and poured out her heart. Sancho, sitting on Flynn's right, sat spellbound, hanging on Chloe's every word. Tyler, on Sancho's left, watched with tears in his eyes.

"Be free, be free as the wind. Believe what I say, Anya; believe what I say. I'm not thirty yet. I am still young, still a student. But what I have been through! I am hungry as the winter. I am sick, anxious, poor as a beggar. Fate has tossed me hither and thither. I have been everywhere, everywhere. But wherever I have been, every minute, day and night, my soul has been full of mysterious anticipations. I feel the approach of happiness, Anya. I see it coming."

Sancho hadn't seen many plays, and never one by Chekhov. He was worried he'd be bored, but he found himself transported. Flynn explained it was an experimental production and that the NOHO Woman's Theatre had an all-female acting company dedicated to producing classic plays with all-female casts. Shakespeare. Shaw.

Moliere. Chekhov. He explained that back when they were first performed, women were forbidden, by law, to perform in the Elizabethan theater. So men played all the female parts in Shakespeare's plays. Chloe's company turned that tradition on its head by producing classical plays with all female casts.

In *The Cherry Orchard*, Chloe played Peter Trofimov, a perpetual student in his late twenties. Every word in the monologue sounded like it came directly from Chloe's soul. The words hit Sancho hard. He too felt that maybe, finally, a little happiness was on its way. He hoped it would push away the tension, fear, and anxiety that haunted him ever since the day he caught that bullet meant for Flynn.

After the show, Sancho attended the opening night reception in the lobby. All the actors and their friends were there. Sancho enjoyed the camaraderie and laughter — actors were an excitable bunch, even louder and more rowdy than mental patients as they all fought to be the center of attention.

The attractive older actress who played Lyuba Ranevsky monopolized Flynn, clearly flirting with him. Flynn charmingly flirted back. Chloe chatted amiably with Alessandra Bianchi as the rest of the cast stared in awe at the elderly movie star.

Sancho took a sip from his plastic glass of red wine as Tyler sidled up next to him. "Enjoy the show?"

"It was a lot less boring than I thought it would be."

Tyler laughed at that. "No kidding. I've seen a lot of friends in equity-waiver shows and it's not always pretty. In fact, usually it's pretty painful."

"Your sister's very talented."

"That's what everyone tells her. Maybe someday she'll even believe it."

"Are you an actor too?"

"I don't know what I am. A would-be director. An aspiring writer. Someday I'll figure it out." Tyler looked across the room at Flynn fending off the advances of the older actress. "How's our friend doing back at the hospital?"

"Good. Real good."

"But he still doesn't know he's in a hospital, does he?"

"No, he creates his own reality."

"Don't we all." Tyler took a sip of his wine. "What about you? Chloe said you're back with your old girlfriend?"

"Kind of. We're taking it a step at a time. We'll see what happens."

"I hope you know I really appreciate what you did for my sister. You and Flynn both." Tyler tapped his plastic wine glass against Sancho's and took another sip. "Jesus, this wine sucks."

Sancho laughed. "It's not so bad if you drink it fast."

Tyler chugged the rest of his wine and made a face as he choked it down. "Yeah, it is."

Sancho laughed again.

• • •

Few celebrities attend the shows at the NOHO Woman's Theater, so Alessandra Bianchi's presence generated a lot of excitement. Chloe didn't tell anyone in the company that they were friends, so when she showed up with an opening night bouquet for Chloe it created quite a stir. Chloe's mother hated her acting ambitions. She wanted Chloe to stay in Wisconsin, find some nice Catholic boy to marry, and pump out a few grandkids.

Alessandra not only accepted Chloe's ambitions, she encouraged her. Supported her. Advocated for her. Alessa told Chloe she never had anyone watching her back when she was starting out and that this was her way to right some wrongs.

Chloe loved spending time with Alessandra. They talked often and had lunch or dinner together once a week. Alessandra even joined the NOHO Woman's Theater as a board member and investor. Everyone was so grateful for her support, advice, and energy. No one more so than Chloe.

As usual, Alessandra looked amazing and elegant. She had this sexy, strong, free, and fun boho casual chic style—kind of Stevie Nicks meets Sienna Miller meets Helen Mirren. Just being with Alessa made Chloe more confident, grounded, and self-assured.

After the show, Alessa stepped right up to Chloe and gave her a big hug. "You were brilliant."

"When you work with good actors, they make you look good."

"Don't minimize what you did. You were wonderful."

"Thank you."

"You were all so inspiring. I might just audition for the next show."

"Oh, my God. That would be fantastic."

"I haven't been on stage since Nixon was President, so I might be a little rusty."

"I'm sure you'd be great."

"I don't know about that, but it would be a hoot."

Alessa watched Flynn approach and grinned. "Good to see you out and about, Mr. Flynn."

"M does let me out now and then." Flynn took Chloe's hand and kissed it. "A magnificent performance."

"Thank you."

"I'm no expert, of course. The world of make-believe is a mystery to me."

Alessa smiled at that. "Isn't every good spy an actor at heart?"

"Perhaps."

"Did Chloe tell you about her new agent?"

"She did not."

"Alessandra set it up," Chloe said.

"She just got a national commercial too," Alessa added.

"For Mountain Dew."

"Good for you!" Flynn said.

Chloe gave Flynn a big hug.

"What's that for?"

"For everything you did for me."

"I did what anyone would have done."

Chloe held Flynn at arm's length. "Not hardly." He was still healing up from the beating Marta gave him. "You okay?"

"Never better."

"I'll come see you."

"Make it soon. Before M sends me on a mission."

"Another mission?"

"The world is a dangerous place and I took an oath to keep it safe. Just a simple civil servant fighting the good fight for Queen and Country."

Chloe kissed Flynn on the cheek and felt a rush of heat and a sudden attraction that surprised her. After all, Flynn was totally delusional. Completely out of his mind. But then again, maybe you had to be a little loony to run into a burning building. Or storm a beach in Normandy. Or save the world from an evil genius.

Maybe every hero has to be a little bit crazy.

THE END

ABOUT THE AUTHOR

Haris Orkin is a playwright, screenwriter, game writer, and novelist. His play, *Dada* was produced at The American Stage and the La Jolla Playhouse. *Sex, Impotence, and International Terrorism* was chosen as a critic's choice by the L.A. Weekly and sold as a film script to MGM/UA. *Save the Dog* was produced as a Disney Sunday Night movie. His original screenplay, *A Saintly Switch*, was directed by Peter Bogdanovich and starred David Alan Grier and Vivica A. Fox.

He is a WGA Award and BAFTA Award nominated game writer and narrative designer known for *Command and Conquer: Red Alert 3*, *Call of Juarez: Gunslinger*, *Tom Clancy's The Division*, *Mafia 3*, and *Dying Light*, which to date has sold over 17 million copies.

www.harisorkin.com

NOTE FROM THE AUTHOR

I was a shy, skinny, bookish, bespectacled, and insecure twelve old living in the suburbs of Chicago when I first realized what I wanted to be when I grew up. I wanted to be Alexander Mundy in *It Takes a Thief*. I wanted to be Illya Kuryakin in *The Man from Uncle*. I wanted to be part of the Mission Impossible team. I wanted to be Jim West, Derek Flint, and Matt Helm. I wanted to be James Bond.

Those men had no fear. They knew karate and could scuba dive and rock climb and skydive and ski and shoot the eye out of a flea at fifty yards. They were confident in any situation and were comfortable in their own skin. I think that was the biggest wish fulfillment fantasy of all for an awkward pre-teen struggling through puberty and that's what inspired James Flynn and his adventures.

At twelve I was terrified of girls. I was always picked last in gym class. I lived a life of perpetual embarrassment. In hindsight, that's probably how most twelve-year-olds feel, but at the time, I didn't know that. So I started lifting weights. I became a gymnast. I boxed. I studied karate. I became a rock climber and learned to ski and scuba dive. I even studied in London for a year and traveled the world.

But I never did become an international super spy. Instead, I became a screenwriter and game writer, creating wish fulfillment fantasies for other nerdy twelve-year-olds. Thank you for indulging in my fantasies. I hope you enjoyed the journey. I do believe Mr. Flynn is just getting started.

Please connect with me on Twitter and Facebook and feel free to ask me anything. This is a two-way conversation.

~Haris Orkin

We hope you enjoyed reading this title from:

BLACK ROSE
writing™

www.blackrosewriting.com

Subscribe to our mailing list – *The Rosevine* – and receive **FREE** books, daily deals, and stay current with news about upcoming releases and our hottest authors.
Scan the QR code below to sign up.

Already a subscriber? Please accept a sincere thank you for being a fan of Black Rose Writing authors.

View other Black Rose Writing titles at
www.blackrosewriting.com/books and use promo code
PRINT to receive a **20% discount** when purchasing.

Lightning Source UK Ltd.
Milton Keynes UK
UKHW041859230622
404858UK00001B/3

9 781684 339679